A
QUIET
KIND OF
CRAZY

SIOBHAN NICOLE

NEWMAN SPRINGS PUBLISHING
320 Broad Street
Red Bank, NJ 07701

First originally published by Newman Springs Publishing 2023

ISBN 978-1-68498-486-2 (Paperback)
ISBN 978-1-68498-487-9 (Digital)

Printed in the United States of America

I'm dizzy.
It's a good kinda dizzy.
Hand's blurry, stretched toward the bottle.
My arm is so heavy.
But my fingers…like tiny little dancers.
They tingle as they reach the glass.
It's funny, the way the bottle rolls back and forth and back again.
My eyes wanna close.
Make me wanna fade away, it's so much easier to just fade away.
This isn't real, it doesn't feel real…and I like that.
It's like I'm the doll version of me.
I'm a Kara doll…but I don't wanna dance for
you. I'm tired of dancing for you.
I wanna drink.
Reach for the bottle, wait…it rolls forward and back…
I take a long slow sip, and it doesn't burn anymore.
My eyes start to close, and I'm not strong enough to care.
Silly Kara doll…
Sleeping pills are supposed to make you sleep.

SLEEP

CHAPTER 1

The door closes, and I can't help but smile as I lean against it. I let go of my old gym bag, and it hits the floor with a loud thump that echoes through the empty space. Kicking it aside, I take the first steps into my new apartment, into my new life. I did it. Mine. No one's watching; it's just me.

I know it's the same apartment I first looked at a few weeks ago, but it's somehow different knowing it's mine. It's better. Enjoying each step, I make my way into my kitchen. Tossing the only other bag I've brought with me onto the countertop, I spin, slowly at first, but then I just give in. I spin for the sheer joy of spinning, the dizziness of the spin, "little girl lost in a field of wildflowers" spin. *Finally.*

Grabbing the bottle I picked up at the store on the corner, I make myself a celebration drink. It's not quite the martini I want, but there's only so much you can do without already having all the fixings in the fridge. I didn't even think to grab ice. Tomorrow's move-in day; tomorrow can be "proper drink celebration" day. Today, club soda and still warm vodka will have to do. Sipping my drink, I walk through the rooms of my new home.

The apartment's dark and still; it's eerily and fabulously silent. It's a whole different kind of silence than the suburbs where I grew up. Chicago echoes of sounds that aren't meant for me: police sirens off in the distance, people talking outside on the street below, the muted beat of some stranger's music. Taking it all in, I close my eyes, enjoying a long slow sip before I continue walking through my new place. I find myself playing with the lights, turning them on and off in each room as I go, smiling as I dream of the treasures that will one day fill the walls, memories of adventures that I haven't had yet.

All of my boxes and of what little furniture I have will show up in the morning. This is the first time I have truly been on my own, no dorm room and roommates, no older brother secretly reporting back to the parents, but truly alone. It did take some doing, but I managed to convince my family that spending my first night here alone was important. I think my mom had visions of tonight being some mother-daughter, tea-sipping slumber party.

Finishing my drink, I lazily walk into the living room wanting nothing more than to collapse and fall into a deep, peaceful, and life-fulfilling kind of sleep. Mom is still trying to make up for the fight about wanting me to live with Rick or at home until I get married—which means she'll be here bright and early along with my brother to help me move in. I'm already wearing sweatpants and a T-shirt, and you can't really change into something more comfortable than that. I grab the one pillow and blanket that I had shoved into my gym bag and curl up on the carpet of my new living room floor. Spending the day packing has left me exhausted; but in a weird, moody way, I feel more alive than I have in a long time.

● ● ●

The sun is invading my sleep. My dreams are now solely made up of the color orange that's creeping in through my closed eyes. Moaning, I roll over, attempting to shield myself from the light, knowing somewhere deep in my psyche that it's far too early for me to be awake. Five minutes later, I give up. There's no hiding from it. As my eyes crack open, I see the light leaking in through the vertical blinds of my fake balcony door. It breaks in through little slats, making my living room look striped. Lacing my fingers together, I reach my hands above my head and stretch—overall sleeping on the floor wasn't as uncomfortable as I had thought it would be; but then again, a little yoga wouldn't hurt right now either.

Sitting up, I take my first real look around the apartment, something made so much easier in the daylight. I wish I had thought it through better and brought my Keurig and some coffee with me; Lord knows it's not doing me any good packed up in the back of a truck right now. The perfect mug of steaming hot coffee, watching the color slowly change from black to beige as the cream is poured in—it would have made this whole moment that much more complete. I know I'm going to have to settle for using my phone to find out where some local coffee bar is, but it's just not the same. Coffee is meant to be enjoyed in pajamas before a brush even touches your hair, not once you're dressed and ready to tackle the day.

Despite the fact that it's far too early, I can't help but feel content in this moment. I'm stuck in the pure bliss of standing on the sidewalk outside my building as the city rushes by. I was prepared to be in a pissy "ain't got my morning cup o' joe" mood, but I don't think that's even possible today. According to Google, I have plenty of options within walking distance that can give me the caffeine I crave. Ignoring the multitude of Starbucks, I head out to a local mom-and-pop place. It's a simple walk of just a couple of blocks, even better since it's finally gorgeous out (even if it is a little chilly). I'm walking in a pre-caffeine, "ain't this beautiful, can't believe I live here" kind of daze.

The door to the coffee bar is propped open, allowing the spring breeze in and the smell of hot coffee and fresh muffins to flow out. I've always loved Chicago in the spring. It's like the city goes through a rebirth after suffering through cold winter days. People are out and about just because they can be. Everything changes from muted, dirty street browns and gray, to a "forty-two shades of green" kind of place, with tulips and daffodils popping out as some type of promise of what's to come.

Apparently the up-too-damn early Kara is sentimental and slightly poetic.

"Good morning! What can we get ya?" Coffee girl is smiling at me. It's one of those "I've already been awake and had three times the amount of espresso you're planning to order" smiles. I know it's immature, but I can't help it. I'm jealous of the caffeine she's already had. I'm sure she's very nice and all, but being that I haven't had my coffee yet, her smile means nothing more to me than her waving her coffee in my face with a nana a booboo.

What I really want to do is slap her with that towel she has neatly folded next to the espresso machine, but the "I'm older than a five-year-old Kara" wins out. So instead, I smile, focusing on my upcoming extra foamy and caffeinated creamy dark heaven, and yes, I am that much of a coffee freak.

"Large dry cap please, and can you throw an extra shot in there too?"

Happy now that I have my coffee, I thank her as I wrap my hands around the paper cup and feel the heat of the cappuccino. I flash my best early morning grin and throw a couple singles into the tip jar as I head back out onto the street.

I may have spent a little too much time wondering around my neighborhood on my way to find coffee. Now I'm worried I'm going to be late getting back. Rick should be showing up any minute with a truckload of my stuff brought over from our old apartment. As much as I'm happy I'm on my own, I'm really going to miss living with him. There's something comfortable about living with someone who knows everything about you, someone you can just be yourself around and feel safe with.

My brother is leaning against the giant U-Haul when I walk up. He seems to have no concern whatsoever about being double parked and blocking half the road, something that would have me in a near panic attack. He looks so at ease standing there; it's no wonder people are drawn to him. He has a confidence about him that has always left me a little envious. It shows in everything he does, even just in the way he's standing—sunglasses covering his brown eyes, his hair still damp from the shower, jeans, and a sweatshirt, actually not much different than me at the moment, but a world of difference all at the same time.

"Sorry, Rick, I didn't mean to leave you waiting here. But you know me, gotta have my coffee."

Looking down at me, he laughs as he holds up two cups, one coffee for me and one of his own. I can't help the smile that now stretches across my face. He just knows me too well—that and he probably didn't want to be stuck with me on a morning where I haven't had any caffeine.

"Perfect!"

I grab the coffee from his hand as I stretch up to give him a quick kiss on the cheek.

"Now I can finish mine and still have one to warm up later, after we find my microwave in all of this shit."

"Hahum… Good morning, Rick. How nice to see you, Rick. Thanks for the coffee, Rick." He's teasing; and just in case it wasn't completely obvious, he flashes me his perfect Rick West smile.

"Sorry, good morning, dear brother." I all but stick my tongue out at him while trying to playfully elbow him in the ribs without letting either of my coffee spill.

"Hey! Watch it there." He dances away. "Don't make me teach you a lesson out here in the middle of the street."

"As if you could." My smile may not be quite as captivating as his, but it has been known to get me out of some trouble too.

"What am I going to do without my mornings including some sad ass attempt from you trying to hit me?" Rick tries to sound exasperated, but I don't buy it.

"Ha-ha, please, you're going to be missing me before you even get all the way home."

"You mean before I fall asleep from being up at the ass crack of dawn to help you move? No, I think your chances are better of me missing you after about three this afternoon."

"Come on now." Rick puts a hand on each shoulder and forces me to turn and look into the disaster of boxes I hastily threw into the truck before driving to the city last night. "We'd better get your shit unloaded before Mom gets here. You know, if we leave it up to her, she'll have your apartment looking like some antique fair instead of some place you and your friends can hang out at."

"Ugh, but I don't wanna. Can't we just close our eyes and have it be tomorrow?"

"Kara…"

"I know, I know."

I grab the first box I see that doesn't look like it will be too heavy and turn to head into the building. Thank God for elevators, or this would have been so much worse. I don't even want to think about how we are going to get the couch and bed up. There is no way that those are going to fit on this elevator, and I am so not looking forward to having to haul them up the stairs. I think Rick can read my mind because he steps onto the elevator declaring, "Shit! How the hell are we going to get the furniture up?"

"I love you, Rick…"

"Kara!"

"It's only the third floor. It won't be that bad!"

He groans as the elevator doors close, and we head up with our first load of boxes.

Two hours, and who knows how many bruises later, Rick is sitting in my living room on my now slightly banged up couch.

"Wow." He looks around my starkly laid out apartment and starts to laugh. "You really don't have a lot of stuff. How the hell did you ever fill up that truck?"

I roll my eyes as I hand Rick a bottle of water. "Sorry, it's not exactly cold, and you haven't been into the bedroom in a while to see all the boxes in there."

"Shoulda known. It was all clothes and shoes, wasn't it?"

"Even I have to admit, I don't want to see any of it right now. I'm dead on my feet. I don't even care about organizing my closet."

Rick mouths an over exaggerated "wow" as I collapse down onto the couch.

"Have you ever noticed how Mom doesn't show up until all the heavy lifting is done?" I put my head back onto the top of the couch and let my eyes drift closed.

"Right, Kara, Mom would have had to have gotten up at, what, 6:00 a.m. to be down here with enough time to help?"

"Five if you count time to do her makeup." I take another sip of my coffee and look over to Rick.

"It's too bad Dad is out of town with work. He would have been here trying to show you how it's done. None of this 'let Kara get the other half of the couch' as we climb three flights of stairs. My poor couch, it was so pretty once." I turn my head toward the large scrape mark on the top of the couch and gingerly pet it.

"Do you hear a phone ringing?" Rick looks over at me grimacing.

"Shit… Where's my cell?" We both force ourselves off the couch and start moving boxes out of the way in hopes of finding my phone before the ringing stops.

"Found it! It's Mom." Rick tosses the phone at me. The pillows in my hands fall as I reach out to grab it.

"Figures, it's like she knew we were done unloading the truck. Do you think she was watching and waiting?" I have to hold in the laughter as I pick up the phone. I swear she would know we were making fun of her.

"Nice timing, Mom, the truck is empty."

"Ha-ha, Kara," she replies dryly. "Get down here and help me. I've got groceries."

All it takes is me mouthing the word *food*, and Rick is out the door and down the hall to help her up with the bags. Nothing can move that man quicker than the promise of a decent meal.

CHAPTER 2

I reach for more...just a little more.
The sound the bottle makes as it hits my glass;
it sounds like keys clinking together.
This is my trophy now.
One deep sip and I push my empty glass back onto the table.
As my eyes close, I hear the pills fall to the floor.

The first couple of days on my own seem to fly by. I spend most of my time trying to get my apartment put together and organized, then reorganized; and on about the tenth attempt, I give in and finally decided to be done. Who knew there were so many different ways you could rearrange what is basically a 650-square-foot box.

We'll go with cozy instead of small; cozy sounds so much better. The walls, in my cozy little box, are a renter's white. The floor is made up of renter's beige carpeting, but the cabinets are a modern dark espresso, and there's some granite-looking thing on the counter-top. At least the lights aren't brass. Does that make me seem bitchy, being glad that if I have to live with white walls at least I don't have brass lights? Rick would say it made me "snooty," snooty like some old-fashioned insult, "me and my snooty non-brass lights." I did get lucky though. I have a walk-in closet, and my view isn't of the El tracks.

When I wasn't unpacking, I was exploring. It's just too hard not to be outside—April, and it's eighty degrees in Chicago! I mean, how does one not go to the beach and go out shopping? It's not like I haven't worked in the city for a while now, and I have always lived close enough that I could come downtown whenever I want; but living down here is a completely different feeling.

The suburbs move slowly in comparison; even when you have someplace to go, the pace is just a little less rushed. If you don't know someone that you are passing by, you probably know someone who does. There is a friendliness that comes with that. It's like everyone is a potential friend or enemy. Down here, it just seems like everyone is a stranger and will always stay that way. No one even makes eye contact as they pass each other, at least no one you would want to. As rushed as it is, it feels more alive. There is a pulse to city life that is hard to explain. It's in the people, the buildings, the pigeons that are everywhere.

It was while I was exploring that I literally walked right into Katie; I was looking up, enjoying the clouds playing peekaboo between leaves on the trees and smack. I was expecting some kind of muttered insult hissed under her breath as she rushed by me, but instead as I muttered sorry, she was laughing.

"Guess that makes two of us that could use some coffee."

That was it, instant friend.

That was two days ago. It's Monday morning; and if I try hard enough, I can still feel the warmth of the sun on my face, although that could easily be the sunburn. The light above my head in the bathroom only seems to make the burn glow even brighter. I'm desperately trying to use makeup to make my newly acquired sunburn look like it could belong to someone professional instead of some idiot who fell asleep on the beach. If I add anymore foundation, I'm going look more like a clown and much less like the financial wizard I want to be. One last look in the mirror and I give up; there is no way to hide the sunburn. My only hope is that I'm not the only one at work who was mesmerized by the first eighty-degree day of the year. I gingerly put my purse over my aching shoulder and grab my cell. It's hopeless to try to get a signal in the elevator, so I'll have to wait until I am walking to the El to try and call Katie. I don't want to be the only one suffering with this sunburn.

"Hey, Kara." Katie sounds far too awake for someone who mainly works nights. Her job, working with a talent promoter for the clubs, sounds so much more exciting than the stack of trade trans-actions that I have waiting for me this morning. I lose myself in the mindless conversation as I walk the rest of the way to the El stop.

It's pointless to try to hear yourself think on these damn El trains, let alone try to hold a conversation. Stepping to avoid the idiotic, overly friendly men that always seem to take the same train as me, I hang up with Katie and climb aboard to wedge myself between other women, ensuring the idiots can't sit next to me again. So fine, not everything about city life is roses and cupcakes, but idiots are everywhere; I'm pretty sure it's not exclusive to the brown line. I'm left with a fifteen-minute ride staring out the window lost in my thoughts, still much better than the car trip from the burbs. Maybe now that my commute is only fifteen minutes, I can find the time to join a gym. It's the city. There seems to be one on every corner. Gyms and Starbucks, it's kinda like the burbs with churches and liquor stores.

CHAPTER 3

There's noise. Over and over again...noise.
It's trying to pull me out of the fog.
Somewhere close by there is ringing...
It won't stop ringing.
I try to get up, but I can't; I push myself up
with my arms only to fall back down.
My head is so foggy; I try to focus...
My eyes close...

It's dark and drizzling, a moonless night. The lights from cars that pass dance as reflections off of the wet pavement and darkened windows. It's the kind of night that love stories are made for.

Somewhere wandering through the streets of Paris, having just been stood up by the man she thought would have been the love of her life, a lonely girl glances down into the river Sein as if to reevaluate her life and the direction it was taking. Unbeknownst to her, a handsome man approaches, her perfect man.

But that would be the script if this were a movie. It's not, it's just life. There is no man; no date to be stood up on. It's just me and a couple bags of groceries going home to eat dinner and read a book on a Saturday night.

Don't get me wrong, I like a quiet evening at home. Getting to enjoy a night to myself, I think it's healthy every once in a while, to just be. Pulling my groceries closer to my chest to keep out the cold and wet, I round the corner, thankful that I'm almost home. Spring is slowly coming to an end in Chicago, and as usual, that means anything goes. It could be hot with sticky humidity or cool and raining like tonight. Sometimes it can be both on the same day. Thankfully, the grocery store is only about a three-block walk to my apartment. I don't know how people do it when it's farther. It took me some time to get used to this part of city living. I miss driving to the grocery store, throwing everything into the trunk, driving home to my garage, and not having to walk blocks with bags of groceries. I'm used to it now though, shopping more often so I don't have to bring home bags and bags worth of stuff. My first trip home I had way too many bags and dropped nearly half of my groceries onto the street. It was horrible. Now I'm able to laugh at it, but at the time, not so much.

I've gotten used to living on my own. It's all about the little tricks like grocery shopping more often. I still miss Rick, of course, but I also get to see him at least every other week for dinner at my parent's house. Life is pretty good. I've determined it's all about finding the perfect balance between work, time with friends and family, and me time, which is exactly what I have planned for tonight.

The two bags of groceries I carried home have left tiny drips of water leading like a trail through my living room and into my kitchen. The wine is chilling in the fridge, and sushi for one is waiting for me on the countertop. I walk into my bedroom to discard the day. After coming home through the rain, nothing seems more inviting than a hot shower. Tossing my clothes onto the bed, I head into the bathroom.

The heat of the water is everything it promised to be. I can feel the stress of the workweek fade away, slowly dripping from my shoulders as the water hits the floor. I don't want to move; I'm enjoying this far too much. I stand in the shower until the chill is removed from my bones. Once the water begins to cool, I get out and dry myself off. I'm walking back into my bedroom with a towel wrapped around my head when the phone rings. I know it's Rick; I think not knowing where I am all the time is driving his older-brother-protective-streak crazy. He has taken to calling me on Saturday nights before dinner to find out my plans "just for safety reasons," or so he claims. Secretly, I wonder if my mom has put him up to this, if she's still clinging to her concept that a woman shouldn't live alone in the city, or anywhere else for that matter.

Reluctantly, I answer the phone. "Hey, Rick, give me just a minute I'm just getting out of the shower." I toss the phone onto my bed, and it settles between the pillows. I quickly pull on my favorite old sweats and T-shirt combination, the same one I wore the night I moved in two months ago. I take a quick minute and dig the phone back out from its hiding place. "Sorry about that. What's up?"

"Just wanted to see how my baby sister is, what she's up to in the big, bad city."

"Uh huh, you know I figured this out months ago right?" I know there is an edge to my voice, but I don't really care.

"Don't worry, I'm not going anywhere tonight. It's cold and raining. I'm just going to stay in with a good book and a bottle of wine. But since we are so concerned about members of our family being out without prior knowledge of their plans, what is it that you will be doing tonight?" I take a deep breath; I can feel my frustration boiling over. "I would love to call the parents of the people you will be with to ensure there will be no girls or underage drinking. Oh wait, we're adults now and that shit is long gone back to the days of high school."

"Are you done now?" I can tell he's trying to keep from laughing at me. He knows me too well; laugh at me now and the phone will be launched across the room, and you can fuck next Saturday's call.

"Yeah…I know I rant. But I know it's mom doing this, and it just kills me. I'm a grown woman, Rick. Why is she still pretending I'm twelve, and it's 1950?" I lean back onto my pillows, pull my knees up, and get comfortable. My wet hair is clinging to my T-shirt; I really should have waited until after Rick called to get in the shower.

"So this couldn't just be me wanting to know you're all good? It is kinda my job as the older brother and all."

"Don't worry, Rick. I will still let you beat up a boy that breaks my heart and put the fear of death into the ones that don't. But other than that, you have got to let me be a little. It's demeaning to be watched like this. It makes me feel like you and Mom don't trust me to not fuck up. At least wait until I make a mistake before you all act like this okay?"

"Okay, okay, Kara…I hear ya. Just promise me one thing, if you do have a date, you give me the guy's info first and where you will be. And I get a text when it's done."

"Would you like his shoe size or just his name and driver's license number?" I can't hide the sarcasm in my voice, not that I'm really trying to.

"Kara, I'm serious. Look I'll even do the same thing okay. That way, you can't pretend that it's a sexist thing."

"Fine, but please talk to Mom before I kill her, okay?"

"Deal. Love ya, sis. Enjoy your book."

"I love you too." I hang up the phone and walk back into the kitchen.

That phone call killed my nice post-hot-shower relaxation. I open the fridge to grab my wine, but nope, I think after that phone call something a little stronger is going to be needed. I grab the vodka and start to whip up a Katie martini. I'm sure it has some fancy long ass name, but for my purposes, Katie martini works just fine. I lean back and enjoy the feeling of the vodka as it slips down my throat, the way the warmth spreads from stomach back up to my head. A few more sips, and I'm starting to relax again. I make the decision to put Rick and Mom out of my head and just enjoy the rest of the night, the way I had originally intended. This was my "me night." The whole purpose is to forget the shit and just relax.

I have a tradition on a night light this, a "no one is watching, pure joy in the moment" kind of tradition. Turning on Adele, while carefully holding my martini, I let the rest of the anger and frustration, whatever it is you want to call it, melt away and I dance my way into the living room. This is me—silly, stupid, carefree, alone and in love with the peace and quiet that being alone brings. Despite my frustration with her, it's my mom's favorite saying that pops into my head. One I had to Google to learn more than just her favorite line, William Purkey's piece,

> You've gotta dance like there's nobody watching.
> Love like you'll never be hurt.
> Sing like there's nobody listening.
> And live like it's heaven on earth.

It's perfection, and it sums up my early post-shower feelings completely. I set down my drink, pick up my book, and flop onto the couch, full-on flop. In the distance, thunder crashes, and lightning sets my apartment aglow. I love a night like this.

I'm about halfway through *Under the Tuscan Sun* by Frances Mayes. My mental bucket list will now be including a trip to Italy. Venice was always someplace I wanted to visit, but the description of life in Tuscany has now moved pretty much all of Italy to the top of my list. I've decided that I could get lost in Italy, in learning the culture, the food, meeting the people and seeing how they live. Sometimes I wonder if I made a mistake by going into finance. It seemed safe at the time, a safe and steady income, a job that someone somewhere would always value. But it wasn't my passion. I love to learn about people, about culture. Sociology, archeology, anthropology, theology—basically put an "ology" on it, and I was in. I never went beyond a couple of classes while in college, being too headstrong to even think I could have picked the wrong major at eighteen wise years of age. But it has left me with a thirst to learn as much as I can about people.

I love trying to figure out why people lived the way they lived. How would I be different if I had grown up somewhere else? Learned something else? Believed something else? I love to analyze a situation. Rick and Katie think I'm crazy sometimes, that I put way too much thought into things, but I have always been comfortable in my own head. Figuring people out is like a fun game. And it keeps me from being surprised in life, keeps me from being hurt.

People are generally rational. Sometimes their rationale is based on emotion, but if you can figure out the why behind the action, the action itself doesn't sting as bad. The downside is that it hurts when people don't put the same effort into figuring you out, most of the time things that I think are so basic, so easy to see, and yet they are completely ignored. It's hard to remind myself that most people don't think the way I do. I know it's probably that they don't have the time in their lives to put into it, but sometimes I feel like it's more like I'm not worth that time. Sometimes I think it's just easier for people to assume Kara can handle it, that she won't let herself fall. As long as they think that way, no one has to be there to catch me, no one has to spend the time trying. Sometimes that makes life feel like a very lonely place to be.

Come on, Kara. I reach down to take a sip of my drink only to find that's it now empty. I have been on the same page of this book for the last five minutes while I have let my mind wander like this. That mind wandering anywhere it wants to is the downside to feeling too comfortable being in my own head; sometimes you don't like the path your thoughts lead you down.

Snap out of it, girl. Definitely time for another martini. I walk into the kitchen and change up my music, turning on a little Lake Street Dive this time. As I become a mixologist combining my vodka with a little of this and a little of that, I remind myself that this is why I love to read. It's also why I like to drink, this mind-wandering, forgetting-what-reality-looks-like thing.

First, I get to see how someone else lives, how they think. But mainly I just get to focus on something else, get out of my own head for a while. The streets of Tuscany had been providing the perfect escape, until my mind took over. I must have let too much time go by since the last time I did a "me night," my mind has some catch up work to do in the relaxation department.

This music is less like a dance my way into the living room and more like a saunter my way there, feeling awfully sassy I sing along while sipping my martini and sauntering my way back to the couch. My eyes drift closed as one of my favorite songs comes on, sitting on a stormy night alone with a martini and listening to Rachael Price sing about her neighbors making love upstairs. Life seems pretty damn near perfect.

CHAPTER 4

*The fog is starting to fade; my eyes blink trying
to make sense of what's around me...
Life is feeling a little more real. I like it better the other way.
I force myself to roll over... I want more.
I reach for the bottle and take a sip.
It hurts, remembering the way life was. I don't want to remember the
good, to see how much I've changed...how much of myself I've lost...
I don't want to remember the bad either. I just want it to stop. I want
to turn it off like you turn off the TV or like you close a book....
I want to be foggy again.
I drink more, faster...the fog settles back into place.*

Katie's late for lunch; I don't know what part of me is surprised by
this. Today, however, it works for me; the reports are piling up,
and I could use a few more moments of work trying to dig my way
out from under them. The more I get to know Katie, the better I like
her. We're friends in the way of opposites. Katie is all bubbly person-
ality and "let me fill you in on the latest drama" kinda girl whereas
I'm more of a "let me sit back and observe, mull it over in my head"
kinda girl. She has a huge heart, and though I haven't known her
long, I think she's the kind of person that would get my back and ask
questions later. That's important to me. I think loyalty, real loyalty, is
hard to find nowadays.

Out of the corner of my eye, I see her blond ponytail bouncing
as she is practically skipping toward me.

"Kara!" She's out of breath and very excited about something. "I've met the man of your dreams. He's tall, maybe 6'2" or so, dark brown hair, and eyes that are so black and beautiful it's like a moonless night."

"Katie, stop it. You're the one searching for the man of your dreams. I'm more searching for the perfect bedroom set." I go back to the piles on my desk, trying to make them appear somewhat organized before we leave for lunch.

But Katie is still looking ahead, unfocused, dreamy. "I bet when he's up to something naughty, he gets a twinkle in those eyes. Umm, I bet he could be naughty."

"Uh… Okay. Earth to Katie! Focus!"

She gives me the perfect Katie disapproval stare.

"Look, Kara…I know you may not be searching for him. But if someone drops the winning lottery ticket in your hand, you're not just going to give it back, are you?"

I sigh. Sometimes Katie is a little too much.

"What am I going to do with you?"

"Take me to lunch." The smile on her face is infectious. I'm trying to pretend to be annoyed with her, but I know I'm smiling far too wide for that to be believable.

She's bouncing down the hallway back toward the elevator before I've even finished grabbing my purse and throwing my cell in it. I could really use whatever energy drink she must be sucking down. Just before she rounds the corner she stops and smiles.

I've learned to be afraid of those smiles. "I told him all about you. He just transferred to your office, some big fancy position, so I bet he's rich too." She ducks around the corner and into the elevator before I have the chance to find something to throw at her. Oh god, this could be bad. What if he's a boss or something? I try to control myself as I walk down the hallway after her, but my mind is already playing out the introductions in my head. This could get interesting. At least in my head, he's gorgeous, untouchable but gorgeous.

●●●

"Katie, seriously! How could you do that to me? What if he turns out to be my boss or something?" I have to shift in my seat to see her beyond the waitress blocking my view as she sets down my salad. Instead of waiting for an answer, I watch, silently, as the waitress walks back into the small café where we're eating. The weather has officially turned to a Chicago summer, and I couldn't be happier. People rush by as we sit only three feet away, separated by a simple black rod iron gate. Our only sense of privacy is provided by the angle of the oversized umbrella that rises from the center of our table to block the glare of the sun.

"Kara, calm your ass down. I swear you could turn anything into something to freak out about. If he's your boss, then at least now he'll remember your name and be on the lookout for you. Someone might just see how hard you work at that place and give you the promotion you deserve. Oh, you're right, what a tragedy! This is definitely something worth keeping you up at night. You should probably just quit now."

How do you even respond to that? I use my salad as an excuse and stuff some lettuce in my mouth to avoid answering her; but I give her my best angry glare as I chew.

In pure Katie fashion, she uses my lack of response to keep talking. "Would you just relax already? Maybe something will come from it, maybe not. I know sure as shit that nothing will come in life if you do nothing. Aren't you the one always telling me that? Telling me what my next step should be? Telling me if I want a change, I have to change something."

"Ya, but Katie who says that I want change?" I've interrupted her rant, and now I'm talking with my hands, a sure-fire sign that I feel under attack. "I've done the whole relationship thing. I suck at it…or they do…or something. I just know whenever I try, whenever I really let some guy in, I end up regretting it later. I just moved down here. I'm trying to make sure I don't regret that decision. The last thing I need is another decision that could lead to disappointment."

"Are you pissed you moved down here?" The tone of her voice is softer now, but just by a little bit.

"No, but…"

"No buts, Kara. You took a big step. You pissed off your mom, stood your ground, went after a dream, and are loving the results. You stepped off a cliff and flew. Well, here's another cliff. You can let it stop you, or you can fly."

"Or I could fall."

"Well, look at the girl who talks all big when it's someone else's life. Talks like fear is something to laugh at from higher grounds."

"Ugh…Katie, stop it. I can't take it anymore. Fine; nothing may happen, something may happen, and who the hell knows what, why, or how, okay. You won't hear me mention it again."

Deep breath, Kara.

"It's just not worth it." I smile up at Katie so she knows she's been forgiven and am met with her laughing at me in return.

"Damn right, and don't you forget it. It's never worth arguing with me."

●●●

My daily to-do list is only half crossed off, and quitting time was already two hours ago. This day feels like it's never going to end. I haven't seen Katie in two weeks and just had to cancel our plans for meeting up later tonight. The office, or at least my little part of it, has been empty for some time now. The nice part of that is it means my music can be turned up, and my shoes can be kicked off; but if I'm going to survive this mountain of reports, the coffee will need to start flowing and soon.

I know it's something so simple, so basic; but I love the feel of a hot mug of coffee with my hands wrapped tightly around it. I love watching the color turn from black to beige as cream is poured in, and I love the moment when you first feel the small burst of energy as the caffeine finally kicks in. My eyes close, lost in the feel of it all, as I walk back to my desk, probably not the best idea I've ever had. But if I had to physically see the chaos of work around me, my little moment of peace would be lost. Besides, I know how many steps it is to my desk, how many before I turn, and when to sit.

I reach my cubicle, and with eyes still closed, I find my chair and sink into it. A few more minutes of peace, a few more sips, and I will acknowledge my workload again, just not yet.

"Well, that was impressive." His voice is smooth and deep, sensual and just enough to put me into a panic. Who the hell is here to have just seen that? And thank God, I didn't wipe out! My eyes blink back at the sudden influx of light while trying to make out who the unnamed face is in front of me. As he slowly comes into focus, I'm glad I've already swallowed any last coffee in my mouth as I'm sure I would have spit it all over him.

Holy perfect. Not magazine cover perfect because that would be someone else's definition of what a man should be. No, this is my own personal wish list taken out of my head and sculpted out in front of me. I can feel the blush warming my cheeks as I run over my appearance in my head. A pen is shoved behind one ear. My hair is everywhere after running my hands through it all day in frustration. My shoes are lying under my desk, and my feet are tucked up underneath me.

Meanwhile there stands my personal definition of masculinity—tall, dark, and oh my god! His eyes are dark, damn near black, damn near the exact color of his hair, and they look back at me with such confidence. His skin looks like someone who spends exactly the right amount of time outside, just enough color, just enough of a glow. He's leaning, relaxed, at the side of my cubicle, blocking far too much of his body for my liking. The one arm that reaches over the side is thick and muscular, one large and strong hand plays absentmindedly with the cup of pens on my desk.

I'm getting nervous as I realize I've been gawking at him a moment too long.

I shake my head in an attempt to break the trance. "Sorry, I thought I was alone up here."

"I didn't mean to interrupt. It's just, a feat such as that, was something I couldn't let go without commenting on. My name is Stephan by the way."

"No." Shit, did I just giggle? A giggle, what am I twelve years old?

Deep breath, no giggle and try again.

"I could use a little interruption. I'm Kara."

He stands a little straighter and smiles—oh dear god, his smile.

"Kara, huh… I think I've heard about you."

It's something about the way he says it, about the twinkle in his eye. I suddenly know exactly who he is and how he would have heard about me.

My mind rushes back through the past couple of weeks, back to the blond bouncing ponytail. I'm going to kill Katie!

"Oh god." My head automatically dips, and my hands reach up to hide the expanding blush that has consumed my face. "I'm gonna kill her." I'm not sure he could make out the words at this point as I'm talking more to my hands than to him.

His laugh is soft and filled with humor instead of even an ounce of anything mean. I feel his hands wrap around mine and gently pull them away from my face. I can feel the heat of his skin on mine, and I like it.

"Blond ponytail girl? Don't go too hard on her. I thought it was sweet. I have to admit it's had me intrigued ever since trying to figure out just who she was talking about. I'm starting to think she didn't do you justice though."

I can't help the look that I know crosses my face. I mean really, that one was a little corny. He smiles.

"Too much?"

"A little," I choke out as I reach for my mug, craving its comfort.

"How about something a little simpler then? I think we can do better than microwaved coffee. Care to join me?"

I think my little coffee break is about to get a whole lot longer. I guess tomorrow night will be for catching up on reports.

CHAPTER 5

I reach out as if he should be there.
But there is nothing to reach for.
My arm is limp as it falls back down, empty.
I feel empty.

A cool breeze is blowing through the open balcony door; it causes the flames on my candles to dance in the dark room. I've gone all out; my favorite collection of chick flicks are awaiting tonight's selection. Vodka is chilling. Brownies are cooling on the oven. Popcorn is ready to be popped, and nail polish is displayed on the table. My apartment is done, and it finally looks like a place that I could live in. Art work is framed and hung. There are candles everywhere. I have even coordinated pillows on the couch to match the artwork, and yes, I am proud of that. To celebrate the feeling that I have officially put "my stamp" on my apartment, I have Katie coming over for the ultimate girls' night.

Leaning back against the couch as our face masks tighten and our nails dry, I let the workweek melt away. Our third round of martinis sit damn near empty. So far, we've covered which new boots Katie should buy, the upcoming weekend wine-tasting trip we want to take, and what new style I should try for my hair. It's what we haven't covered that I know is killing her. I know, at any minute, it's coming, the inquisitions will begin. I'm loving making her wait, putting it off just a little bit longer until she bursts. It's far too much fun.

"So have you met him yet?"

I look over at her, giving her my best evil eye. "I could have killed you, Katie. I had my eyes closed when he comes strolling up. He scared the crap out of me. I thought I was alone in the office!"

She knows better. "Um, hmm, and…"

I take a moment. Stretching, I settle further into the pillows on the couch and try to empty the last few drops of my martini into my mouth, the least I can do to her is drag it out a bit. She's practically bouncing, one more exaggerated sip. "KARA!"

I can't help but laughing. "And he's pretty damn perfect, okay! I keep waiting to find out he keeps mummies in his closet or something. He's funny, he's sweet. He held the door open for me, and he pulled out my chair at dinner."

"And gorgeous, Kara, don't forget gorgeous. I mean, did you see his ass?"

"Katie!"

She's smiling up at me, thoroughly enjoying this. "So… dinner…"

"He took me to a little Italian place. It was perfect…candlelight, wine. I laughed most of the night away. He teases in this way that's fun and light, yet you can tell he could be so much deeper."

I know my voice sounds far too dreamy to be coming out of someone my age. I sound like a high school student with her first crush, not someone who's twenty-four.

"He has a confidence about him. Every move he makes he seems so sure of ahead of time. But he isn't the least bit egotistical either. The whole time we were out, he barely noticed anyone else. It was like we were in our own little world. It was great, Katie. I absolutely hate to admit it, but you did good, damn good."

"Yeah, well, it sounds that way. Guess I should just give up the day job and take over match making permanently."

She's lying on the floor with her feet up on the couch, wiggling her toes as the red polish dries. She swirls the last of her martini around in the glass.

"I wish I could have met someone for me." Her voice is quiet, wistful. She shakes her head as if to shake out the thought, carefully placing her smile back on her face she looks up at me. I try to make her laugh by offering her the invisible man I swear has been following me around. It's nothing but a feeling but one that, normally, Katie loves teasing me about.

She doesn't bite, rolling her eyes she focuses back on Stephan. "When do you see him next?"

"We're going out with a group of people from work on Thursday after we all get off. Does that count?"

"I don't know? Are you going as his date or just like you will both be there?"

"I think I'll be his date. I'm not sure. It's with a bunch of people I don't really know. They were all going, and Stephan invited me to join them."

"Sounds like you're his date to me. So yes, it definitely counts."

● ● ●

Scanning the bar for Stephan, I feel a desperation start to build; I can't find him anywhere. I'm trying to tell myself he just got held up at work, that he's not blowing me off already. People are looking back at me, the lonely girl in a room full of groups. With wishful think- ing, I look down at my cell to see if I missed a call. I keep my head down, eyes focused solely on the blank screen of my phone, as I walk past the staring faces. Mr.-All-That is trying, far too desperately, to get me to notice him leaning against the bar. Convinced that I have been ditched, and seeing that Mr.-All-That has started his boy band strut toward me, I make the decision to leave the bar and wait out- side. It's too stuffy in here anyway. It's a day of thunderstorms, and the humidity hangs in the bar and mixes with the smell of stale beer. Turning, I just miss walking into the darkest and most beautiful eyes I have ever seen, although I am getting to know them well. These eyes are smiling at me, well, more like they are laughing at me. I try to hide my embarrassment with a laugh of my own.

"That time your eyes weren't even closed. One of these days you're going to see me coming." He brushes the hair from my face and looks down at me.

"It was so humid and sticky in here that we decided to head to another bar. My phone died, so I couldn't call you. I couldn't even get your number out of it."

He leans in a little closer, and my whole being becomes aware of his every move.

"But I like it better this way. Now we can walk together to the other bar."

Stephan puts his arm casually around my shoulder and leads me out of the bar. The steady pace of the rain has finally let up, leaving a light drizzle behind. We walk silently, not an awkward silence, but as if in perfect peace with the moment, just enjoying the walk. I think back to the last rainy night I had, walking home with my bags of groceries, feeling as though I should have been in some romantic love story.

We're about two blocks away from the bar where the rest of the group waits when the sky opens, and the rain falls. I can't help the screech that escapes my lips as I leave the warmth of being tucked under Stephan's arm and run for cover. Water is dripping from my long brown hair as Stephan strolls toward me, apparently oblivious to the downpour that surrounds him. I'm sure that I now look like a wavy-haired wet dog—not quite the look I was going for when I straightened every last strand of hair this morning. He's smiling at me as he ducks under the window awning to escape the rain.

Just perfect, here I resemble a hosed-off Lassie, and he still looks amazing, even soaking wet. My clothes are tangled and hanging all wrong, and his just seem to be hugging every last muscle on his body. He leans toward me, laughing, while shaking the drips of water from his hair, adding more water to my already soaked outfit. I open my mouth in protest when without warning, he grabs my shoulders and gently presses his lips to mine.

At first, he's careful, soft, as if he's expecting me to stop him. Then he deepens the kiss and wraps his arms tighter around me. I'm lost in the feel of his lips on mine, the way his hand pushes into my lower back, the other hand wrapping around the base of my neck. I'm lost in the way my body melts perfectly into his, in the way he smells and tastes. He's like a mix of water and whiskey, deep and earthy. My world stops spinning. The rain disappears. There is only Stephan and I and this moment, and it's beyond anything I had spent the past two weeks imagining.

CHAPTER 6

Even asleep…even lost in these memories, I can feel it coming on.
My eyes open far too quickly.
I'm going to be sick. I can feel it in the pounding
of my head, the rolling of my stomach.
I reach for water…there has to be water.
I don't think I can make it to the bathroom.
I roll onto my side and push my feet to the floor.
I'm surprised that I can stand, proud that I can stand.
I take my first step and see the ground rush toward me.
That doesn't seem right.
My arm reaches forward…it's like slow motion.
I watch, I see it reach to break my fall.
I see…black.

Who would have thought that walking with eyes closed could lead to something as good as Stephan. There has to be some kind of life metaphor in that…some "blind yourself to the chaos around you and good will find its way in" concept. Slowly and with eyes closed, I lean against the kitchen counter and listen to the sound my nails make drumming against my glass. I feel peaceful, content seems too simplistic a word, too boring, but it's the perfect description nonetheless.

Stephan and I have been seeing each other for a couple of months now; I never thought my move downtown would lead to this. A relationship was the last thing I was wanting to focus on. I was all about proving to everyone else I could do this on my own, maybe a little of proving to myself. Now instead, I have Stephan. I still find myself waiting for the floor to drop away, for the fight that will wedge itself between us. It always comes, that fight that happens from being too honest, from showing too much of who you are. But being with Stephan calms me. It's like I can lean on him for the confidence I sometimes have to pretend I have.

Having him near me gives me something to focus on. It turns off the extra thoughts that can play havoc on my mind—the little things I find myself getting worked up over, the bills that are always higher than I think they should be, the days there seem to be no way out of the paperwork at the office, the hang-up calls at my desk that make me want to lose it. Stephan has a way of making all of it disappear the moment his arms wrap around me.

I know Katie feels slighted. I know I haven't spent as much time with her since I met Stephan. She has been nothing but supportive, but I think she's jealous too. We have gotten to the point in life where you want to have more than a weekend worth of parties to talk about on Monday. With her job at the clubs, I think she's starting to feel stuck in a life that is starting to pass her by. She has a new man in her life, and I only hope it's real, that it's not some guy just to have a guy. I drop my glass into the sink, close enough it won't break but far enough to hear it clink against the bottom of the sink. I have to be done daydreaming about Stephan and being concerned for Katie. I have to finish getting myself ready for a night with both of them.

Katie will be here in twenty minutes, and then the two of us are off to dinner. In a very jute box-soda shop-1950's kind of style, we will be double dating tonight. I know she is wanting my opinion of whatever his name is, and I'm really hoping to like him as my mind is already playing out the afternoon barbecues we'll have this fall. In a very Sandra-Bullock-movie type of way, I imagine bonfires with marshmallows browning on a stick and afternoon wine tours followed by a dinner at some quaint little diner. It would be great if I didn't feel like I had to pick between the two of them all the time, let alone the ridding I get from my family for missing too many dinners at Mom and Dad's.

●●●

I would be perfectly okay if the fire alarms started ringing, or maybe there could be a rolling blackout, anything to make this dinner date end. My ability to pretend, to play along, is quickly fading away. I don't know what she sees in him. It's not like he's bad looking, under different circumstances (like one where he doesn't open his mouth). I might have even found him attractive. He could never be hot; he tries too hard for that, but handsome maybe, brown hair that reaches just past his blue eyes. You can tell he works out, and it's obvious by his overly darkened glow that, when he's not running at the gym, he's lying in a tanning bed somewhere. I just never thought of Katie as someone who would date based on looks.

John.

He has that Vegas-like way of saying it, "I'm John," with one eye brow cocked higher than the other and that little side to side head bob. It's like he's watched one too many movies about Vegas sleaze balls without realizing they were being made fun of—not longed after. He plays with the ring around his finger as he talks, and when he laughs, it's deep and throaty. He sounds like someone who has smoked for half his life. As if that's not enough, I swear I know him, or at least enough of idiots like him, and it's driving me crazy trying to figure out which one it is.

Katie looks over at me with that "what do ya think?" look in her eye. I know when she excuses herself to use the washroom that I'm supposed to follow. I know it's so she can get my opinion of him. I know this, so I don't make eye contact when she stands. Instead, I feign a sudden interest in the cheesecake that is placed between Stephan and I.

The sad thing is, I don't have a reason not to like John. He's not really a jerk or anything. There's just some vibe about him that I can't stand. He would be fine for someone else. I just don't like him for her. She seems happy though, downright glowing whenever he gives her any attention. Maybe I'm being too protective. I mean, Katie found me Stephan, and I do want her to find someone just as special. Only, does it have to be him?

I reach under the table to find Stephan's hand. So far, all this double date has done is to make me appreciate my man that much more. Stephan is trying to make conversation with John. He's trying to find some common subject that they can relate on. So far, the conversation has covered football (briefly, John finds it "too simplistic"), construction (John would just rather hire someone than do anything himself), and music (shocking but John likes old school Vegas Rat pack. I'm not sure I believe he even knows who was in the Rat Pack). Stephan is still trying, but I have tuned them out; I take the occasional sip of my martini and mumble an "umm interesting" when it feels like the moment is right.

All I really want is to leave, to curl up into Stephan's chest, wrap myself in a blanket, and pretend to watch television while sitting on my couch. I want to fall asleep feeling the warmth radiating out of his body, to have him wake me with a kiss while laughing that I have fallen asleep yet again. We both know I will, but somehow he always acts surprised when I do.

"Have you ever been Kara?"

Shit.

I heard John ask the question, but I have no idea what the topic is. I look up into Stephan's eyes hoping for some help. He winks, knowing full well I wasn't listening.

"Yeah, she has mentioned it to me before. You loved Colorado, didn't you, Kara?"

Oh thank God. I nod my head up and down, a little to eagerly.

"It was great. We went in the summer though, more hiking than skiing." I try to smile at John as I talk. Instead of coming across as friendly, it just seems to egg him on more.

"John likes to go in the winter." Katie's chair screeches against the floor as she pulls it out to sit back down. "He's quite the skier."

"I'm sure he is." I quickly take another sip of my martini before the sarcasm in my voice betrays my real thoughts. I can almost feel the relief flowing from Stephan, skiing—finally something he seems to have in common with both of them.

Soon Katie and Stephan are off and comparing the slopes from different ski resorts they have stayed at over the years. John, it appears, doesn't have as much skiing experience as he has led us to believe. He shifts in his seat, uncomfortable that he can't seem to steer the conversation back toward how wonderful he is. As much as I would love to stay and watch his discomfort grow, I'm officially out of a drink; and if I'm to make it through the rest of this evening, I will definitely be needing more. Standing, I excuse myself to head to the bar for another martini.

"Can you get me one to?" Stephan looks up from his conversation with Katie. I'm glad at least the two of them seem to be getting along so well. I lean down with a "You bet, ya babe" and a kiss to his cheek. John looks from Katie to Stephan, and eventually his eyes fall upon me. Fearing he will decide he needs a drink as well, I start walking quickly toward the bar. I hear him talking as I walk away, thankful that he has decided his drink is full enough. I breathe a sigh of relief, a sigh of peace, as I round the corner. I'm not expecting the slap on the ass or the arm that flops down around my shoulder.

"Guess it's just you and me for the drinks, huh, beautiful."

Great, just great. I shrug out from under John's arm and mumble, "Guess so."

●●●

"Katie, I just don't see it. I mean he's fine and all I guess, but you could do so much better." I know I'm coming across like a bitch, but I can't help it. Last night's dinner disaster is still too fresh in my mind. I'm sure if this were a conversation we were having in person, she would be able to tell it's only out of concern for her that I say anything at all. Instead, the phone seems to steal any sign of empathy from my voice.

"What the fuck is that supposed to mean, Kara?" Her voice is flat, and there's no hiding the anger in it. "Gee, sorry, ya know, we can't all have the perfect man. So sorry mine couldn't be a Stephan."

"Katie, stop it. You know that's not what I mean. I just…" How do I even start explaining this without it sounding like an insult? Doesn't she see he's just a spoiled child who is trying to prove how special he is? I guess what I really want to ask her is why. Why does she have to have a guy right now? Why can't she just be Katie? Why is it not enough for her to just be her?

"I don't understand why." The words are out of my mouth before I can even realize that it's only half a question. It's not even clear to me how she's supposed to answer it. My-not-a-question is met with an angry puff of air. Great, now I've really pissed her off. Wedging the phone between my shoulder and ear, I pour a glass of wine in hopes it will help to take the edge off this conversation. My mind is racing with what to say next, how to fix this. Is there anything I can say to make her realize she's forcing a relationship just to have one?

"He loves me, okay, Kara. He treats me good. I would have thought you would have wanted that for me. You don't have to see it because I do. I thought you could have been supportive. I was excited to have you meet him, excited to have someone to double with, something we could share, but I guess not." The phone goes dead, and I know she's just hung up on me.

Great, Kara, just wonderful.

I refill my glass thinking of all the drinks Katie and I have had together, of nights spent on her couch or mine, deep conversations, and even deeper secrets shared. The phone sits on the counter like a beacon. The more I try to ignore it, the bigger it seems to grow until it's all I see. Dialing her number, I try to figure out what I will say if I can even get her to pick up. With my back pushed against the wall, I slide down until my butt is settled firmly on the ground. I hear the beep from her voicemail, but I can't seem to find the words. The phone lies facing the ceiling, still recording. The message left is the sound of me breathing and the sound of wine sloshing in my glass.

● ● ●

Rick can tell that something's wrong. He won't come right out and ask, but I know he can tell. Mom must have called him; I don't know why else he would have called tonight. "Your sister." I can hear her now. "I only ask for one thing out of you two, one dinner a month, one time to see my family, to catch up with the people I love. Is that so much to ask for?" Yes, yes, it is. Today it is.

I just don't feel like going, sitting there, pinkies up, pretending that everything is great. That city life is like walking on a cloud, a noisy, overpriced, "filled with people who either stare or don't make any eye contact at all" kind of cloud. I'm pissed off and halfway to drunk, and that's never the right combination to be around my mother.

I can't tell her that things aren't perfect. I know it's stupid. I know that they must know things can't always be candy and rainbows, but it's like if I admit to anything less, it lets her win. It lets her sit across from me with that obnoxious look on her face that says, "See, you never should have moved away. It only leads to problems." So here I sit listening to Rick try that old "Just show up and deal. We all have to. It's worth it just not to hear about it later" crap. I want to scream no! No, it is worth it. I want to stomp my foot and yell, "I don't wanna go." Real mature, I know. So well, maybe it's the vodka that wants to do that part, but I won't argue with it.

I hang up with Rick, probably a little too quickly, a little too bitch-like. I can't even really remember what I told him, and that will suck tomorrow. It would help to know if I told him the truth or if I'm supposed to be sick. I pour another drink and become one with my shitty ass, self-pity mood.

It sucks questioning if things will ever be normal with Katie again, if I will ever feel like I can really just talk to her without having to overthink what I say. Stephan can tell how it's wearing on me, these past three days of her not picking up the phone when I call and not texting me back. When we're together, he just sits silently, letting me be in my own head as long as I need to. He's my strong, silent, unmovable man. He agrees with me that John is nothing special, and Katie could do a lot better. But he would be really stupid right now to disagree. He's my one light in this whole mess, my one happy place right now.

Happy, I can't stand that it takes me so long. I kinda hate it about myself; but I know I'm the kind of person that when one thing in life gets fucked up, it feels like all of life is fucked up, at least for a little while. I have to give myself time to be one with my mood, to surrender to it. Stephan seems to understand that, and although for me, there is normally no separating everyday life and a funk like this, this time there seems to be. This time, Stephan is my separate.

He is strong enough to be separate. He can hold off the "whatever he needs to" part of life. Just thinking of him makes me feel better, picturing his arms wrapped around me. My head rests against him. I stumble back toward my room lost in the thought of Stephan, of the way it feels to lay against his chest after we've made love. Listening to his heart racing, his breath slowly returning to normal, trying to make my breath match his same frantic rhythm, I lean back onto my bed, with lights off, craving the sound of his voice. I reach for the phone to call him, desperate for the feel of him, desperate for him to come over.

At first, I think the phone is dead. There's no dial tone, no noise at all. I'm about to hang it back up to try again when she starts talking.

"Hello?" Her voice is hesitant.

"Katie?" All the days spent hoping she would call; and now, now my mind is reeling, trying desperately to switch gears. Shifting through feeling gaga for Stephan, to the anger at her avoidance, to the frustration that all I was trying to do was look out for her, and of course, the "oh shit I'm sorry I hurt her." Countless phone calls to her, silently praying for her to pick up, and yet I never thought of what to say.

"John told me I should call." She's talking quickly, like she doesn't really know how to get it all out.

"He said I was throwing away a friendship that was too good to toss away. I just thought you should know that. Mister 'not good enough for me' is the only reason I'm even talking to you right now."

What the hell do you say to that? I want to shoot back just as hard, to yell, "I thought I was just being a good friend!" But I know if I did that, it would only make this fight so much worse. It just sucks to think of apologizing when I know I'm right. I know she could do better, should do better. Instead of going on the defense, I try to calm myself with a deep breath. I close my eyes and listen to myself breathing, counting, focusing solely on the breath. I can picture her holding the phone, waiting for me to respond. I picture John in the background trying to tell her to be patient. With one last breath, I start to say the words I know she wants and needs to hear. I say the closest thing to the truth that I can.

"Katie, I should have supported you. That's the bottom line. You like him and that should have been enough for me. I never wanted to hurt you, and for that, I am sorry."

"Damn right you should have supported me!" she's yelling now. "All I wanted was your damn support. You never heard me say what I don't like about Stephan. No, all I ever did was organize that whole relationship for you. If it wasn't for me, you would be alone right now, or did you forget that?"

The phone is like an anchor in my hand. It must weigh one thousand pounds. I can hear John in the background whispering to her, the tension in his voice proving to me this whole thing has been hard on Katie too. "Katie, relax. You don't want to lose her. You two need each other. Let her apologize."

I hate that he is going to bat for me. I hate that he is the reason she's calling now. I just hate this whole damn situation.

"Katie." I sound so small, so weak. "Katie, I am sorry."

I hear a long sigh.

"I know, Kara. I'll talk to you later okay."

I sit, long after she has hung up, listening to the dial tone, not really knowing what else to do.

CHAPTER 7

My wrist hurts. My head hurts.
I try to remember why, but everything is jumbled together.
Stephan. Did I see Stephan tonight?
I can't remember. My eyes slowly open, trying
to make sense of where I am.
It's dark.
I don't like the dark.
My heart begins to pound...

I'm dancing through my apartment listening to music as I finish setting everything up. I want tonight to be relaxed but easy. I've already taken out everything needed to pull it off—popcorn, bowl, soda and beer, so similar to the girls night I had spent with Katie all those months ago. It's kind of hard to believe that my life has changed so much in such a short amount of time, that I've fallen for a guy this hard.

Thumbing through the closet, it's clear I need to do some shopping. Jeans and a T-shirt is all I can really find. But he claims he loves me in a T-shirt, something about the way my neck hits my shoulders, the way my shoulders flow into my chest. Grabbing the shirt, I quickly throw it on. I bend over and run my hands through my hair giving it a quick shake for that purposely messy look, the one where you can't tell if someone was just fucked or if they're ready and waiting. I'm ready for him to get here, like now.

I wrap my arms around myself and imagine, just for a moment, that they're his arms. Looking into the mirror behind my door, I picture him standing there behind me. It brings a smile to my face thinking of how at ease he is around me. The other night, he was leaning against the bathroom door just watching me as I did my makeup, teasing me about how long it took me to get ready.

Beyond what I'm feeling, the missing him while he's gone, dreaming of him while I sleep, and thinking of him damn near every moment of the day, things became a little more real for me when he told me how being around me while Katie and I were fighting, it made him see just how quiet of a person I really am, how much time I can spend just being still.

No one sees that.

I'm sure it's something that somebody else wouldn't understand, but to me, it means he took the time to figure me out. He can see me for who I am without me writing it out like a script. He sees me, and he's still here. Isn't that everyone's dream? To be loved for who they really are by someone who really knows them?

We haven't said the word yet, but I think it'll be soon. I know I'm feeling it, and it kinda took me by surprise. I wasn't looking for love; I wasn't looking for him. I was so fixated on being on my own. Love, Mr. Right, that's all more of what my mom wanted for me. I mean, I'm still figuring out what I want for my life. I don't have it down completely, but I'm pretty sure it includes him. I think he's at the same point too. He's thirty-four, so he's been out on his own longer than I have. It seems like he already has what he wants out of life, but I think he's starting to include me in his future. Now I guess it just becomes the game of who will say they love the other one first.

Okay, Kara, getting a little deep here with the pre-date jitters. But it's only because I think I'm ready to tell him I love him, and I'm terrified by it. What if I'm wrong, and he's not feeling it too? What if he doesn't say it back? What if he does say it but only so I don't feel awkward? What if I scare him off? It has only been a couple of months since we met.

Breathe, Kara.

I need to calm down or instead of a relaxed night at home ending with I love yous and maybe some mind-blowing, "just said I love you" sex, I'm going to end up in the fetal position rocking back and forth as I give in to nerves. Katie martini special times two please.

Feeling much more relaxed, I flop onto the couch and wait for my man. Damn this can be easy, well, easy after a couple martinis. But this is how it is with Stephan; it's easy. Laughing, I think of my friends. Their dates seem to be hard, full of men who need to prove something. John is the perfect example. Look at my car, look at my clothes, and look at where I eat. See this drink; it is the drink of a man.

The conversation going on in my head is quite amusing, and I smile at the blank-faced suit I picture trying to be everything the world says he should be and being nothing at all. Stephan isn't that way. Feet on the coffee table, bowl of popcorn sitting nearby, his arm around me, and a movie on that neither of us ever watch—that's Stephan, relaxed and at ease with himself and his surroundings, confident and safe.

It seems like I have been waiting for him forever, but finally I get his call from the lobby. Leaning against the door, I wait for him to get off the elevator. I smile as he walks slowly toward me. When he's finally close enough, I grab his hand and pull him the rest of the way. He wraps his arms around me and presses his lips softly to mine. I feel the world stop spinning as I melt into his kiss.

"How's your friend?" I struggle to think of his name. Mike? Jim? Does it really matter?

He had taken the day to help this nameless friend of his.

"Fine, I got him all set up in time for the game tomorrow."

Pretending to panic, I can't resist the urge to tease him. "You mean he could have missed the Bears game. Thank god you got there in time."

"Funny." He's smiling as he strolls past me and sinks down onto the couch.

"It's a nice TV though. We may have to head over there to take in a game or two."

"Oh joy." I close the door behind Stephan before turning back around.

"So what are we watching, I assume it's not sports?" He's smiling up at me as he beckons for me to join him on the couch. "You know, I may just get you to be a football fan yet."

"Good luck with that. My brother's been trying for years." I nestle into his arms with my feet curled up under me. Straining my neck up to meet his lips, I find them warm; and waiting, he kisses me back. "We aren't watching anything, are we?" He smiles and wraps his arms tighter around me.

I'm leaning up against him, wrapped up in the heaven of his legs, my head pressed up against his chest. We breathe one breath, the rise and fall of our bodies are in unison with each other. So what if I'm a dork and did that on purpose? I like it. It makes me feel even closer to him. A movie is on in the background. I half hear it, half see the actors walk across the screen. I'm too in this moment, too lost in his arms to care who Jason Statham is trying to kill now.

"Kara," Stephan has taken one arm away and plays with my hair as he talks to the back of my head. "My mom wants to meet you."

As much as I hate moving, this is one I need to see his eyes for. Sitting up, I twist until I'm facing him. His eyes look far away. I was expecting to see something playful in his expression, but I see pain instead.

"What's that look for, Stephan?" I reach up, and my fingers barely touch his skin as they trace the crease that has suddenly appeared on his forehead. "I thought you were close to your mom? Why do you look…"

I hear him take a deep breath, our breathing is no longer in unison. He's looking through me, not really at me but more like at the wall behind me. "I'm worried about her meeting you." I can't hide the pain that is on my face, and I know he must see it. Why doesn't he want his mom to meet me? He brushes his hand across my cheek, but his eyes are still far away.

"For Mom, for so long, it's just been her and I. I'm not sure how she's going to take me being serious about someone." The last few words are spoken as one long sigh.

"Where's your dad?" The question is out of my mouth before I realize it, before I can be more careful about what I say. His voice turns hard.

"Dad left when I was twelve. He said he had enough. He couldn't pretend to love her anymore." He closes his eyes to hide the pain that I saw flash in them at the mention of the memory.

"But what about you?" *Damn it, Kara, stop with these damn questions.*

"He didn't need me anymore. He has a new family now…new kids I guess."

"He left you too?"

The look in Stephan's eyes turns cold, kind of an icy strength.

"That was a long time ago." Stephan closes his eyes, and I can see he's trying to calm himself back down. I don't know what to say, so I say nothing and just wait for him to continue.

"That's why I'm worried, Kara. Please don't think it has anything to do with you. I don't want Mom to think I'm leaving her too."

For a long minute, I just sit there looking at him. I can't imagine what that would have been like, what that would have felt like. I'm trying to figure out what it is I want to say, how to put all the thoughts and images running through my mind into words. Stephan pushes me back against his chest and wraps his arms around me once again. I know him well enough to know this is his way of saying he's done talking about it.

"She's flying to Chicago in a couple of months for Christmas. We'll plan something before all the holiday stuff begins. I told her I would ask you to meet her, and now I can tell her I have. Let's just get back to us."

I lay nestled up inside his arms. I feel like I have emotional whiplash. His mom wants to meet me. That's a big step. This information about his dad, how he was so honest with me, that seems even bigger. But I don't feel like I can tell him I love him now though. I mean, I love him even more than when I met him at my door two hours ago; but I don't want it to seem like I'm saying it to take the place of the memory of his dad, to take the place of the pain I know he must still feel.

●●●

We stand in the entryway of my building. I hate this part of the night, the part where I have to say goodbye. I don't want to pull away from him. He's trying to end the hug, and I just hold on tighter. I can hear the people behind me waiting for a cab stifle a laugh, but I don't care.

"Kara, I…I really do have to go."

"Hmmm…I can't hear you." I press myself even tighter against him.

"Kara." I can hear his smile in his voice. He takes his hand and gently tilts my head up so that he can look into my eyes. Reluctantly I start to let go. He's laughing again; I think it's at the pout that's set on my face.

"Thank you for listening tonight. I don't really like to talk about it, but thank you."

"Thank you for sharing it, Stephan." I reach up on my tiptoes and kiss his waiting lips. I want to nestle back into him, but I think he has other plans. He's still looking into my eyes. It's like he's trying to penetrate my soul.

"I'll never leave you, Kara. I'll never walk away. I won't abandon you."

"I know, Stephan. I know." I wasn't ready for this kind of depth tonight. Sure, I was ready for I love yous, but I was thinking more of the laughing, tickling, "just said I love you sex" kind of I love yous. I feel like I should have been better prepared for a deep honest conversation like this. I should have had something to share with him too.

I stand there, feeling kind of awkward, not really knowing what to do next. He's just looking at me as if he's trying to decide what he wants to say. The look in his eyes start to soften until they are back to the moonless night. Let me get lost in them, eyes that I'm used to. I think he's decided whatever it is he was thinking about because his shoulders relax just a little, letting go of tension I didn't even notice he was carrying. His arms wrap just a light tighter around me. He leans in to kiss me but instead whispers in my ear.

"I think I might just be falling in love with you."

What! I'm sorry but what!

Did he really just say that? I mean, I'm in jeans and a T-shirt for damn sake! Why this pisses me off, I have no idea. Didn't I put on these clothes planning to tell him I loved him? Didn't I pick these clothes because of how much he loves me in a T-shirt? But shouldn't I be better dressed for this moment, the first *I love you*? Jeans and a sidewalk, standing outside my building on a fucking sidewalk!

But this is who we are. We are jeans and a sidewalk.

I can feel myself begin to breathe again. This is the perfect moment, the perfect I love you. I can feel his words start to sink in. I've heard them before in my life, from different people, yet this moment means more than all of those previous times added up together. This I love you has more emotion, more real heartfelt meaning than any three little words have ever held before.

I look up into his eyes, and I can feel moisture starting to form in the corners of mine. I will not cry; even if it is tears of joy.

"I love you, Kara." His eyes are holding mine, waiting.

I realize I haven't said anything, and here he's just told me he loves me twice.

I smile a stupid, goofy "joy at the world" kind of smile.

"I love you too, Stephan."

Now there is no way I'm letting go of this man. The strangers on the street can go ahead and laugh all they want. I tuck my head into his chest and listen to his heartbeat; I'm totally and completely content.

"You know what this means, don't you?"

Huh? My mind draws a blank. I can tell I have a look of total confusion and maybe slight panic on my face as my eyes meet his. *Where is he going with this?*

"You'll have to tell Katie she was right. I really am the man of your dreams."

I smile, looking up at him. "I told her that weeks ago."

CHAPTER 8

My mind fights against the fogginess of sleep…
I hear someone close by talking.
But no one should be here. No one can see me…not like this.
Stephan? It's with a chilling fear that I realize it's his voice I hear.
"Hey, baby, it's me… We need to talk. Call
me when you get this. Love you"
It's the machine, just the answering machine… I
lower my head, and my eyes close again.
Love you.
Love you.
It echoes in my head. He would be so mad at me…

The sky is glowing green, threatening to soak me with rain as I step through the glass gym doors. There's something about the light right before a good Chicago storm. It's hard to describe to someone who hasn't been here to see it themselves; it's the way the sky seems to glow from within. It was one of the things I missed most about this city when I was away at college. I love a fierce storm, so this threat of a shower before I get home is only adding to my good mood. Today I managed to run five miles, and that's been a goal of mine for some time now. As a reward, I'm thinking sushi, a tall glass of wine, and enough alone time to finish the book I started last week.

I can't wait to be able to tell Stephan I finally did it. The day I joined the gym, I could hardly run half a mile. But between my time on the treadmill and promising myself I would walk to the gym from work instead of taking the El finally paid off. Stephan hates the nights like this where I am here later than normal, and I had to completely hide it from Rick, which I hate doing. He would kill me if he knew I was walking through half empty streets after dark, but what can he expect? It's Chicago. It gets dark at like four. What am I supposed to do? Lock myself up once the sun goes down?

Most days, Katie will meet me, and we try out different classes. Working out is never as much fun as trying not to laugh as your best friend is telling you how all her attention is going to not peeing on herself as you try some new fucked up Zumba move. There have even been occasions where the guys will meet us for a quick workout, although I hate being in a sports bra around John. It always feels like he is looking just a little too long.

Tonight was special though, just me, proving once and for all I can do it on my own. I set a goal with moving down here, with running five miles, with building on my career. Now I have all of that plus the love of my life, and I did it.

Me.

I pause to enjoy the moment just a little longer, eyes closed and head turned to the sky. The breath I take is a thank you to the universe, to God, to just being. I know I am blocking the door. I can feel it in the occasional hand that pushes me aside or whisper of words as people walk by. I don't care. I earned this moment. I deserve this interruption to their day. After one hand grabs just a little too much, pushes just a little too hard, I give up and move on. You almost have to plan your exit to make sure you don't walk into someone as you join the masses on the sidewalk.

The streets are crowded as people rush past, trying to make it home before the skies open and the cold October rain falls. Walking through the city at this time of the day always leaves me feeling a bit like cattle being led to the slaughter. In the day-to-day congestion of people, it's not rare to be run into or have an arm hit as someone passes you by. So I'm not surprised when I feel someone hit me from behind. It's the voice that throws me. I hear him whisper sorry as he skirts past; his voice is rough and throaty. It's cold and angry and sends shivers down my spine. I try to laugh it off, finding it pathetic that just a voice can manage to freak me out, but secretly I'm glad

I only have five more blocks to go. Turning the corner, I instantly begin to feel better. The street is dark but not overly crowded.

The few people that walk by have their heads down, trying to shield their faces from the cold autumn wind. It already feels more like home, less like the cattle drive. The occasional streetlight plays with shadows, and I've grown accustomed to the patterns they create. The sky has a tinge of green as lightning cracks in the distance, and the rain begins as a slow drizzle. I tilt my head toward the sky and watch the first few drops fall, fat with the weight of the storm to come. I smile, knowing the storm tonight will be a powerful one.

● ● ●

I picture the old evil witch from Snow White, the hand that reaches out with an apple. Only this hand is empty.

Dirty nails scratch at my arm as I'm pulled off the street and into the dark narrow alley.

Shocked, I yell out and try to push back against the faceless form hiding in the shadows. "What the fuck, asshole!" But the words are barely out of my mouth when my head is slammed against the bricks. I feel my body start to sway. I feel my heart begin to pound, and time begins to pass very slowly. My eyes flash black only to be followed by bursts of bright orange as I struggle against the stars forming behind them. I struggle to stay awake, terrified at what will happen next.

A knee pushes forcefully into my back pinning me against the alley wall. I feel a hand at the top of my head, and it forces my face further into the bricks as though it's expecting them to give.

Something sharp is cutting at my cheek, something in the wall.

His hand moves slowly down my head, leaving a trail of grime and sweat across my face like a dog marking his territory. It moves down my back and stops as he grabs me roughly. I force my eyes closed, wanting to block this moment from my life. It's not long before he continues to push his hand down my leg… It's fire, the feel of his hand on me is like fire.

"Hello, little bitchhh…"

His breath is dirty, and he smells of sweat and cigarettes. It's with a slow and chilling clarity that I realize it's the same voice that whispered sorry on the street only a few minutes ago.

A single tear escapes my eye and mixes with the blood from the cut on my cheek.

I have to move. My hands try to find a way to push against the wall, to push myself further into him so I can find the room to run. He just pushes against me harder.

"Tsk, tsk, little bitch"

I have to fight. I have to do something. I picture Rick silently begging me to be smarter, to be louder. Telling me if I can't fight, then I have to find help in someone who can.

I try to scream, but my voice is gone. His hand is at my throat. A new fear takes over as my mind begins to picture everything that could happen in the next few minutes.

"Do you want to scream for me, bitch?"

His words make me fight harder. Twisting and turning, I push back against him with all the strength I can muster, but it seems to do nothing. It's like I'm pushing against the bricks of the wall instead of a man. He forces his knee even harder against my back as he presses his lips to my ear.

"Do you want to die for me, bitch?"

I stop fighting. I stop moving. My mind stops working.

● ● ●

I'm sitting on the ground. My back pressed to the brick. My hands are flat against the pavement. I can feel blood dripping down my face. I watch as my hand reaches up to touch it. I watch myself as I lower my hand to look at the blood on my fingers.

It's slow motion. Life is slow motion. I'm alone now. I don't know how long I've been sitting, how long I've been alone. He left; he left me here, shoved against the brick.

I didn't think he would leave. I had started to accept that shoved against the brick would be my last moment, my last memory.

"Do you want to die for me bitch?"

I can't stop from shaking.

It's dark.

I hear a noise. Someone is coming.

My mind takes a moment to process this information before the panic sets in.

Oh my god! He's coming back.

Move, Kara! Move!

I want to get up.

I want to be ready to fight.

He's coming. He's really going to do it this time; do all the things he whispered in my ear. I'm watching myself. I watch as I sit, wishing I would get up, wishing I would fight.

I watch as I prepare to scream, as I prepare to die. I hear laughter. Now I start to really move. The thought that he's coming back, coming back but not alone, gets me moving.

I try to stand, but I fall. I'm making too much noise; he's only going to come faster now. But I can't seem to stand. My legs are Jell-O. I'm crawling now, crawling my way to the street; it's the only fight I have left.

I see them. Three people stop to look at me. I watch, and it's as if I can see what they see. I'm just a girl crawling down the alley, crawling to the street.

"Drunk ass bitch." It's not him. The voice, it's not him. I feel the blood return to my body in a wave of relief. It's not him.

The sky opens. The rain falls.

CHAPTER 9

Bitch...
Scream for me, bitch...bleed for me, bitch...
Drunk ass bitch...
Bitch...
Make it stop...

The words rattle around in my head, pulse with every beat of my heart. I'm drowning in words, in the talking of people on the street. I'm drowning in the hissing of his voice as it whispers in my ear. I'm cold, so cold.

I wrap my arms around myself, and I'm surprised to find that I'm still solid. I feel blurry, like a picture taken too fast, frozen in time but forever lost its shape.

I just want to be home, but I'm afraid of how to get there. I walk with my head down, shoulders slumped over as if they could protect me. I walk looking at the pavement, counting each crack as I step over them. I don't want to see the faces looking back at me.

What if he's there, what if he's one of them? He could be one of the blank faces watching me, and I wouldn't even know. I don't know what he looks like. He is a shapeless mass formed from the shadows, nothing but a black blob made up of nightmares. The not knowing sends a new wave of terror through my bones.

What if he's waiting up ahead, waiting for me again? I jerk my arm away at the mere thought of him grabbing me and end up elbowing some poor stranger on the street.

"Sorry," I mumble my apology as I keep walking, head down.

"Bitch," I hear her angry hiss as she passes me.

"*Bbbiittcchh…*" The wind blows cold against my skin. I'm shaking. I can't control the shaking. I can feel the blood begin to dry on my face. It itches, where my cheek had been against the bricks.

I feel the bruise forming on my back. It burns where his knee had pushed me against the wall.

"*Biiitttccchhh…*" hissing air like acid. *Do you know what I'm going to do to you, bitch?* I can hear him in the wind; I can smell him on my skin. He smells like my gym. I'm running now.

Just get me home, God. Please get me home.

● ● ●

I'm shaking so hard that my key won't fit in the door. Water drips off my arm and starts to form a little lake in the middle of the hallway. The other side of this door is warm. It's safe. I just have to get through this door. I stand alone, terrified that at any moment someone will walk down this hallway. Someone will see me. He might see me.

I'm desperate to get inside, desperate to force my key into the lock. I'm damn near manic with fear, and I'm pushing so hard I'm afraid the key will break in half. And that would leave me stuck here, on the wrong side of the door, the opposite of safe, alone and exposed where anyone can walk by. I lean my head against the wood of the door and focus on breathing, focus on trying to stop the shaking. *God, please.* All I need is one second, one easy little second to get the key in the lock and get inside. Tears begin to roll down my face as I silently pray. *Please, God…please.* I try to clear my mind and focus on the safety of my apartment, of knowing exactly how many steps to the table where I put my keys, how many steps until I reach my bedroom door. With one, last, deep breath, I shove the key into the door lock and stumbled into my living room.

A crack of lighting lights up the inside of my apartment, but otherwise, it's dark. I don't make it to the table where I keep my keys. I reach my hand up, lock the dead bolt, and I crumble, right there in the doorway. I fall to the floor. I curl up in a ball, just like when I was little.

It had always worked to calm my fears when there was a storm, when I couldn't climb into bed and nestle between my parents, but tonight it does nothing.

My parents…

My brother…

Some part of me is wanting to call them, to call Stephan, to have someone here with me so that I'm not sitting by myself, alone and in the dark. But I can't seem to move. I lay in a ball, and I can't force myself out of it. The events of tonight replay in my head like a bad movie. Everything he said to me, the threats, the promises of what he was going to do. The sound of his voice at my ear, the heat of his breath on my neck. Why did he leave me shoved against the brick? I don't understand. I thought I was going to die there in that alley. I really thought my last memory would be the feel of the cold brick against my cheek, the feel of him at my back.

It seems like I've laid here for days, how many hours that really equates to I have no idea. But I'm weak and cold and alone in the dark, just a ball on the floor. This must be shock, right? I feel trapped reliving every moment of tonight over and over again, trying to find something I could have done differently, something that would have stopped this night from ever happening.

I watch as I leave the gym. I watch as I walk down the street, totally ignorant of the danger that is to come. I see every moment as separate and complete. I'm stuck in this replay, totally stuck. There has to be some way I could have escaped him, some way I could have hurt him, instead of me being the one who bleeds. There has to be something I haven't seen yet, haven't noticed. But by the time my mind has caught back up with itself, by the time I watch myself collapse into this ball on the floor, I feel totally and completely drained of all energy. I feel drained of anything resembling life, and I hate it.

I hate that I'm shaking. I hate that I can't seem to control it. Every inch of my body is shaking, even the tips of my fingers are tingling. I can't get the smell of him off of me. My cheek itches, and my back burns. I don't want to be alone, shaking on the floor barely in my doorway. It feels like I'm waiting for him to find me here too. I know I should call someone, but right now the mere concept of seeing or even talking to anyone is just too much. I don't want to feel like this, and I don't want to be seen like this. I don't even want someone to hear it in my voice.

The occasional crack of lightning is my only sure way to tell that time is passing. Each time my apartment fills with light, just for a moment before the darkness takes back over, each time I can see the framed print that I have always cherished from my dad, "Do not go where the path may lead," it's laughing at me.

Look where my trail has led me. I tried to go out. I tried to leave the path and walk on my own. This is what I get for trying. Well, fuck the path and fuck the trail too.

I'll be stronger than both of them. I will bushwhack my way through the fucking jungle if I have to.

I'm still shaking, but this time, I'm shaking out of anger, out of pure rage. I stand up and walk through my dark apartment; head held high, and shoulders back. The glass on the frame shatters as it bounces off my renter's white wall. I walk through the tiny shards, listening to them crack under the sole of my shoes, and into my room. Crawling into bed, I'm emotionally drained, but I feel strong.

CHAPTER 10

I'm in the comfort of my room, in the safety of my bed, yet every time I close my eyes I see an endless stretch of old brown bricks. I see the crevasses that time has worn away and the dirt that has built up within them. I see his hand, his nails dirty and yellow, trying to scratch at me.

I won't close my eyes. I can't take what I see behind them. There are three spider webs that need to be removed in the corners of my ceiling, one blackened scrape across the wall above my closet door, and the light that is in the center of the room needs to be dusted. I can't sleep, and strong is the last thing I feel like anymore.

My knees are drawn to my chest. My arms wrapped tightly around them. I'm rocking myself as I lay here like a baby. All I'm missing are the tears, then I could truly hate myself for this moment of pure weakness.

Hate myself for being everything I despise in others, the weak little girl who cries to get her way, cries to get attention, the one who cries to manipulate others into acting how she wants them too because she knows they are afraid of her tears, afraid of her emotion.

I see myself lying here; I see myself as though I were someone walking in the door and looking down at me. I see myself. *God, please don't let this be me.*

I can't feel like this, and I don't know how to change it. I close my eyes, and I see him. I open my eyes, and I feel him. I feel his hot breath on my skin like a rash. I feel the burn his fingers left on my arm. I want him gone; I want his touch off of my body.

The water is hot as it cascades over me, hot as it pools at my feet. I'm scrubbing at myself; if I had steel wool, I would use it too. The water burns, and the burn replaces his touch on my skin with something new. My nails scrub at my arms, at my legs.

They scrub until it hurts and the pain starts to feel good, starts to feel like relief. Pain shouldn't feel good. But pain is okay, even the strongest person feels pain.

Now I'm scrubbing everywhere, scratching at myself with my nails as I clean him off of my skin. I scrub to the point of blood. Mesmerized, I watch as it drips off my skin.

"Bleed for me bitch…" I'm frozen as I watch. *"Bleed for me…"* No. *I bleed for me, asshole! I do this. Watch me. I bleed for me.*

It's peaceful, standing here, watching how the blood mixes with the water, how it makes patterns as it swirls. It reminds me of lying in a field and watching the clouds, trying to find pictures in their shapes.

I watch as the blood flows down the drain. I watch, and it calms me. It's as if it's his blood that pools at my feet, as if it's him that disappears down my drain. I no longer feel his touch on my arm. I no longer feel his breath on my skin.

I don't have the energy to leave the bathroom, let alone the shower. The steam that surrounds me seems to have taken any energy I had left. My back finds the wall, and I slowly allow myself to slide down until I'm sitting on the wet shower floor. It's a small space, and that works for me. My feet are flat to the ground, my knees drawn to my chest to warm me; I wrap my arms around them and balance my head against my arms. Embracing myself, wet, and raw, I somehow find the peace, the solitude, which had eluded me tonight. Maybe it's pure exhaustion. Maybe my mind has snapped. I don't care. One second my world is black, imageless and perfect, the next not so much.

My neck hurts, my legs are asleep, and I'm freezing. I wish there were a moment of fog, a moment of trying to remember where I am and why, a moment to remember that just a second ago, there was nothing: but there is no haze, no fogginess to my memory.

I know where I am, and I know why. My hair is stuck in clumps down my back, still wet but not to the point of dripping. I feel like an idiot for falling asleep in my shower, not to mention totally nuts. Who the fuck does that?

My legs don't want to cooperate as I try to stand up. I have to grip at the walls, climb my way out of my own shower. Grasping onto the edge of the sink, I wait as the blood returns to my legs, as the tingling gives way to steadiness. Carefully I comb out my hair and walk back into my bedroom. There are clothes on the floor, discarded from some other day. My room gives the appearance of comfort and warmth, but I can't lay in that bed again; I can't spend another minute staring up at a white ceiling looking for the spiders that belong to the newly found webs. I collapse onto the couch with a warm blanket finding distraction in the television.

It's 2:00 a.m., and sleep seems nowhere in sight. It's 3:00 a.m., and I'm scared to close my eyes. By three thirty, I cave. I need sleep. I want the black imageless world from a few hours ago back. The sun will rise soon. Rick is expecting me; we're supposed to have breakfast.

Stephan, we have a date. Stephan…I need to sleep.

I walk slowly to the bathroom. There are still traces of blood in the shower. Turning my head, I look away; I can't face that right now.

There must be something I can take. PM something, some flu, cold, gonna let me sleep, pill I can take, but there is nothing.

It's not until I'm holding the glass that I even realize what I'm doing. Am I really going to drink this? I'm an "Apple martini, tastes more like Kool-Aid, thunder cracking, good book reading" kinda drinker. I tentatively sip at the vodka, and it burns. I can feel exactly where it's at every second as it slides down my throat.

The first sip burns. It burns like the water from the shower. It burns, and I like it. The second sip soothes. I pour a larger glass and listen as the ice clinks off the side of it. It doesn't burn anymore.

●●●

I wake up to the sun shining in through the slots of my blinds; the vertical lines it creates reminds me of my first morning here. The stark difference between this moment and that one is overwhelming.

I'm on the floor. The glass is still in my hand. The sip I take is mainly melted ice, but I can taste the vodka too.

My phone is ringing. My head is ringing.

"Rick?" My voice cracks as I answer the phone. Shit, breakfast.

"You okay, Kara?" I can hear the concern in his voice. I'm not one to be late, let alone a no-show. "You sound like death?"

"I'm sorry, Rick. I have a killer headache."

My voice is now barley above a whisper. It's the only way to hide the guilt I feel for lying. Well, not so much lying as not sharing the total truth.

"I…ah…I must not have heard the alarm. What time is it?"

"About eleven. We were supposed to meet at ten thirty. I was getting nervous."

"I'm sorry. Can we reschedule?" I try to sound stronger, but I don't think it really works. I sit up, hoping it will help me to focus, to sound like I didn't lose it last night and drink myself to sleep after a quick nap on the shower floor.

"Sure, no problem, but are you sure you're okay?" I hate hearing the tone of his voice, the "I don't believe her but what else can I do" tone.

Do I tell him? I want to. I desperately want someone else to take these emotions from me, to watch them play out in someone else's head. If I could just give him some of this, just to make it easier for me to breathe.

I'm almost there, I'm almost ready to tell him. The long stretch of quiet confirms that Rick is waiting for some type of explanation. I slowly stand up, holding on to the arm of my couch as the blood returns to my head. I keep him waiting, pacing around the small room, ten steps to the wall, ten back again. The silence on the phone is getting awkward; I can almost hear Rick's impatience with each breath he takes. I open my mouth finally ready to start as I catch my reflection in the mirror hanging on the wall.

No. I don't even recognize the splotchy cut across her face, hair in clumps, and bags under her eyes, girl that looks back at me. He can't see this; no one can see this. I don't want to see this.

The breath I release is one of defeat. I close my eyes and pace in utter blindness.

"I can come over if you need me to, Kara. I'm going to come over. Do you want me to drop of some breakfast, some toast, or oatmeal?" I hear the real question mixed up within these other ones. I hear the concern. I hear the fear, the doubt, the "what's wrong with her," at least I think I do. But he *can't* come here now, see blood in the shower, smell the booze on my breath. He can't see the scratches that are like a road map of red crisscrossing over my arms and legs. I don't want to admit that this is me.

"No!" I'm sure he could hear the panic in my voice. Taking a deep breath, I try to sound calm.

"I'll be okay. But thanks, Rick."

I hang up the phone before he has time to argue with me. I hate that I've lied to him like this, and I hate that he didn't push what he clearly didn't believe.

I walk into the bathroom to splash some water onto my face. Flipping on the light, I see the splatters of blood in my shower. Quickly, I turn the light back off and sink to the floor, kicking the door shut as I reach the ground. I know that I'm sitting perfectly still. I'm in my home, and I know that I'm safe. But I'm shaking again. My insides are shaking, blurring as though they are not sure where reality lies, shaking as though I may break at any moment. I hug my knees tighter, hoping I have the physical strength to stop the shaking. But by now, I should know it doesn't help. I focus instead on breathing; each breath shows that I'm okay, that time is passing. I'm surviving on the hope that the further I get from this moment, the better I'll feel, that the shaking will eventually stop. I start rocking back and forth, and I'm surprised that the dark seems to help. I would have thought that the dark would just make it worse, but somehow the dark keeps me from seeing, seeing my surroundings and seeing my own face in the mirror. Shaking and rocking, sitting in the dark, this seems to be the new Kara. It seems to be all I am.

From far away, the phone rings, but I don't think I have the ability to answer it. I know I should; I can feel the thought forming in my head, *Get up, Kara. Pick up the phone, say hello.* I pause, momentarily, in my childlike, "baby in a momma's arms" rocking. I pause long enough to look at the door, to picture where it is the phone lies after I hung up with Rick. But by the time my body catches up with the thought to stand and walk into the other room, the phone has stopped ringing.

● ● ●

I feel like an idiot sweeping up the broken glass from the frame I shattered last night. I loved this stupid little picture; I had carried it with me since high school. That asshole made me break something I loved. I hate that I gave him that power. I've never felt hate like this before. It burns in me so much hotter than his fingers had burned on my skin. It's a soul crushing, anger-fueled hate. I hate him for making me feel scared, for making me feel powerless. I hate him for making me lie to Rick this morning. The hate, the rage, it might be the only thing that is making me move right now. It's taking on a life of its own. It's not Kara that takes a step. Kara is still shaking, is still blurry. It's the hatred that walks, the rage that cleans. I take the broken glass straight to the garbage shoot in the hallway. I don't want it in my apartment. It's something he caused, and I don't want anything about him near me.

I walk back through my apartment door and into the kitchen. My thoughts are singular and focused. Last night only one thing made it stop. Only one thing made it better. I need my heart to stop pounding; I just need to be able to breathe. I have two choices, only two, and I don't want either. The rage keeps me moving. The hatred knows my plan, hatred at him, at me for feeling like this. I don't give myself time to think it through. I don't want to stop long enough to question it. I pour the cool liquid into the glass and bring it straight to my lips, swallowing it in as few sips as I can stand.

● ● ●

It's 1:00 p.m., or at least that's what the clock in my kitchen says. I find myself questioning that. Rick said it was eleven when he called. There's no way I spent two hours sitting on my kitchen floor. Reluctantly I get up and check my cell; not only is it really one, but I have two missed calls, one from mom and one from Rick. I don't have it in me to call either of them back or even listen to the messages. I'm not really sure I even have it in me to see Stephan tonight, but I long for the feeling that being in his arms brings. There has never been a place I felt safer then when wrapped in his arms. I crave that feeling right now. I need to feel safe.

I have five hours before he gets here. I sit on the corner of my bed. *Do I tell him? How do I not? How would I even go about hiding this?*

Looking at my reflection in the mirror, I question everything. My hair has the look of someone who slept with it wet. My eyes have the hollow look of someone who didn't sleep at all. I have a bruise that starts at my cheekbone and angles down to just below the edge of my nose. There is a matching cut that seems to outline the top of the bruise as if it wants to draw even more attention to it. I close my eyes and focus on breathing. I don't want to see anymore. I know my arms have scrape marks from where my nails scratched at them in the shower. I'm sure that under my pants, my legs look the same.

I can't see him tonight; Stephan can't see me like this. I don't want to know how he would react. I couldn't hide the scratch marks, the bruise. He wouldn't want someone like this. He wouldn't want it. I want him here like I have never wanted anything before; for the sake of my own sanity, I need him here. But I can't; he can't. I just can't let him see this. I'm a mess right now, physically, emotionally, and there is no way to hide it. I need a few days before I can keep it in, just not yet. I told Rick I was sick; it would be easy to do the same thing to Stephan. It's Saturday afternoon. That gives me the rest of today, and all of tomorrow before I have to pull it together enough to see him at work.

CHAPTER 11

I try not to think about my decision as I pick up the phone. If I think about it, I'll change my mind. If he were to come here now, if he were to see me like this, I have to force my thoughts from progressing any further. I can't face my reaction from last night, my reaction this morning. It just shows how weak I really am; it shows that I'm not strong enough for any of them.

The phone rings twice before Stephan picks up.

"Hey, baby." Just hearing him speak, the breath I didn't even know I was holding in is let out as one long, deep sigh. I can hear the happiness in his voice that it's me calling. I picture him sitting at home. It's the afternoon, so he would have just finished his run after getting to sleep in this morning. I picture his dark hair wet from the shower, his shirtless chest glistening with the water that drips from his hair. I picture his bare feet up on one chair while he sits on another, a cold glass of water in his hand. This image of pure relaxation, of calm and of strength; it makes me want him here with me all the more.

But the picture changes. I imagine myself standing behind him, half hidden from view in fear of someone seeing me right now. I see the cut on my cheek, the blank look in my eyes, my hair hardly combed. It makes me shiver to picture the differences between us right now; it makes me feel sick to my stomach. I have never felt so distant from him, and it makes me hate the alley man that much more. The hatred gives me the strength I need to lie.

I take a deep breath. Putting on my best "I'm fine, and I swear I'm not losing my mind" voice, I prepare myself to outright lie to the man I love.

"Hey, honey." *Stay calm, Kara.* "I think I'm going to have to cancel on you tonight."

"Why? Is everything okay?" I hear the concern, the slight edge in his voice. I'm going to have to do better than this if he is to believe nothing is really wrong.

"I'm okay, just…not feeling all that great." Reaching up, I touch the cut on my cheek; this is going to have to be explained somehow. It won't be gone by the time I have to go to work on Monday.

"I fell at the gym yesterday when I was done running. I got my five miles though." I try desperately to give him something else to focus on. After all he had been the one helping me to reach my goal.

"You fell?" The concern I already heard in his voice has multiplied. "Are you okay? Did you see a doctor or file a report at the gym?"

"No, relax, I'm okay. I just cut my cheek a little that's really all." I'm trying to downplay the fall concept to keep him from panicking, but now I'm also killing any excuse I had for canceling on him. I take a deep breath. It's harder to lie to him than I thought it would be.

"It's just my head's killing me, and I didn't really get to sleep at all because of it last night. I don't think I would be good company. I'm sure I'll be fine by tomorrow or Monday." I spit out the last part, afraid that he would try to reschedule our date for tomorrow night, and I need the extra time to pull myself together.

"Kara," I can hear the disapproval in his tone. "You probably have a concussion. That's why you have the headache. You should have filed a report and gone to the hospital. You should have at least called me."

"I'm sorry, Stephan."

Wait, am I really apologizing right now? It makes me feel like I'm apologizing to him that this whole damn thing happened, apologizing for the man in the alley like it was my fault, and that does nothing but piss me off. I can feel the anger starting to rise in me, and it takes me a solid minute to calm back down.

"Look, I'm just not feeling good. I'll see you at work on Monday okay. Love you." I hang up the phone before he has the chance to say anything else. But it's already ringing again as I open the fridge door.

Closing my eyes, I focus on the concept of just one more. I need one, one more to help control the rising anger and the bitter taste of my apology on my tongue. I let the phone ring as I pour the vodka over the ice, and it's amazing to me how quickly the sound of the ice clinking off the glass calms me. I almost don't need the first sip, but I take it anyway. Feeling better, I reach out for the phone. It doesn't take a genius to know it's Stephan. I don't say anything as I answer.

"Hey, relax, okay? You just told me you have a headache, and the last thing you need is me yelling at you. But you really can't ignore it if it's a concussion."

I have nothing to say. What can I say that would work with this lie? I'm not really mad at him. I know it was never him I was mad at to begin with, but my silence must make him think I'm still angry because he keeps talking.

"Please understand, baby. I'm just worried about you. If you have a concussion, you really need to watch yourself. I know you're not feeling good, that you're worried you won't be good company, but I'm coming anyway. I love you, and part of that means that I want to take care of you when you need me. You don't have to entertain me or worry about what type of company you'll be. You can just lay there, read, sleep, whatever, I don't care. But I'm coming."

He hangs up the phone before I have time to think of anything to say that can keep him away. Shit.

I stand in the kitchen holding my glass completely freaking out. Is he coming now? Or is he keeping our original date and coming tonight?

Thankfully I had swept up the glass; I had tidied up at least a little. Trying to combat my racing heart, the feeling of time speeding up as I stand still, I slowly finish my drink and carefully wash the glass, as if trying to wash away what I was feeling as I drank it. I hide the half-empty bottle of vodka in the back of the fridge, not that he would notice how much was missing; he didn't know I had just bought it.

I throw my hair in a ponytail and find a long-sleeved sweatshirt to hide the marks on my arms. Thank God it's October, and the longer clothes make sense. I add a pair of heavy socks and try to put some makeup on my cheek. But the bruise hurts to touch, and I start to worry that the makeup getting into the cut could cause an infection. I settle for lining up a row of Band-Aids horizontally across my cheek. I look like an idiot with them there, but I'm past the point of really caring.

Just as I step out of the bathroom, I hear the phone ring. I'm silent as I pick it up. I still have no idea how to handle him being here right now.

"Hey, baby, I'm in the lobby. Can you buzz me up?" I take a deep breath and try to steady myself. I'm supposed to have a headache and be exhausted, so I don't have to be perfect. I just have to make sure I don't fall to pieces.

"Ah-huh." I push the button that lets him up and stand holding the phone, just looking at it. I know I need to make it to the door before he gets up here. It just seems to be such a long walk. I find strength in letting the doorway hold me up as I wait for him to get off the elevator. I'm nervous. Fuck that, I'm completely terrified that he will see right through me, that one look at my face and he'll know I've been lying.

Part of me still wants to tell him, for him to take some of this anger on for himself. Part of me wants to see what his reaction would be, as if that would give mine some validation. But a bigger part of me is afraid his only reaction would be to wonder why I was so upset. It's not as though anything really happened. The man in the alley didn't try to kill me. He didn't rape me. He didn't even hit me. What if Stephan can see through me and can see I have no real reason to act like this? What if his only reaction is to think I'm weak, weak for caving at simply the threat of something happening? I put all of my focus on the elevator doors and try to make my face look calm.

You're just tired, Kara. You have a headache. You fell down.

Stephan gets off the elevator and stops. He's standing in front of the closing doors just looking at me. My hand instinctually rises up and touches my cheek. I don't dare take my eyes off of his as I watch the different emotions flash over his face—doubt, anger, concern.

It feels like forever before he starts walking toward me again. He reaches out for me, closing the gap between us, and wraps me in his arms. I'm glad that he ignored me, that he came anyway. This moment is worth it.

I know it hasn't even been a day, but it seems like forever since I have felt this safe. I nestle deeper into his chest and never want to leave his arms again.

"Kara, are you sure you just fell? That you're okay? You look horrible, baby."

"Gee, thanks." I mutter it to the soft fabric of his black shirt. I can feel his chest rise and fall as he laughs at me. He places his hand on my lower back and leads me into my apartment.

"Lay down, baby. Let me get you a pillow and a blanket." Stephan leaves me at the couch and walks into my bedroom as I sink into the cushions. Maybe I will really be able to sleep now that he's here. My eyes are closed, but I can I hear him walk back into the living room. I feel him gently lift my head and place the pillow underneath it. I feel the blanket as he tucks it in around me. He sits on the floor next to me and places his arm over my chest.

"Sleep, baby. I'll wake you up in a couple of hours."

I open my eyes to smile at him, feeling more at peace than I have since leaving the gym yesterday. He hasn't asked for another explanation; he hasn't mentioned our phone conversation or me not going to the hospital. I haven't even said more than two words to him since he got here, but as I drift into sleep, I feel safe.

● ● ●

"Kara, open your eyes." It's more of a command than the soft whisper I wish it was, and I find myself having to blink a few times before he comes into focus. He's standing over me with his hand gently shaking my shoulder.

"Sorry, baby, but you were out cold. And if you do have a concussion, I need to wake you up every few hours."

"Okay." I sit up rather confused. It had been a good sleep, a deep, dreamless, wandering-in-the-black peaceful kind of sleep. Why did he have to wake me?

"How's your head?" He reaches out, and his fingers gently run a line down the side of my face, stopping where the bruise begins. The memories reach out across time and scratch at me. I'm no longer confused. I remember why he's here. I remember it all.

He leans down and plants the world's softest kiss on my bruised cheek. The difference between the softness of his kiss and the roughness of last night's brick is almost too much to take.

"Sorry." He backs away quickly thinking the moisture building in my eyes was pain at his kiss. "I couldn't help myself, baby. I want to make it feel better."

I try to nestle myself against him, try to get his soft lips back to my face. "You already have. You're here." I smile up at him, and despite my best effort, I know it doesn't seem sincere. And I'm sure he notices.

"Your head must be killing you. Let me go get you some aspirin." As Stephan heads into the bathroom, I snuggle deeper into the couch, praying to get the comfort of a peaceful sleep back.

After only a moment, I hear Stephan walking back into the living room. I open my eyes to see him carrying some Advil, a glass of water, and a wet washcloth. But the look on his face has changed. It's more focused, more concerned. He places everything on the coffee table, picks up my feet, and sits on the couch, putting my feet back down over his lap. Turning to look at me, his eyes are full of questions. This is the moment I realize I never cleaned the shower. It's still spattered with drops of blood.

"Let me see your face." His voice isn't exactly icy, but he's not asking a question either. His hand is already reaching for the Band-Aids on my cheek. Gently he takes each bandage off. I have no idea what a cut from falling at the gym would look like. Does it match the marks I have on my face? Taking the washcloth, he slowly starts to clean the cut. He does it with such care, such love, that I can feel the moisture welling up in my eyes again.

"You should leave the Band-Aids off, Kara, let some air get to it so it can heal."

I can't tell any longer if he believes me.

"Did you get hurt anywhere else?" He's staring at me, daring me to lie to him. There is fear behind his eyes. I don't know how to respond. I'm looking at him as he watches me, and I'm lost with what to do. I don't want to admit I lied to him, even though I think he is starting to figure that out.

"I saw the blood in your shower." Watching me for a reaction, he takes my hands and checks the palms, looking for the scrapes that should have been there from trying to catch myself from a fall. If he pushes my sleeves up right now, he will see the marks I made with my nails last night as I tried to get the feel of the alley off of me.

Stephan kisses each hand and, thankfully, puts them back across my chest. I can tell by the look on his face he no longer believes my story, at least not all of it.

I hate that I lied to him, that I still am. His fingers gently wipe the tears from my face.

"I love you, baby. You know nothing can change that, right?"

He's watching me, waiting. I don't say anything; instead, I close my eyes. I can't look at him knowing I'm lying when all he wants is to love me and to hear the truth. Eventually he sighs and shifts his eyes to the wall in the back of the room.

"Go back to sleep, Kara. I'll still be here when you wake up."

I'm not sure if that's a threat or a promise. When I wake up, will he want to know why there are no marks from trying to catch myself? Will he want to keep talking?

How do I sleep now? He clearly knows I'm lying. Can I trust him, or will he poke around my apartment? Will he see the half-empty bottle of vodka in the fridge? Will he check my arms, my legs? My mind is racing, trying to come up with what I should do now. I lie here, clearly not asleep; as he watches me, it feels like we're playing some sort of sick game, me knowing that he thinks I'm lying, him waiting for me to sleep so he can prove the lie. Eventually he stands up, kneels by my head, and kisses me. "Go to sleep, Kara." He smiles trying to reassure me. "That's an order."

I wake up on my own this time. I open my eyes just enough to look at him without him noticing that I'm awake. He's sitting at my kitchen table just watching me sleep. There is an all-too-familiar glass in front of him, drained of all liquid, only ice remains. He looks worried. I can see his mind working, trying to put together the pieces of the puzzle I've just left him. I raise my arms above my head in an overexaggerated stretch. I have to do something to keep him from putting any more thought into this. As I sit up, he watches me but doesn't say anything. He's just looking at me. Beyond the concern I see in his eyes, there's a new look on his face, focused and hard.

I rub the sleep from my eyes and try to make myself appear refreshed.

"Thanks for the Advil and the sleep. It seems to have worked. My head isn't throbbing anymore."

I talk because I don't know what else to do. I talk to fill the eerie quiet that has settled over my apartment, to cover up the fact that all he is doing is silently staring at me. I know I have that "guilty of something so I can't seem to shut up" thing going on. But I can't lie here anymore, not with him looking at me like that. I'll end up cracking, and it will all come pouring out. The mere concept of that has me struggling to breathe, has my heart pounding in my chest. The blurry is coming...the shaking that won't stop. The anger that is back puts an edge on my voice. "Come on, weren't you supposed to take me out to dinner or something?"

Stephan doesn't say anything. I sit up and match his stare, daring him to say more. He's still just watching me; the look on his face is like fire. It has me checking to make sure my arms are still covered after my stretch, that he can't see the scratches. After forty-eight seconds, I know because I counted, he forces a smile onto his face. It's tight and controlled and comes nowhere close to reaching his eyes.

"Dinner, sure, where do you want to go?" His voice is still tight, but I will take it over the fire and betrayal I felt in his eyes any day.

"How about pizza and beer?"

He walks over to me offering me his hand to help me off the couch. "How about pizza and soda? You might have a concussion, remember? Let's skip the beer." The sarcasm in his voice isn't hidden as much as either of us would like.

"You got it, pizza and diet coke. Let's make it a casual place though. I'm too comfy to change." My attempt at being cute fails, but at least it seems to have sliced into some of the heat of the moment.

Hand in hand, he leads me out the door. I know in my heart he hasn't bought it; I can't even begin to imagine what he must be thinking. At least for the moment, he is letting me get away with it.

CHAPTER 12

The clock says 2:00 a.m.
The bottle is empty; the night is longer than my bottle is deep.
The fog has lifted…
I want to cry for the life that's gone, my life…the way it once was.
But there are no more tears.
"Never let them see you cry, Kara."
Too many voices are in my head, and none of them are mine.
"Never let them see you cry."
After dreaming of Stephan, he's all that I want right now…
I want to call him, but I know I can't.
It's 2:00 a.m., and there's no way to hide anything at 2:00
a.m. He would know something is seriously wrong.
I need to sleep, not just drift but sleep, real sleep.
I'm afraid of sleep.
I can wake up if I'm just drifting…napping. But sleep,
real sleep…there's no guarantee of waking when I need
too. There's no guarantee I can handle the dreams.
I swallow my last couple sleeping pills…
Please, God… I need to sleep.
Please, God.
I don't remember my eyes closing, but they do…

The past week has been tense to say the least. If nothing else, the invisible dance between Stephan and I have kept me focusing on him instead of everything else. Maybe that's why I haven't told him, haven't had to say the words out loud. Maybe he doesn't really want to know, doesn't want to think that the woman he loves would lie to him. No matter what it is, neither of us have brought it back up. I can tell it's there though, still stuck out there, infecting the air between us.

That's why I came to the decision I have. It's just done, nothing more and nothing less. I don't want to talk about it. I don't want to think about it. I want to be able to sleep, to dream without it being a nightmare. I'm putting it behind me, behind us. We are moving on now; I'm going to show him that everything is just fine, that I am still me and that we are still the same couple we have always been. I want to be wrapped in his arms, listening to the sound of his heart beating. I want to feel calm and safe and loved. Instead, life rears back its ugly hand and uses it to slap me across the face.

The steak is getting cold as it rests, sitting out on the counter-top. The corn is in a pan of now cooling water, and the zucchini is still on its cookie sheet inside the oven that's since been turned off. Of course, it wasn't until dinner was done cooking that I saw his text.

"Sorry, babe. Client forgot the world doesn't revolve around him. Running late, be there as soon as I can. Love you."

It's these moments that always leave me feeling like why do I even bother? I had felt like such the little Suzie homemaker as I bustled through the kitchen in my cute little apron. I was drinking a martini as I waited for my man to come home from his already late client meeting; it felt like if you put me in pearls, I would be straight out of some 1950s commercial for laundry soap or something. Now, just moments later, I wonder why the fuck I bother.

The cut on my cheek had almost healed; and while I was changing clothes after work, I had felt so in the moment, so much like me again. They say karma is a bitch. I say fuck it, tonight just proves the opposite; the more I try, the worse it gets.

When it's Kara the bitch who is up and running, things are great. When it's Kara the "let me think of you, let me do something for you"…well then; doesn't life just suck. I know it's not his fault. I know it's his job. I knew it was his job when we started dating. His clients own him; life comes at that cost when you make the kind of money that he does. But that knowledge doesn't make these moments any easier.

I've been trying, overdoing it really, but trying to make everything better, to make it as close to perfect as I can. I want things back to the way they were before, before Stephan figured out that I had lied to him, before that fucking alley. He hasn't brought it back up, but every once and awhile, I catch him watching me with that same look on his face that he had that night a couple of weeks back. I don't know if it's my imagination seeing it because of the guilt I feel or if things really have been more strained since that stupid night. But I want it back, I want us back, and even more, I want me back.

I gave in and canceled my gym membership last week. I haven't had the courage to go again. I'm afraid that just the smell would bring it all back to me; and besides, I won't walk down that street anymore, no matter how far out of my way I have to go. But other than that, I really have decided to just put it all behind me, move on and all that good stuff. It took a lot of forced moments at first, but now I feel like I'm getting the hang of it. Rick bought my falling story so much easier than Stephan had, so had everyone else at work. The only thing I can't move beyond is that Stephan knows I lied, and it's eating at me.

I place out portions of the dinner onto plates and wrap them with plastic wrap. It's seven forty-five when I finally sit down on the couch with a bowl of cereal. I had planned for dinner at seven; Stephan was supposed to be here at six thirty. There's really nothing on TV; as I flip through the channels, I lean back into the pillows trying to get more comfortable. By the time I have finished my bowl of Cheerios, I've found an old rerun of Friends; hopefully he will be here before it's over.

I don't remember falling asleep, but I clearly I did. I can hear Stephan laughing quietly, and I feel a blanket being tucked around me; I feel his lips brush against my forehead. "Hey there, sleepyhead, sorry I'm late."

I smile. This is exactly why I had given him a key, these moments. He had thought the keys were just for in-case moments, in case I get locked out, in case I fall down again and need him. I'm sure he thinks it was some sad attempt to make me feel better about lying to him, and in some ways, it was; but it was in hope for these moments too.

"I'm not sleepy." I hear him laughing again.

"Oh, okay, sure, then why where you sleeping?"

I keep my eyes closed but snuggle my head up against his chest as he's now sitting next to me on the couch.

"Because my boyfriend stood me up for his snooty clients, and I got tired of waiting."

"I'm sorry, baby. I didn't mean to ruin our evening. Did you eat? Can I take you out to make up for it?"

"What time is it?" I ask him as I rub the sleep from my eyes.

"About eight thirty. How about dinner, and then we can find some bar with a band for drinks?"

"Hmm. Are you sure your clients won't be there? Will I need to dress up to compete with them?"

I look at Stephan. He's concentrating; he can't quite tell if I'm really mad or just joking.

"I'm just giving you shit, baby. I know you didn't want to have to pick them over me. I knew what your job meant when we first started dating. I guess I'm just not that good at sarcasm when I'm first waking up." I stand up and bend back down to him to give him a quick kiss.

"Give me ten minutes, and I'll be ready to go."

●●●

Dinner was perfect—candlelight, jazz music, flowing wine—perfect. I settle into the tall, straight-backed bench at the bar. I can't believe we managed to get a table. Stephan is sitting across from me; he looks tired, but he's hanging in there. I think he's still trying to make up for missing the original dinner; but the way the night is going now, it's even better. The bar is dark, and the music's loud. It's the kind of loud where there's no point to even try to talk; I would be pretending to hear him and nodding along, smiling when I think I should, and agreeing to God knows what. The music is good, the type where you have no choice but to move, dance on the floor or

74

dance in your chair, but you-gotta-dance type of music. Not a single song I recognize, but since when has that stopped me? I'm trying to be supportive of how tired I can tell Stephan is, so I sit instead of dragging him along behind me to dance.

After three songs have played and we still haven't seen a waitress to order, Stephan heads up to the bar to get our drinks. I'm watching him as he walks back to our table and thinking myself a very lucky girl. A blond-haired woman with too much makeup on and a slinky black Band-Aid for a dress is following behind him as though she were staking her claim. I smile, knowing she won't get anywhere close to my man; he will blow her off kindly, but blow her off nonetheless. She bumps into him, nearly spilling my drink and pretends to be surprised and apologetic, touching him just so on his arm, the "oh my, you are strong under this shirt" pathetic crap that I'm sure is flowing from her desperately red, painted on, fuck-me, whore lips.

Stephan says something short and sweet in return, and I'm wishing he was facing me so I could read his lips. He turns and slides in next to me, no longer across from me as he was when we first sat down. This would be his real response to Miss Red Whore Lips, the "I'm with her, and you ain't getting in here" response. I can't help it; my possessive inner bitch shows up. I look right at her and smile, then lean in and kiss my man, a deep, sensual, "wrap my arms around him and press my body into him," soul-melting kiss. Stephan backs away and looks at me, a stupid grin plastered to his face.

"I'll have to make sure to be hit on more often with you around if this is your reaction."

I can't stop myself from laughing. "Sorry, I couldn't help it."

"Babe, you never need to apologize after a kiss like that."

"Hmmm, that's something I'll have to make sure to remember."

I'm practically bouncing in my seat to the music. Stephan is laughing at me, again.

"Go dance, baby. Don't let me stop you."

That's all the encouragement I need. Stephan moves aside, and I'm up and off to the dance floor. They still haven't played a single song I know, but that's fine by me. I'm having the time of my life just moving to the beat of the music. I know Stephan isn't big on dancing, and that's okay. It's that he doesn't expect me to sit there with him that I love. He just lets me be me. I look back to our table and see him watching me. I start to dance just for him and the rest of the people seem to disappear. I can tell he only sees me on the dance floor, that the rest of the world has melted away for him too. I close my eyes and let the music become one with my body.

The dance floor is busy but not packed, and I have a decent amount of space to myself. I rub my hands up my body from my hips, up over my chest, and through my hair. I feel his hands join mine and his hips push into me from behind, and I'm in love. He doesn't like to dance, but here he is, dancing with me anyway. I open my eyes planning to turn to look into his face before I lean in to kiss him my thanks. I see him looking back at me, moving across the dance floor toward me. It takes my mind a minute to catch up, just long enough to hear a voice whispering in my ear. It's not the same voice, but it doesn't have to be. It's scratchy and hot and whispering in my ear. I can feel the color drain from my face as my mind brings me back to the brick. I'm no longer in the bar; I'm on my knees crawling out of an alley. Everything starts to blur, and I feel myself start to fall.

Just before my knees hit the ground, I feel Stephan's arms grab me. His eyes had been mad as I watched him walking toward me on the dance floor. Now when I look up, they're filled with anxiety, the anger toward my whispering stranger long gone. He picks me up and is carrying me like a baby. People are moving out of the way for him, laughing at the girl who they think had had too much to drink. I can hear them as I'm carried past. "Drunk…" *Drunk ass bitch…* Despite my best efforts, I'm shaking in Stephan's arms. He's looking into my eyes, searching them trying to figure out what has just happened.

"Kara, I need to put you down so I can pay. Can you stand?"

I nod my head yes. I wish I could talk, but the words are stuck, as if they were being stepped on and forced down, stuck in the pit of my stomach. I'm embarrassed, scared, and desperately racking my brain with how I'm going to explain this to him.

Outside, he waves down a cab and gently places me inside of it. It's started to rain. I know my eyes look terrified. I know my breath is coming in gasps. I curl into myself and lean against the door as Stephan gives my address to the driver and settles in beside me. The look in his eyes is one of weary panic. He doesn't say anything on the ten-minute drive back to my apartment. He has turned his head away from mine and is looking out the window. His hand is on my knee, and occasionally his thumb brushes the skin softly across my knee and up my thigh. He's lost in thought, and that terrifies me almost as much as the whispering in my ear.

I had known I was safe; I was with Stephan. I was in a bar full of people. My reaction makes me angry, leaves me feeling completely disappointed in myself, and leaves me terrified. I have no idea what to tell Stephan. I can't say I drank too much. He was with me, and he knows I didn't. I can't say I was just tired because I was asleep when he got to my apartment. There is nothing I can tell him to explain this. I look out the window and watch the city streets pass me by, praying for God to give me a way out of explaining this.

Not nearly enough time has passed since I was first set into the back of the cab, and we're already pulling up to my building. I still have no idea what to tell Stephan, how to explain all of this. Stephan pays the driver, silently takes my hand, and leads me inside. I'm following behind him, half walking, half stumbling as we head up the elevator and to my apartment door. He stops, frozen in front of the door, and turns to look at me. At first I don't know why. I know he has his key. He let himself in earlier tonight. In cowardly fashion, instead of meeting his eyes, I look down finding sudden interest in the carpeting on the floor. He reaches his arm out slowly, slow enough that I can see it coming, slowly like he is afraid he will scare me. He tilts my head until I'm forced to look up at him. His eyes are full of anxiety and fear or concern, anger? I can't really place all the different emotions I see reflected back in them.

"Kara?" Closing his eyes, he takes a deep breath and slowly, deliberately begins again. "Kara, what was that?" Another breath, the "please, God, calm my soul" kind. I recognize it; lately it's the only way I breathe.

"Are you okay?" His thumb is rubbing tenderly over the now fading scar on my cheek. The love and concern etched onto his face

77

hurts my heart. It leaves me feeling pathetic and guilty that I haven't explained why I've been behaving weird the last few weeks. I feel weak because I don't know if I ever will.

I want to tell him. I wanna feel like I can. I want to explain myself and take away the lie that is standing between us, but all I can do is nod a weak yes.

My nod seems to be the spark that sets off the explosion.

"Bullshit," Stephan spits the words at me. They slap at my face and sting in their truth.

He turns to unlock the door but instead places his hand up against it and just stands still for a long moment. He runs his hand through his hair as he finally turns back toward me, the door still locked behind him. His eyes are wild, and I can see how hard he's trying to control himself.

"Two weeks ago, you call to cancel our date saying you fell. I came running over here to take care of you, only to discover you lied to me."

I open my mouth to start to argue with him. I don't even know why. We both know I lied. Stephan holds his hand up and shakes his head no. The control over his anger is starting to fade.

"Don't even try to feed me some line of shit, Kara. We both know you were lying. There was blood in your shower, and you had no marks on your hands from trying to catch yourself from a fall."

He's glaring at me, just daring me to lie to him again.

I have nothing for him, nothing I'm willing to say. I stand there like a weak and wide-eyed child, looking up at him while he waits for me to say something, anything. He's just looking at me, desperate and waiting for me to provide some type of reason, some explanation. Eventually his eyes close, and I hear him sigh. I can see the exact moment when the look in his eyes change from anger to a look of defeat. It leaves me afraid that he has given up on so much more than just the hope that I will answer him. I watch as Stephan slowly turns back to the door, unlocks it, and heads inside. The realization that the love of my life has just left me standing in the hallway begins a slow and creeping march straight to my heart. What have I done?

I watch as Stephan walks into my kitchen and hastily pours himself a drink; it goes downs in one angry smooth gulp. He doesn't quite slam the glass down onto the countertop, but there's nothing careful about his movements either. I quietly enter my apartment and find him leaning against the wall.

"Do you care to explain any of this? Explain what the fuck has been going on with you?" He's focusing on breathing again, eyes closed, trying to calm himself down.

"Kara, why are you lying to me?"

I can feel the moisture building in my eyes; I turn my head so he can't see me break.

I want to fall to the floor. I wanna scream. I want to hit something. I want to physically be the storm that's raging in my head right now. I want him to see it. At the same time, I'm scared of what would happen if he ever did.

"I'm sorry." I say it to the wall as I walk away from Stephan, too much a coward to say it to his face. I keep walking down the hallway and into my bedroom. I close the door and collapse on the floor behind it, hidden from view.

● ● ●

I hate how I feel. I hate knowing I did this to Stephan. I hate the alley man. I wanna make it go away, to let it out as one primal scream, one desperate act. I need release, the kind that came as I watched all the pain, all the anger flow down the drain of my shower, the calm feeling I got as I watched my blood mix with the water, as I watched it make swirling dancing movements, and flow down the drain, the feeling of power that came knowing I did that and no one else. I know that I can't; I know that it's sick that I even want to. I hate that thought. Just add it to all my hate. I hug my knees tighter to my chest. I hate this, all of this. I'm rocking back and forth like a child, rocking in the fetal position lying on the floor of my bedroom in the dark after leaving Stephan alone in my kitchen, and it's all too much.

I tiptoe out of my room, afraid I'll find Stephan sitting the couch; but he's nowhere to be seen. The apartment is dark. I have to turn on lights as I walk. There's a pad of paper and a pen out on my table, as if Stephan were going to write me a note, but it's blank and I'm not sure what to make of that. The vodka is sitting on the countertop with his glass next to it; the dishes from the dinner I had made are still piled in the sink. My fingers dance over the top of the dirty plate, feeling like my Suzie homemaker moment was another life ago, not a mere four hours. For the second time this month, I'm left feeling like my life has changed suddenly and in so many ways I can't seem to control.

Stephan's glass in my hand makes me feel a little closer to him in this moment. I hold it to my chest and breathe in and out, calm and slow. This is me breathing. As much as I was hoping it would calm me down, it does nothing. I watch as my hand pours the clear, now warm vodka. I raise the bottle higher and enjoy playing with the liquid; it makes a small waterfall as it flows into my glass. I start to feel the calm settling over me. I try to line my lips up to the exact spot Stephan's were at, the marks from his lips are like a ghost calling out to me. I'm sure I'm not as graceful as he was when he finished his drink, and instead of putting the glass down, I pour another. I try to remember exactly where it was that he had stood, where he had leaned against the wall and waited, although standing here like this with the now empty glass in my hand leaves me feeling even more pathetic and sad rather than closer to him. I could have been as close as I wanted, if I only had the strength to tell him the truth.

My glass is empty, and it rolls away from me. I couldn't quite get it to stand up straight as I tried to put it back on the countertop. The bottle is empty now too.

I'm drunk. I giggle to myself, but it stops short as my mind plays back memories I want to forget, drunk and alone.

Drunk...

Drunk ass bitch...

Only this time it's so much worse. This time, it's Stephan's voice I hear, Stephan's angry eyes I see. And that's just too fucking much.

I grab my empty, rolling glass and cling to it as though it was a life jacket in a storming sea. I stumble and fall into the wall as I try to make it into my bathroom. I know I need more to forget, more to get through this night. It hadn't been as hard as I thought it would be to get my doctor to give me something to help me sleep. A simple work is getting stressful. City life is noisy and keeping me up. I miss my family. Pick an excuse and I had a shiny new bottle of pills. It's these pills I look for now, these "make it all go away" pills. I know I'm making a god-awful mess in my drunken rush to find them. The little orange bottle is almost empty, but it will do its job tonight. One hand clutches my glass, one hand holds the pill bottle.

I make my way slowly back to the kitchen, walking carefully so I don't fall and spill my pills. I hold the empty bottle of vodka high in the air, up and over the glass, watching as the last few drops fall, not even enough for a single sip. I add some tap water and swallow down two pills. The watery vodka concoction doesn't really do it for me. I know somewhere in the back of the fridge I had hidden another bottle. It's not full, but it's there. And it doesn't take long to find. I carry my little collection back to my bedroom and attempt to gracefully collapse onto my bed. I beg for sleep. I pray for unconsciousness, and I'm terrified of what dreams will come.

AWAKE

CHAPTER 13

"Kara, you won't answer your phone, and we need to talk about last night. I know you lied to me, but I need to know why. I know you're there. Just talk to me."

I'm in the alley, crawling on my knees when I hear his voice. It stops me cold. It stops me before I meet strangers who laugh. It stops me from thinking alley man is coming back. My mind is reeling against the sound. His voice, it doesn't belong here. I know this dream; it runs through my head like a well-read book, and Stephan doesn't have a part in this scene.

"Kara!" His voice sounds angry. I knew he would be angry with me. I think he's getting closer. I turn my head in a desperate panic looking for the voice, looking for Stephan. But I can't find him anywhere.

"No! Kara! No!"

How can he not see me? He sounds so close, but now he sounds scared too, not just angry anymore. He must be scared that he can't find me. Where is he? Why can't I see him?

"Kara! Please!"

I can hear him more clearly now, but it's like something's over my ears. There's panic and fear in his voice, and it scrapes rough against the image in my mind.

"Kara! Can you hear me? Open your eyes, Kara! Please!"

My mind is starting to clear. I'm lying on something soft, not crawling, not on pavement. I'm home. I'm in my bed, and Stephan is here. He's here. He's here, and he can see me.

Shit.

My eyes blink quickly, trying to find the way back between the dream and the real.

"Kara, look at me." It's more of a command this time. "Open your eyes, and look at me, damn it!" He is so close that I can hear him breathing. It's hot and heavy.

"What the fuck have you done? Kara!" His voice is rife with fear and anger, lots of anger.

"Stephan, no…" I think I said it out loud; I think the words made it out of my head, out of my mouth. I'm trying to open my eyes, but it's like they don't want to face the scene playing out before them. The sound of my sleeping pills as they rattle against the side of the little orange bottle helps to pull me out of this fog. It brings on a new, sharper fear than what I felt while crawling out of the alley of my nightmares, the fear that it's too late now; Stephan can see me for everything I am. I left it spelled out right in front of him to find— weak, drunk, scared.

Out of everything I want from Stephan, everything I want him to think I am, nothing could be further than the moment we are currently stuck in.

"Go…just go, Stephan."

I say it as though it were a prayer. Go and take this moment with you. Go and let me hide. Let me make this so you could never see.

I feel his arms on me, pulling at my shoulders, as he rolls me over, trying desperately to look in my eyes. I can't take looking at him right now, seeing what he really thinks of me reflecting back off his face.

"Go away, Stephan."

My words are laced with anger, anger that my little prayer hasn't been answered, anger that I will have no choice but to face him, to explain this, explain me, and I'm too raw right now to handle any of it.

My emotions are still fresh from that stupid dream; and when I finally wake, it's to Stephan seeing everything I was trying so hard to hide, proving even more to him that I had lied. It's just too much. I try to roll over again, but he has me pinned on my back. The pillow behind my head is gone, and whatever blanket I had over me has been ripped violently off. I can't seem to move.

I can feel my heart start to pound. I know the dream is gone; I know I'm here safe and with Stephan. But it's too much, being held down like this, not being able to move is too much. My eyes burst open, and I struggle against him with everything I have. I can feel the pure emotion pushing through my limbs, pushing him off of me. I can feel the fear and panic building, burning. I can only imagine the look that must be in my eyes; I can only imagine what Stephan must think of me right now.

One look into my face, and Stephan lets go of my shoulders and jumps off of me. With his hands up in the air, he backs away slowly, just watching me. I can't get away from the look in his eyes; they are so full of anger and concern, full of fear and panic. And it's all just a little too raw for me; it's too real. I turn my head to look at the wall, anything but having to look in his eyes. Our little standoff continues this way for seventeen breaths, his deeper than mine.

"What did you do?" His voice is flat and controlled.

Looking at the wall, I say nothing. His hand on my cheek, he cautiously turns my head until I'm looking at him.

"Just go away, Stephan." I repeat it again and again, annoyed that he has the audacity to be here now, to push it now. I'm trying to force my head past his arm, desperate to be able to turn away from him. He seems to get the hint and let's go of my face only to reach for the cup on the table at the edge of my bed. I can feel the emotions rolling off of him, waves of anger he is barely able to control. In case I had any doubt, it vanishes as the remnants of the cup spill slowly down my chest while he pours what little remains over me.

"How much of this shit have you had?" He holds the glass directly in front of my face. "How much, Kara?" The pill bottle gripped tightly in his other hand. It would be easier if he were screaming at me, giving me something to react to; but his voice is steady, controlled and cold.

"Leave me alone, Stephan. What the fuck do you know about me anyway?" I lie back down on my bed and curl in on myself. After twelve more breaths, I hear him walking away, footsteps down the hallway. Fucking figures.

He doesn't leave like I think he is. Instead I hear the water in my shower turn on.

I sit up in my bed trying to make my brain work well enough to figure out what exactly Stephan is up to. It's no use. I'm sure I'll know soon enough. With a "yeah, well, whatever," I flop back down once again, bringing the blankets with me. As I roll over, I pull the blanket back over my head, cutting out any of the light, and I lie waiting in the dark.

"Nice try, Kara." And once again, my covers are gone. I lie in the same clothes that he had left me in after the bar, still wet from where he had spilled the remnants of my drink. I glare up at him, hating this position, hating everything about life right now.

"What the hell is your problem Stephan?" I know I sound like a child, but I'm passed the point of caring.

He stands over me, looking more like a giant figure from some horror story than the man I love.

"I am done talking with you right now." I know somewhere in my head I should be processing everything that is happening, but all I can think is, *Huh, so this is Stephan angry.* This is Stephan very, very angry.

With that, I'm lifted off the bed and thrown over his shoulder. He doesn't say a word but walks out of my room and down the hall into the bathroom. I wouldn't quite say he threw me down, but it wasn't as gentle as I would have liked, not that any of this was to *my* liking. I look up at him, to continue to fight him, but the cold water hits my face. And all that comes out of my mouth is shrieking screams. He walks out, straight out of my apartment, leaving me fully clothed sitting on the floor of my shower, cold water pouring off of me. I reach up and turn the water off, too weak to do anything other than stay sitting on the cold and wet shower floor.

My mind can't wrap around what has just happened. Did he really just leave? Did he really come back just to walk out on me again? I pull my knees up and put my head down, resting it against my legs, rocking back and forth. I don't know how much time has gone by. It could have been five minutes; it could have been five hours. I never heard the footsteps in the hall; I never heard the door open. But I feel a towel being set around my shoulders. I feel his hands lift me off the floor, gentler this time. He carries me back into my room and sits me down on my bed. I don't move. I don't speak; I don't even feel like I'm really here. Stephan kneels down onto my floor by the base of my bed and gently starts to talk to me.

"Kara, you can't sit here like this. You need to get changed. I'll wait for you in the kitchen. I won't leave."

I don't respond, I still can't seem to get my mind to connect to my mouth. What is he doing? Why is he doing this? Ten minutes or so after, he has softly closed the door to my room and walked out. I'm still sitting on my bed, still sitting in wet clothes. I can feel my teeth chattering, but I don't move. I hear the door open again.

I hear him sigh. He kneels beside my bed. For a moment, he just looks at me, looks me in the eyes, looks through me. He sighs again and begins to remove my clothes. I know I should be shocked, should say something. I'm too lost inside my mind, too lost inside his actions. There is nothing sexual in the way he undresses me, even as I lay naked before him, still wet on my bed. He covers me up with my blanket and begins to go through my dresser, trying to find clothes, as I try to work my way out of my own head. I start to find my voice.

"Stephan." I sound weak. I sound as empty as I feel. It's all I manage to get out, but it seems to be enough. Stephan stops riffling through my clothes and comes to sit by me. My teeth are chattering again, and he puts his arm around me, rubbing my arm trying to get me to warm up. It seems Stephan doesn't have anything left to say either; he just sits with me in silence.

●●●

I wake up wrapped in my blanket with another one placed over it. The curtains are drawn tight, and I can hear voices talking in the next room. I blink a few times, trying to place what's going on. My head feels foggy; it doesn't want to let me focus. I sit up, my arm bumping my nightstand as I do. I look down to find a glass of water and two Advil sitting on the table top. Taking them quickly and gulping the water down, I start to climb out of bed. As I stand up, the blood rushes to my head. My legs feel weak and unsure. I reach my hands out and grab my nightstand with both hands to catch myself before I fall. I count my breaths in and out, deep and slow. After a moment, I feel more sure of myself. I stand and walk past my door without looking; seeing my reflection right now is the last thing I want to do.

Rick is sitting at the table just outside the kitchen while Stephan roams through my fridge. My mind is instantly in panic mode. Stephan called Rick. I feel completely betrayed and frozen. I have no idea what to say to either of them.

"Hey there, sis, feeling better?" Rick looks up at me and smiles. *Smiles?*

Not angry, not accusing, not demanding explanations. I look to Stephan, hoping to find answers, something to explain why no one is yelling at me at this moment. He looks back at me with no emotion; his face is a carefully constructed mask. It hurts into the very edges of my heart. It is so different from the way he normally looks at me.

"Your brother stopped by while you were sleeping. I was telling him about our little dinner party last night where someone got slightly over served."

I take a deep breath and feel my limbs de-thaw. He's lying for me, and he's not happy about it at all.

Rick spins around in his chair to look at me. "Ouch, Kara…my heads hurts just looking at you." He's laughing at me, light and carefree, totally oblivious to the tension between Stephan and I. I have no idea how he misses it. I look from Rick to Stephan and back again. The difference between these two, at this moment, is huge. Rick represents everything I feel like I lost—stupid, goofy, laughing. Stephan is everything I am left with—disappointment, uncertainty, anger.

"And, sis…"

It takes a moment to be able to focus completely on Rick again; my mind is still waking up, still foggy.

"You gotta watch it when you go out. It's a good thing Stephan was there with ya or who knows what could have happened. I never gave you the big bad city talk. Do I need to?"

Rick is half joking and half looking at me with that older-brother-protection love in his eyes. I can't look at him; I can't take this train of thought any longer. I force a tight laugh at Rick, trying to sound like myself and failing, hoping he takes that as simply hungover. I turn around and head back to my room mumbling something about getting changed and brushing my teeth.

When I finally gather enough courage to walk back out, Rick is gone, and Stephan is sitting in the dark at my table, the empty bottle of vodka sitting in front of him, the other bottle in his hand. I walk as quietly as I can. I barley breathe. I sit down on my couch behind Stephan and just look at him. We sit like this for a few minutes before I hear him.

"I know you're there."

He never even turns around to look at me. He talks to the wall. I guess I have taught him well.

"I don't know what has happened, what's going on with you. Why you won't talk to me? I know this isn't you." He pauses and takes a deep breath.

"I just lied for you. Don't make me sorry I did that." He stands up and walks out. He never even looks at me, and he takes the bottle of vodka with him.

The sound of the door closing echoes through my brain. I sit still on my couch, afraid to move. I'm not sure how long I sit there. It's dark before I finally move. Nothing feels right. Nothing feels real. It's because of him. Because I'm not sure where I stand with Stephan the past twenty-four hours, the past two weeks, it feels like my life is over, like the Kara I had known is forever gone, and I have no idea who this person is that now fills up this empty body.

I know I need him; I know it like I know I need to breathe. He is where I feel safe, where I can almost feel whole and sane. Without thinking, I walk over to the phone and dial his number. The phone just rings and rings. No one picks up, not even the machine. He is avoiding me. I drop the phone, and I break. I begin to sob uncontrollably, barely breathing sob. It comes out like one swift kick to the stomach, one primal scream. I scream at the phone lying on the ground, "I'm sorry!" even though I know no one can hear. I grab the phone and whip at the wall screaming, "I'm fucking sorry!" The phone shatters into pieces as it hits the ground.

CHAPTER 14

Shut it off… Please, God, shut off my mind. I
have nothing left to turn it off… Please…

I lie, arms wrapping around my knees, on the carpet of my living room. My shoulder is digging into the floor as I rock back and forth. The November afternoon sun is keeping the inside of my eyes a reddish orange color when all I want is black.

Please, God…life hurts too much right now. Please just make it stop.

●●●

My eyes open, adjusting to the morning light as it pours in through the windows. It's a cold, soon-to-be-winter light, the kind where you have to live somewhere it gets miserably cold to understand the difference. I'm stiff and chilled to the bone, but I slept sound, no dreams to terrify me. I slept simple black moments slipping through time. Maybe losing it last night, not the fight with Stephan, but my stupid weak sobbing into the carpet, maybe it was what I needed. I slept through the rest of yesterday; I slept through the night. I haven't been able to say that in weeks.

With arms stretching overhead, I think back to my first night here; sleeping on the floor of my new apartment, everything seemed so happy and hopeful. I can't believe that was only seven months ago. So much has changed for me. So much feels different. How does Rick not see it, all these little things that have changed in me? Am

I really that good of an actress? Can my brother, who knows me so well, not tell that something is drastically wrong, that I am slowly losing my mind? The only one who seems to be able to see me is Stephan, and now he won't talk to me.

I lie in the cold light replaying yesterday's drama through my head. Yesterday…the day before…whenever the hell it was we were at that stupid club—I had felt like me again. I had felt happy and goofy. I was content with the imperfections of life. Stephan's meeting had messed up the night, but it was fine. We rolled with it. We still had fun; and then one fucking moment, one fucking stranger asshole man, changed all of that for us.

Why! Why did that have to happen? Why did Stephan leave me alone only to come back when it was too late? Why was it that moment he saw instead of all the others? He didn't see the moment I was cooking for him. He didn't see when I was nose to the grindstone, working my ass off being everything I'm supposed to be. Doesn't he not realize that I'm more than what he found last night?

Does he really think that all I am is weak? All I am is someone he has to lie for? And who the fuck was he to take my vodka? I'm not a fucking child! I'm sorry if I can't be as perfect as he can, if I can't react the way he would react. Well, fuck him and fuck his high horse too. One mistake, one glimpse into who I can be and he walks out on me, the one thing he promised never to do. What kind of man is that? Fuck him! Who needs him? I can be strong; I can do this.

I get up, hit the shower, and get dressed into the most comfortable clothes I own. Blare, and I do mean blare some music, as I start to clean. I wipe away every last ounce of anger, loneliness, desperation, and betrayal. The cleaner my apartment becomes, the better I feel. See, I don't need him. I needed one night of just living my emotions, one night of allowing crazy to rule. That's all I needed to be me again.

I make a big breakfast, with pancakes and bacon and an endless supply of coffee. I really wish I had the fixings for a mimosa but plain old OJ will have to do. Feeling very content with myself, I sit down, stare out the window, and begin to eat. The remnants of the broken phone are in the garbage, my apartment is clean, and I'm full. I need a day to celebrate all that is me once again. It's been too long. I can't even remember the last book that I read, the last new movie that I saw, and my nails still look like what you would expect after crawling out of an alley. Chick flicks, mud masks, comfort food, and one big comfy blanket, I don't need the martinis that normally accompany such a night. I had last night. I don't need more. I just need me, just being me.

But it's too quiet now. My nails are painted. I've had more than my fair share of mint chocolate chip ice cream, and my blanket keeps getting wrapped around my legs. It's annoying. My comfortable chick flick backfired; I couldn't find a new one that I wanted to see, and I've seen this one too many times before. I practically know it by heart, and it isn't giving me the distraction I need. I can't get my mind to turn off.

I hate to admit it to myself, but I want Stephan here, sitting next to me, wrapped up in this annoying blanket, making stupid comments about the color I painted my toes. Instead, he's off doing who knows what, mad because I didn't have scrapes on my hand to match the cut on my face. If I had known to think of that, I would have scrapped up my damn hands up for him. I could have stopped all of this from happening. I could have stopped myself from feeling like this.

I know; I could have told him the truth too. There are so many different ways I could have changed the way this weekend has ended up, the way this whole mess has played out, so many ways that would have ended with Stephan sitting next to me where I'm wrapped in his arms, warm from him instead of this damn blanket. Fuck this damn blanket. I throw it to the floor and kick it away from me, trying but failing to take all of my frustration, all of my hate, out on this piece of cloth instead of feeling strong and capable, the whole "fuck you, world, I got this" feeling that I was going for. I feel weak. I feel alone. I feel the hate that comes on so easily now. I stand in front of the television after turning it off, looking at my reflection in the now black screen as it hangs on my wall.

Come on, Kara, make the decision. What are you going to do?

Do I go out, at night by myself, afraid of every stranger on the street, in order to replace the booze Stephan took from me, or do I stay home sober and slowly go crazy? Which demon do I want to face tonight?

CHAPTER 15

My reflection is daring me to be strong, shit talking me out of leaving the house.

Don't be weak. Don't be pathetic. If you leave, if you drink now, you're everything they think you are... "Drunk ass bitch." Be stronger than that. Show Stephan you're stronger than he thinks you are. Who do you want to be, Kara? Be it now.

After my little conversation with the TV reflection version of myself, I give in and decide to try to be good. I'll stay here. I'll find something to do, some way to control the thoughts and the hate that's slowly consuming my mind. I used to love to be by myself. I loved the freedom it gave me. I could be quiet; I could be goofy, dance in my underwear with no one watching. I had a great routine to "Celebration." I resort back to my old staple—my I can't sleep but I really need to—a nice hot mug of decaf coffee and a long documentary. As much as I admit I love ancient history, nothing can put me to sleep faster than the history of the pyramids.

When I wake up, a little stiff from yet another night in the living room instead of my own bed, I decide to try to keep being good. I skip out on the morning coffee (can you believe it), do a few stretches, brush my teeth, and head out for a run.

Oh wait, that's right, I don't do runs anymore.

Okay, so I walk briskly to the coffee shop and get a cappuccino. I also apparently don't do the no-coffee mornings. At least I'm outside, sunshine and fresh air and all that good for you stuff. There is a small dog park not far from my apartment, so I head over to watch the puppies play.

It feels good to sit in the sun, feel what's left of the warmth hitting my face. I'm not sure how long I sit like this before my phone begins to ring, a silly stupid ring, the one that belongs to Rick.

I don't know how to answer the phone, the words to say.

What the fuck is wrong with me?

"Kara?" He pauses just a second too long.

"What's going on, Kara? I don't want to pry, but… Stephan called today to see if I had heard from you, to see if you were all right? What does that mean, if you are all right? Did he do something to you?"

Did Stephan do something to me? Stephan called him! What the fuck does that mean? Where did he even get his number?

"No, Rick…he didn't do anything." Although I have to admit I like hearing "the big brother I will fight for you honor" tone that he has taken.

What do I have in me to tell him right now? I'm starting to get the lies mixed up. What have I already said?

"Then what, Kara? What the hell is going on. Don't pretend like I'm not supposed to notice that you don't show up to Mom's dinners, that you missed out on breakfast, that now something is clearly up and you have nothing to offer as an explanation."

Fuck. Think, Kara, think.

The first thought is mean, but it's one I know will shut him up, will stop the questions, and get him to leave me alone, at least for a little bit. I swallow against the taste it leaves in my mouth.

"Excuse me!" I sharpen the edge in my voice, raise the tone to barley below a yell.

"What the fuck, Rick? Yeah, I haven't gone to dinner, haven't gone to breakfast…why the fuck would I? Should I sit there in the clothes someone else has picked out, sit there and smile when I'm supposed too, just to get you and Mom the 'let me breathe for a fucking moment?' Should I sit and let her tell me how I live life wrong, watch you pretend like you agree! I'm not you! I'm not going to sit there and play at someone else's life. If you can't find the courage to say shut up, then I will. Shut. The. Fuck. Up."

I hang up before he has a chance to even absorb the words.

I don't know what to do. Stand, sit? Cry, yell? I have enough stored hatred to run a lap around the world and no energy left to leave this bench in the middle of the city. I curl my feet up under me and slowly sink until I am laying on the bench like a child just missing her mother's arms.

I'm not asleep, but I'm not aware either. I am stuck between two worlds, as the world I live in passes me by.

I'm not sure how long my phone has been buzzing before I finally turn my hand over to see it.

"At your place, we need to talk. Where are you?"

Then the next text. "Hello…"

Then the next. "Never the hell mind."

They are all from over an hour ago; I'm kicking myself that I missed them. I send him a quick message back. "Sorry, I was out jogging." There, take that asshole, see I can be good.

"What do you need?" I wait, but he doesn't return my text.

Instead of heading home I make the only call left that I can.

● ● ●

"Katie? Are you home?" I wish it was her I was talking to, not some soulless recording that's spitting back the numbers I had just called—you know, in case I had forgotten since I dialed them all of two seconds ago.

"I need to get outta here. Call me back, okay…please."

Twenty minutes later, and I'm sitting at my kitchen table, drumming my fingers, without any clue how to spend the rest of my day, when she texts me. "I'm downstairs. Get your ass down here… Where we going?" I love Katie. No questions asked, she's here and ready to provide me with any type of distraction needed. Not having to think twice about it, I do as I'm told and get my ass down there.

"So where to?" Katie asks. We sit side by side in my car, heading out of the city. The smaller the buildings get in my rearview mirror, the better I'm feeling, the easier I'm breathing.

"Woodfield?" I quickly glance over to her. "Some retail ther-apy?" I don't really want to shop, but I know Katie won't turn that one down. She doesn't have her own car, so I know she doesn't get out to Woodfield as much as she would like.

"Oh hell, yeah." It's hard not to smile when I'm around Katie. I don't know what I did right in a past life to deserve this friendship, but whatever it was, I'm glad I did it.

"You took the words right out of my mouth," Katie continues. Her smile is almost contagious. And with that, we're heading to one of the larger malls in the suburbs. It's about a forty-minute drive or so, and I know I've been to quiet for too long. I won't be able to avoid the subject forever.

"Stephan's mad at me." I say the words, keeping me eyes perfectly straight ahead but just saying them out loud I feel like a weight's been lifted.

"I thought it might be something like that. Anything you wanna talk about?"

I take a deep breath and think for a minute about how I want to word this. I'm tired of all the little white lies. But I'm not ready for the whole, deep, dark truth either.

"I think it's to the point where we're starting to see who the other person is and I'm not sure he likes what he sees."

I look at Katie out of the corner of my eye, trying to judge her reaction. "The other night, he saw me drunk…really drunk. He walked out on me and took the bottle with him, like I'm some sort of child he can punish. It just made me so mad. Who does this control freak think he is?"

Katie doesn't say anything; she's just looking at me, waiting for me to continue. But I don't, I don't know what else to say, what else I'm willing to say. Instead of talking, instead of watching the road, I'm now looking at Katie, almost daring her to respond.

"He loves you, Kara. I know you love him back. Talk to him. I know you, and I know you want to run right now, but don't. You don't have to make up your mind either way yet, just talk to him and then decide."

I have to admit it. I'm kind of taken aback by what Katie said. I didn't think she paid that close of attention to me, to trying to figure me out. I also kind of didn't take her as smart enough to put it together. Don't get me wrong, I love the girl, but she's always come off a little ditzy to me.

"Well, I can't talk to him right now anyway. I missed his text this morning. He showed up at my place to talk, and I wasn't there. Now he won't even text me back."

"He will, Kara, just give him some time." She puts her hand over mine with a little squeeze.

"If you need to talk, then I'm here. Otherwise I need some new jeans and a killer pair of heels, something that says casual dinner out but also says 'fuck me later' to John."

Okay, my thoughts are now officially elsewhere.

"I do believe those are called 'fuck me' pumps."

"Yep, we should get you pair while we are at it."

The vision of me walking in a four-inch heel, now that would be a sight. "Sure, Katie, I give it all of four steps until I'm flat on my face!"

"Okay…how about some bright ass red lipstick and something to show off that ass! That will knock some sense into Stephan!"

I have to admit I like that idea, showing up dressed to kill. I think back to the morning on the El, of how I felt. Fuck that, alley man came at me while I was sweaty and in old workout clothes. But am I really ready to draw attention, to purposely make people look at me?

I think Katie is a mind reader. "Kara, shut up."

"But I haven't even said anything!"

"Yeah, but shut up the conversation in your head. First, it's not fair because I can't hear it to make fun of you. And second, you're overthinking whatever the hell that conversation is about! This is an outfit for Stephan, well, him and you. But I don't want to think of you in the part you're gonna enjoy!"

"Katie, you are truly something. Shall we say 'special'?"

"Yes, ma'am! And that is why you love me!"

Rolling my eyes in her direction, I manage to glimpse my reflection in the mirror. I look like me.

"How is this color?" We've been playing in the makeup section for long enough that the salespeople are starting to get pissed, but I don't care. This is too much fun. The lipstick I had just "tested" is a lavender, carefully outline with a plum-colored lip liner. One eye is covered in gold shadow, and the other is ready for St. Patty's day in a festive green. Katie has on the red lipstick she was wanting me to buy. It is beautiful, but it's the contour pack she has been playing with that has me trying not to pee from laughing so hard. She looks like a tan skeleton with bright red lips.

"Oh. I love it! It sets off the green eye shadow so perfectly." We are planning on making a purchase; I mean, we're not that bitchy. But for these prices, we're paying enough to have fun playing.

Katie has a couple of bags at her feet. The ultimate pair of heels and some skinny jeans that don't leave much to the imagination. She claims she has the perfect shirt to finish off the outfit. I don't even want to think of what that might be. I have tried on everything Katie has thrown at me, but I haven't brought myself to buy any of them. Some foundation and mascara seem much safer at the moment.

"Come on, Kara, you at least have to get the lipstick. He can do without the clothes." I feel like I'm thirteen as I double over from laughter. It's as though we were sitting in our eighth grade classrooms, and someone just said the word *boobie*.

It's while we're at lunch that Stephan finally decides to text me back. No reason or excuse on why it took him half the day, just a "Can we talk tonight? I can come by your place at six?"

No, not my apartment, not where all this started. I have a feeling I might want to storm out on this little conversation, and I can't exactly get up and stomp out of my own apartment.

I text him back, a very short and simple "Not at my place." I probably should have named someplace else we could meet. I'm sure the "not my place" text seems rather bitchy, but I don't have much left at the moment when it comes to dealing with him. I'm still hurt it took him so long to text me back, hurt that he ever walked out in the first place.

"Okay. How about my place then? I have plans with some friends, but I can meet you there at six."

"Fine." I hold the phone in my hand, trying to decide if I should add anything else. I can't really think of something beyond wanting to send him an image of my middle finger, and I don't think that one will help right now. So I wisely put the phone away.

Katie's looking at me, waiting for me to tell her what all the texts were about; but I really don't want to share right now. I flag down our waitress and turn my watered down iced tea into a Ketel One and cranberry as I smear my new red lipstick over my tightly drawn lips. She wisely doesn't say a word.

I'm silent as we start the ride back to the city. I feel horrible. I feel like I ruined Katie's day out. It was fine until the texts started coming in. We were having fun. We did our shopping, managed to do makeup that left us looking like drunk clowns. The first half of the day was spent making plans for the next few weeks, plans for dinner, and maybe a show at the Chicago Theater. John had called to check in while we shopped and even made sure I knew that if Stephan was being too big of a dick, that he would take both Katie and I as his date. Between Stephan pissing me off and John now being nice, I'm stuck feeling like maybe I don't understand men at all. Maybe I'm the worst judge of character there is.

Don't get me wrong, it had been great forgetting about this fight with Stephan for a while. But after lunch, after those stupid texts came in, it got awkward. I knew I wasn't good company; I was pissed off and quiet. Katie had dealt with it well. She kept the conversation going by herself; commenting on people's outfits as they walked by, a "can you believe she would wear those shoes with that skirt" kind of conversation. All I had to do was provide the occasional "yeah" or "wow" to keep it going, to not feel like the piece of shit friend I was acting like.

"I'm sorry, Katie," I say as I'm pulling up to her building; I couldn't not say something.

She grabs her bags, gets out of the car, and pauses. "Kara, give him a chance. He cares about you. He might just be everything you need right now." She looks at me and smiles. It's a sympathy smile. I hate those smiles. "I'm here if you need me."

How do I respond? That's sweet and all, but what does she really know about it? And now I get a sympathy, poor-Kara kind of smile.

I force a smile back at her as I mutter, "Thanks." She nods her head, shuts the car door, and heads into her building.

It's only five when I pull away, even with the drive over the Stephan's house, I'm going to be early, really early. I head out nonetheless, thinking, *What the hell else am I gonna do that's not going to get me in more trouble right now?* The drive gives me time to think, which really only gives me time to get worked up. I love Stephan, probably more than I have ever loved anyone. I know this is all just me being scared. I can't face it if I tell him I need him, and he's not there. If I explain to him why he found me drunk, why I feel like I need to drink, and he still tries to stop me, still doesn't understand.

I can't live with my head running like this. My mind is in a nonstop spin, like some full-speed, out-of-control roller coaster running off the track. If he really knew anything, he wouldn't give me such shit about needing an escape. If he could spend ten minutes alone in my head right now, he would do anything to stop it. He would pour the fucking drink for me, if he only knew what it felt like.

I knew I wasn't going to explain it; I'm starting to doubt that I'll ever say it out loud. I don't think I know the words that could make them understand. They would act like they got it, and then they would walk away thinking I'm nuts. And if I thought he watched me too closely now, it would just get so much worse.

I need to close this up. As much as I hate the thought, I need to keep him at a distance right now, just until I can figure this out, until I can learn how to control my head. He can see through me too easily, and I can't have that. I can't. I won't explain myself. I'm twenty-five years old, well past the time of having to explain my actions to someone else. Isn't that the whole point of moving out to this stupid city anyway? Oh joy, the wonderful experience this move has given me. If only I could go back and change it. I would never have made the move if I knew then what I know now.

Well, fuck this move and fuck him too.

I see his house coming up on the right, but I can't seem to make myself stop. I drive right passed it and just keep going. How many times, driving home from one function or another, have I wanted to keep driving, no idea of where I was going, just drive until the roads ends, for the sole reason as to see what is there when it does? Well, now I can. I don't need this shit, his shit. He walked out on me yesterday; well, now he can see what that feels like. I feel powerful as I drive down his street and past his house, a little bitchy but powerful nonetheless. Fuck him; it's like a song running through my head. Fuck him, fuck him, fuck him. I get about five miles away before guilt gets the better of me, guilt and the truth. Fuck him for making me push him away, for pushing this fight with me. Fuck him for making me love him and making me need him.

"Fuck!" I scream it at no one but myself. A primal scream, a scream for the sake of screaming. I do a quick U turn, horns blearing out behind me as I speed back down the street toward his house.

Its five forty-five by the time I park and walk up to his place. I know he's not home yet, so I take the time and try to settle myself down by sitting on a bench in the cool night air. I'm right out front of the row of brownstones, his house one of many in a line. He'll have to walk right by me when he gets back.

It's cold, and I'm shivering. So I'm not really surprised that this whole settling down thing isn't working for me. I'm mad at him, and now I'm pissed at myself for my little outburst in the car and driving away in the first place. Sometimes I swear it feels like I'm the only one getting in the way of my future; sometimes I don't care at all anyway. The way I feel at this moment makes it one of those I don't care much anyway moments. I lean my head back against the bench and let my eyes slowly close. Taking a deep breath, I try to focus only on calming myself down. I'm looking for anything else to focus on, but there doesn't seem to be much that will still the thoughts in my head. I settle on making shapes out of the bursts of color and light behind my eyelids. I never hear Stephan walk up.

"Kara." He sits down next to me. "Kara, open your eyes and look at me."

But I don't want to look at him, not now. I may be here, but I'm not ready for this fight. My head is turned away from him; and if I were to open my eyes now, they would be looking at the dark sky, the last of the purple and dark blue colors in their final appearance before they fade to black, something that would be far too peaceful for the way I feel at this moment.

"Kara, look at me please. Please don't make me beg," Stephan whispers the words in my ear. His tone and warm breath are seductive despite my anger at him. But his words, the very concept that he's trying to guilt me into looking at him, seem cruel.

"Kara, please. I'm worried about you. I'm scared for you. Please talk to me." His hand is on my thigh. My eyes glance down at it, staring a hole through his spread fingers. It's as if time itself has slowed. My mind is confused, and his words make my heart burn. There's a part of me that wants to lean against his chest and tell him every last thought and fear I've ever had. But there's this bigger part of me. It feels like if I told him, it would be like handing over the little bit of control I have left. That's the part of me that's scared and really angry.

"Stephan," I'm trying to control the sound of my voice, to keep it from quivering and to keep it from betraying how close I am to losing any little bit of strength I have left.

"You really know very little about me, to sit here and tell me you're scared for me." My voice is beginning to shake; I can feel my anger growing, feeding the bitterness inside of me. "It's beyond ignorant. You know nothing of my mind or my past and very little of my present. Are you really so egotistical as to sit on your high horse and judge me?"

I push him away and stand up. I can't bring myself to turn and face him. It would just be too much to see the look on his face.

"You know shit." I spit it out. I can't help it. I never turn to look back at him as I walk away.

I want to run. I wanna scream. I want to hurt. I want him to stop me. I want him to force me to turn, to force his arms around me. I want him to hold me and never let me go.

But instead I focus on putting one foot in front of the other, on making forward motion. By the time I reach my car, the tears are streaming down my face. But I keep my back straight. I know he's watching, standing in the same spot trying to figure out what just happened. I won't let him see me break. I slowly sink into my car. I can see him in the rearview mirror, still standing alone by the bench.

There's no hiding the look of pain and disappointment that's etched onto his face. Buckling my seatbelt, I pull away.

I've been driving far too long. The fifteen-minute drive back to my house has taken over half an hour. I blink twice, trying to blink away the tears as I drive, trying to see through them. I'm not quite home yet, but at least now I know where I am. I know where I was too lost in my own head, lost in thoughts I don't want to remember, but one thought keeps breaking through.

I was wrong. I was wrong to lie to Rick; I was wrong to run out on Stephan. I don't want the world to think I'm strong. I want the world to know how weak I am, to see the real me, who I am right now at this moment, and to love me anyway.

I'm just so scared. I'm terrified of what I'll have left if they don't, if instead of loving me, they leave. I'm tired, so damn tired. I don't know how much longer I can do this.

●●●

I'm standing in front of my table, the brown paper bag sitting like a present on Christmas morning. I really don't want to drink it, but I need to do something, anything to keep me from feeling like this. I grab at the vodka, frantically bringing it to my mouth before I have time to talk myself out of it. The glass bottle is smooth and cool to my lips. The first sip burns, and so does the second. I slide my back down my kitchen wall until I'm sitting on the floor, fully dressed from my day and knowing I've left Stephan wondering what just happened. It burns to the pit of my soul, knowing I can push people away like this when all I want is for them to love me. It matches the burn from the booze; the vodka is scorching my throat as it slides its way down, burns as it hits my stomach. The punishment from the burn is a weird comfort, but I know it'll be short-lived.

God, make it go away, I can't handle this. Make it stop…please. It burns. What would Stephan say to that?

"Kara, please call me. Please, what don't I know?" His voice is pleading with my machine, as if it could answer his questions.

I know this ploy, and I'm not impressed. I've seen it all before. Make me think you care, make me think you want to hear me. You'll get me to admit it all, then…then it will be as if you never heard me, as if I never told you anything. I will be ignored, and you will be indifferent.

Kara can handle it. Kara will be fine. Kara doesn't need the attention, the care; you can leave her be. You can give it all to someone who needs it.

I've heard it all before. I've felt it all before. I hit erase, and his voice is gone. I walk back to my bed and climb under the covers. I know I'm hiding, and I don't care. It's 10:00 p.m., and it's Sunday. I have nowhere to be. No one is counting on me, no one can see me. I don't want to drink, so I lie in bed. I'm not tired. I close my eyes. I close them, but it's not the black nothingness that I crave. I close my eyes and see the alley.

But this time, I control what happens…

This time, when he leaves, someone will find me. This time, they will care. This time, I fight. This time, they won't laugh at me. This time, they're angry at him. This time, they can fix me.

CHAPTER 16

The alarm goes off, and my hand slaps it as if it were any other morning. I know it's time to get up, that it's time to head to work. Instead I lay and look up at my bedroom ceiling thinking of yesterday. I think of all the ways I can play out in my mind what will never be. People will never care; they have their own problems, their own drama, and that will never change.

It's not possible to go back in time, and no one can fix me. It creates a desperation that I can't calm. This feeling, this desperation, it's become too much of who I am lately. It's like a warm, fucked-up blanket; it comforts me when I'm lost, and no one can make me feel lost like Stephan can.

Thinking of him just confuses me more. I know I have to see him today, that there really can't be an escape. I know if I call off work, he'll show up here, and that would be even worse. At least at work, even though I can't escape him, I can escape the questions he'll have. He won't risk a confrontation where everyone could see it. He won't let that control go if it means he could be embarrassed.

Last night, he came at me like he knows me, like he has always known me. How dare he be scared for me now? I'm fine now. I needed him to be scared for me when it happened, to push me when it happened. I find myself getting angry again. Why couldn't he have seen through me then? Just because he knows a few family stories, he thinks he can understand me. This is who I am. No one saw me, and this is what it created. No one saw me then, so deal with it now. Deal with it and leave me the hell alone about it.

Even as tears threaten, my anger seems to be providing strength. He wants to claim he is scared for me? He wants me to trust that? He, of all people, should know the way the world works. He watched his dad close the door on him and never come back. He wants me to trust that I can open myself to him, to let the thoughts and fears that whip and churn though my mind out, to lay them down on the table like something to be shown off and bragged about. Here is Grandma's best china. To the left we have the history of our family, and back there we have Kara and her insanity. Why would I? Why should I open myself to that, just another person who can show me I don't mean enough to take the time to give a shit? Well, I'm not going to give him that chance. If I haven't done a good enough job at hiding, then I just need to do better. I will show him I am nothing to be scared for, that I am stronger than he thinks I am.

The shower is hot, and as the heat cascades over my body, I feel the control return, the plan form. My hair dried and straighten, I walk slowly into my room, with one decision echoing through my thoughts. The best defense is a good offense. If nothing else, I'll have the look of strength and control today. Come hell or high water, I will leave him spinning and feeling as unsure of himself as he has left me all weekend. I won't say a word to him, the occasional nod to stay professional, but other than that, nothing.

I dress in my best sexy, yet still work appropriate outfit. My black skirt skims the top of my knee but has a slit that reaches midthigh. I add a crisp white button down top, the type where the first button is dangerously low on my chest. I finish the outfit off with pumps that I know I will regret wearing the first time I have to get up and walk anywhere at all and a wide black leather belt. I add his favorite perfume, one that he had given me after hearing me compliment Katie one afternoon.

I feel powerful as I walk toward the El, sipping on my coffee along the way. It's not until I'm sitting in my seat that I question what I've really done. The slit in my skirt and the low cut to my blouse are gaining attention from those sitting around me. I don't really do good with attention from guys anymore; it doesn't take much to leave me in a complete panic. It's the morning rush so the El is plenty busy, and the crowd provides a sense of security for me. But I still don't feel completely comfortable, and it has me questioning the walk home. It will be dark by the time I get off the El after work today, and it's almost a three-block walk back to my apartment building, not too long but long enough. I find myself wishing for my old holey T-shirt and sweats.

My cocky "I'll show you" attitude has already been thrown through a loop by the time I get to work. I'm even more deflated when I hear that Stephan has been called away for a meeting. There's one red rose on my desk with three little words written on a card beneath it.

Talk to me.

I can feel the anxiety building within me. I only make it to lunch. I make up having a migraine; I think the look on my face helps to sell it. What my boss reads as pain is really pure panic and anxiety. I have to get home wearing this damn outfit. Stephan still wants an explanation, and I psyched myself out for nothing. I feel like a deflated balloon doll, one of those special "dress up your balloon to look like a whore, hole where the mouth should be" kind of doll.

I can't do this. I'm practically hyperventilating by the time I'm home and leaning against the inside of my apartment door. I lock it, unlock it, and lock it again, just to make sure the dead bolt really did turn. I strip off this stupid shirt and skirt and wad them up. I try to throw it at my garbage can, but both go flying in separate directions like large pieces of cloth confetti now decorating my living room floor. The shoes are left tossed every which way on the carpeting near the front door, and my belt is draped over the corner of my bed. My old baggy clothes feel safe, like a uniform for me now. If it's really going to be a uniform, only one thing is missing.

The first sip burns, and lately I find comfort in that burn. It means that soon my thoughts won't be as loud; soon I'll be able to turn it off in my head. I lean my back against the counter and slowly empty my glass in one long sip. Today I don't pour another; today I just needed something to take the edge off. I still have a few things left to do before I can be completely free and lost in the fog. I pick up the phone and call my doctor for a refill on my sleeping pills. It's not that I'm planning on taking them, but I'm not willing to go another night playing the "let's wait and see if Kara's going to go crazy tonight or not" game. Two weeks ago, I could barely keep it together when it was just alley man I was running from. It's painful to admit that now I run from Stephan too.

CHAPTER 17

It takes a while before I start to feel normal again. It's requiring more and more of an effort to get everything to turn off in my head. Now that I'm calm, I'm afraid to lose it, like any movement too quick, or even the mere thought to turn off the light, might take away the calm and bring back my mind in all its glory. I can't seem to get my inner self to shut up.

I know that people wouldn't like my reasoning for why I drink. I know they say it's bad to use booze like this, but if they knew that a couple drinks could give me peace, wouldn't they be okay with it? Wouldn't they want me to be able to be the Kara that people need? I wouldn't be "girl who can't look at you on the bench" or "girl who makes up migraine." I could show people who I really am. My mind will never turn off completely, but at least it's calm now, rambling waves of nothing thoughts—but it's calm here. I can get lost in these kind of thoughts. They're not scary like my dreams. They're not as sharp and painful as my regular emotions. I find I don't need to be as careful around them.

An hour can go by in the blink of an eye; the best part is I don't even remember what it was that I was thinking about. It makes me feel like I must have solved something, worked something through; like they say with a dream, you never remember the ones you finish. So those thoughts must be finished, if I can get lost enough, maybe, eventually, all these thoughts and fears will be finished too.

The sound of my phone chiming, telling me there's a new text, is slowly pulling me back toward the real. I know it will give up after the third alert, but it's too late. Blinking against the afternoon light streaming in through my windows, I stumble my way toward the table to reach my phone.

"I'm done playing games. I love you, and I know something is wrong, very wrong. I know you won't talk about it if I ask, so I'm not asking. I give up; I'm on my way over to you. You WILL be there. We WILL talk." Shit. Shit, shit, shit.

Jumping up, I run into the bathroom. I'm picking up clothes along the way to shove into the hamper, at the same time trying desperately to get a comb back through my hair. After ten minutes of running around like an idiot, my apartment is almost clean, and I look halfway decent. I'm sitting on the arm of my couch waiting, waiting and thinking. This is not a good combination for me. The nerves and excitement that I normally have for seeing Stephan are gone. They have been replaced with annoyance and anxiety. I finally reached a calm, and he's coming to interrupt it all.

Well, fuck him. I need this calm. I walk slowly, and very calmly I might add, into the kitchen and pour my second tall drink of the day. The glass feels cool on my lips. Pouring yet another one, I start to feel sexy and free. Fuck him. He thinks he knows me, knows what I need. I don't think so. I can hear him fumbling with his keys in the hallway outside my door.

I'm leaning against the wall, my drink pressed tight to my chest when he finally gets the door open. He stands halfway in the apartment, halfway in the hall, staring at me, not saying a word. It feels like forever that he's just watching, like he's looking for something to be wrong with me. I hate him looking at me like that; I break the silence, finding my inner sassy bitch is more than just slightly annoyed at this interruption to our evening.

"Well, you wanted to talk, so go ahead...talk."

His eyes narrow at my tone. "Stop it, Kara, just stop it. I can tell that something is bothering you. It's obvious to anyone who knows you. You haven't been yourself in weeks; it's crazy how much you've changed in such a short amount of time. You won't talk to me, and I don't know why. I thought you loved me too." He runs his hand through his hair as he says this. "Why won't you talk to me?" I expected anger, yelling, something much more explosive. You can hear the anger in his voice but more than anything else I hear the hurt that's there too.

His response throws me through such a loop that it leaves my resolve spinning on end. I hate knowing he is taking this personally, that he's doubting the way I feel for him, that he thinks it's *him* I won't talk to. I want to take his hurt away; I want to be able to give him what he wants from me. But then, I imagine the look on his face as he sees me for who and what I am right now. I picture the hurt in his eyes slowly turn to disappointment, and it feels as if it will kill me. This imagined disappointment has me trying desperately to find my sassy bitch self again. I would rather lose him over anger than have him walk away regretting he ever loved me. I close my eyes.

Sassy, Kara, bitchy Kara. Come on, don't let him see through you, Kara. Breathe.

"Well, which is it? Are you so worried about me, or are you worried because whatever you think we have you're no longer sure of?" I'm trying to be graceful and smooth, as if it enhances the new sassy me that seems to want to make her presence known. But my sexy low sinking into the couch is truly more of a drunken flop.

"What are you drinking?" Stephan asks, suddenly paying more attention to the drink in my hand than the words coming out of my mouth.

"Nothing you need to worry about. Why, would you like one?" The blurry is starting to return, and I like it. A giggle escapes my lips.

"Kara, seriously…"

"Seriously what, Stephan! This is my night, my house, my night."

Oops, I said that one already.

"You want to tell me I can't have a few drinks in my own house! You don't like what you find here, you can choose to leave whenever you like. The door is right behind you."

I stand up too quickly and sway slightly. Stephan's hand is there to steady me, which of course does anything but.

"What are you doing, Stephan?" I look up at him, my inner sass long forgotten; his touch stopping it cold. He looks down at me and takes a deep breath, and for a moment it's as if we are breathing the same breath again, like we're back laying on my couch wrapped in each other's arms and the alley never happened, like it never came between us. He bends in slowly, painfully slowly. It makes me want to yell, "Take it, take what you want, take it all, I don't care. Just love me again." But instead of kissing me, he pauses. He looks at me with deep eyes that seem to go on forever.

"Kara," he is barely whispering to me now. "Kara, I want to kiss you."

Since when does he ask for permission?

I don't respond, but I don't move either. I take another breath while trying to quiet the confusion in my head and just enjoy the way the air tastes, the way I know Stephan tastes. He moves in and slowly closes the gap between us. His lips are warm and soft on mine. He feels powerful and gentle all at the same time. I take a step into him and wrap my arms around his neck and pull him against me. His arms circle around me, and they feel safe. They feel protective. He runs his hand up my back with just enough pressure that I seem to melt into him. He runs his other hand down my back, stopping for just a moment at my hips, as if asking permission again. The slight groan that escapes my lips seems to be all he needs, and his hands continue down cupping my ass, slowly his kiss gets deeper. I'm lost in the moment. The softened edges of my vodka-soaked mind leave me a creature of pure feel, pure touch, and now pure pleasure. Stephan's hands are kneading into my back, grabbing at my shoulders, and then in one fierce movement, he has pulled away from me.

Is this a joke to him? Is he seriously trying to just leave me completely shattered? No. I see it in his eyes. He wants to know we're okay. He needs me as much as I need him. He wants to know he's still mine. But he doesn't want to play with me either. He doesn't want me broken. I can see the disappointment in his eyes for what he did, for kissing me just to see if I would kiss him back. I hate him for how the disappointment looks in his eyes. He should be mad at me, but now that it's aimed at him. All I want to do is take it away. I don't want to hurt him, and I know that's all I've been doing. I know at the end of it all that this is my fault.

He is standing a few feet away looking at me with such confusion and pain. I step back into him, melt back into him, pushing him against the wall, trying to reclaim the feeling of a moment ago.

"Stephan," I whisper. I push back into him and look up into his eyes. He is looking down at me, studying me, as if deciding what to do next. He holds me and slowly starts to kiss me. First, he's on my lips; but after a moment, he's trailing an imaginary line down my jaw, behind me ear, down to where my shoulder meets my neck. Oh god, it feels so good.

His hands are tugging at the back of my shirt, trying to pull it up over my pants, up to my shoulders. It sits discarded and crumpled on the floor at my feet. He has left me standing in my bra, cupped up against him and breathing heavy. He continues his imaginary line. Leaving my neck, he traces his line across my chest and down. His breath hot against me, and I have no choice but to react. I am moving against him, lost in the moment. In one swift movement, he is holding my hands behind my back. He pulls away and stands there looking at me once again.

"Kara, I can't do this, not now. I need you. God, do I need you, but I need to know what's wrong first."

What! What's wrong now? Are you kidding me? Are you fucking kidding me? Oh yeah, sassy ass bitch, welcome back. I give Stephan one hell of an icy cold look, turn around while kicking my shirt toward the couch, and walk into the kitchen.

"Door is straight ahead, Stephan. Feel free to use it."

CHAPTER 18

I can feel the panic creeping its way into my soul once again, ready to curl up in the spot it now calls home, leaning up against the counter I grip onto it as though it were a life raft in a stormy ocean. I concentrate on slowing my breathing, to focus only on the breath. In and out, one, two, three, one, two, three—each breath is proof that I'm still here, I'm safe, and I'm okay. If I can control the breath, maybe I can learn to control the thoughts.

I slowly begin to let go of the countertop. I want another drink. I know if I drink enough, quickly enough it'll all go away. I can ride out the storm, and by the time it really matters, it will have passed and I can function again. It feels as though there is a tidal wave permanently on the horizon, always ready to crash into shore. I can see it coming, and I'm trying to push it off of me, to push it back the way it came. I know once it hits, I'll drown in it; it will have its way with me. So I fight it because I have no other choice.

I'm afraid, and it's not just of drowning in the emotions and fear that I know will come. I'm afraid of being left alone in them, of saying out loud, "Hey! Over here! I need help!" and no one comes. What happens in that moment when you realize you're truly alone? Not that they wouldn't be there, watching and waiting in the background for the storm to pass, only to come swooping in to try to pick up where they think everything left off. But in the meantime, you are clinging to a lifeboat alone and in rough waters, everyone on the beach waving to you while they sip their piña colada and complain about their tan.

What about the friends that realize you're just not worth the drama that comes with breaking down, with letting people see the crazy? So I stand on the shore, not quite with the group sipping their frozen drinks, but close enough that they really don't sense the separation. I stand here watching the tidal wave come and fighting against it. It makes me so tired, too emotionally drained to do much of anything, and too much past the point of caring either.

Fuck this "I don't need another drink" thing, I grab what's left of the bottle and head into my room.

Stephan had come over tonight telling me he loved me, telling me we were going to talk, demanding it in fact and leaving me no choice at all in the matter, and part of me really hoped I would be able to talk to him, that I could be everything he wanted me to. But when I couldn't, he left like it was nothing at all. It was so easy for him. Okay so it was when I told him to leave, but still, he never even looked back. I don't know what it is that I expect out of him. The words coming out of my mouth are telling him to go. I don't know why I get so hurt when he does exactly what I have asked.

Holding onto the bottle of vodka, clutching it to my chest between sips, leaves me feeling brave; without it, I'm left with the reality of it all. I know I'm anything but brave. I'm scared shitless, scared of falling asleep and what I will dream but even more afraid of staying awake and what I will think, scared of what will happen if I truly admit I love this man more than I have ever loved anyone. What happens if I actually tell him?

It's easy for me to pretend he would care. Sometimes I play out in my mind what could have been, how Stephan would find me, how he would have protected me; wrapping me in his arms, he would tell me how brave I am, how well I'm handling it all. But if I were to actually tell him and he does nothing, then I can't pretend anymore. It would no longer be a question of if he would care. It would be an unarguable fact. He doesn't care.

Then I really would be alone, alone in the dark and alone in that alley forever, and I can't take that. So I say nothing and I doubt I ever will.

It's taken longer than I would have liked, but now I can start to feel the heat from the vodka begin to warm me from the inside out. My thoughts start to lose their edge, and I slowly feel my eyes close. I'm rewarded with the gift of a dreamless sleep.

CHAPTER 19

The sound of my alarm buzzing, over and over again, it's annoyingly attempting to pull me back into reality. But I'm too damn tired, and my head is pounding. I'm just done with all of this, beyond done, and clearly I'm not as good at pretending as thought I could be.

I roll over, trying to will myself back asleep. But instead, I find myself staring at the wall, getting angrier and angrier at the clock that won't shut up.

"Fine! I'm up, you stupid piece of shit!"

Apparently, I yell at inanimate objects now. Sitting up, I turn off the alarm and hold it in my hands, my blankets still twisted around my body. Looking down at the clock, I find myself rationalizing all the reasons I should stay in bed and all the reasons that I shouldn't. It really boils down to facing Stephan at work. No escape, nothing to make my mind lose its focusing and nothing I can run too when I really need it. Giving in and flopping backward onto my awaiting pillows, I do a half army crawl toward the nightstand. I find my sleeping pills and shake the bottle over my open hand. I'm not sure how many I pop into my mouth. And I'm not sure I care, grabbing a cup off of the nightstand I swallow them down. It tastes like I'm drinking watered down vodka; I can't remember when that would have been from.

"Stupid f'ing clock. I know how to fall back asleep." I smirk. Great, I'm talking and making faces to objects now.

I can hear the phone ring, but I just roll over.

I can hear someone knocking on the door, but I just roll over.

When I do wake up, it's dark in my apartment. It's dark outside. I pick up my phone. It's eight, and I have slept through work. Hell, I've slept through the day. My phone shows ten missed calls and four messages.

I look through the missed calls: Stephan, work, work, Stephan, work, Stephan, Katie, Stephan, Rick, Stephan. I don't want to hear what the messages say, not now at least. I know that after blowing off work, one of those messages will be along the lines of "unless you have been in a major accident you're fired." I don't need to hear it to know that it's there. I don't need to be told that the life I have set up for myself is suddenly gone; I can feel that it's gone with every fiber of my body. I've known it for weeks. All that has happened is that reality has finally caught up with what I have known all along. I walk into the kitchen and open the fridge. I don't know what it is that I'm looking for. There's nothing in here I want right now; but apparently I have looked one second too long because the stupid door starts its beeping, reminding me that the fridge is open. No shit it's open. I'm standing right here. I know it's open. I close the door and stand there, just looking at the closed door. I walk slowly into the living room, as if I were sick. I make it as far as the couch; sinking to the floor, I lean my back up against it.

I hear my phone ringing again, but I left it in the kitchen. It's all of ten steps away, but I stay where I am. I feel like I might be in shock, shock of what something as simple as sleeping away the day really means. What did I really accomplish by turning off the alarm clock? I've probably lost my job. I've probably lost Stephan, if I hadn't lost him by my actions from the past couple of weeks already. Katie and Rick, well, who knows what they think. They probably just figured that I'm having a busy workday. I hear the phone ringing again; but this time, I also hear banging, not knocking, but banging at my front door.

"Kara!" It's Rick's voice. "Kara! Open the door!"

I'm frozen at the fear and panic I hear in his voice. I hate knowing my actions put it there, that yet again I am the cause of a person I love being hurt. Begrudgingly, I get up and start to head to the door to let him in. As I walk, I take a quick look around my apartment, and it's as if I see it for the first time in who knows how long; I realize I can't open the door to him.

It's not that my apartment is a mess. I had just cleaned up for Stephan yesterday. It's more about the little things that are out for him to see. There are three half-finished drinks scattered about, and I know they don't hold water. There is an empty bottle of vodka sitting on my table, and the few plants I have look like they've been through a drought. I freeze in my steps and hope that he didn't hear me get up, that somehow he'll assume I'm not home. I have no idea what he'll do. I'm hiding, and whether he thinks I'm home or not, he has to realize I'm avoiding him. He starts to talk through the door. I can tell from the tone of his voice he's not sure if I can hear him. It's obvious he's hoping I'm not here listening to him beg through the door, that he's hoping his sister is someone who would never do that.

"Kara, please…please, Kara. Please let me in. Let me help you. Are you sick? What happened? Please, Kara." His voice is desperate. It's barely above a whisper, but I can hear him perfectly.

I can picture him standing there, one hand at his side in defeat and one hand on the door hoping it will open. I picture his head leaning against it. The thought of him falling into my apartment if I were to open the door puts a smile on my face. Shit, I really am crazy; how am I smiling right now? Now, when my older brother, who has always been there for me, is begging for me to open the door. I start to move to let him in, and then his words stop me in my tracks.

"Stephan called me."

Oh shit.

"He's on his way here. If you don't let me in, we'll use his key. He called Katie too."

How the hell did Stephan get these numbers! How could he do this to me! More importantly, what did he tell Rick? Rick's voice is desperate but still managing to get angrier and angrier.

"Don't make me break into your house, Kara. Please don't make me. Don't do this to me. Don't do this to Stephan. He really does care about you, and I don't know what is going on. But I know he's scared for you."

Tears spring to my eyes, I can't help it. "Damn it, Kara!"

I hear his fist hit the door in frustration. I hear his footsteps as he walks back down the hall. I know I don't have long. Stephan's house isn't that far from here. If he's already on his way, I have even less time. I'm not even really thinking, just going through motions. I start to clean up the apartment, but as I move past by the bathroom, I glimpse myself in the mirror. It stops me cold in my tracks. My hair is matted and stuck to my shoulders. Old makeup is under my eyes. I have a bruise on my forehead, but I have no idea where it came from. I don't have time to fix the apartment and me. Even if I did, how would I explain today? How would I explain to Rick why I sat inside and listened to him beg for me to open the door? How do I explain the last month of actions to Stephan? I can't face him, face them, not today, not like this. It's even worse since I know Katie and Stephan will be here with Rick too. I make a decision, and it's one I don't want to focus on.

I start running through the apartment holding my gym bag as if it has the power to save me. I throw my toothbrush, a couple changes of clothes, and my wallet in it. I grab a piece of paper to write a note to Rick, something to tell him that I'm okay, that I just need a little time, something to tell him not to worry, not to let Mom and Dad worry, something to Stephan to say I still love him, and I'm sorry, even something for Katie to say I'll be back soon. I sit drumming my fingers on the table knowing that with each passing moment, I get closer to the time that they will be letting themselves in, and I will have no choice but to face them. I have no words, no idea what to write. I can feel the panic starting to rise like bile in my throat. I can't face them. I end up writing a simple note, a pathetic, I know it's a "nowhere good enough" note.

> I'm sorry.
> I just can't do this right now.
> I'm so sorry. I love you.

I can hear their voices come from around the corner as I shut my front door. I don't bother to lock it; I know they have the key anyway. I can hear Stephan telling Rick and Katie about how he found me that one stupid night, how he was sorry he had lied to Rick, how he felt like this was now his fault. He tells them how I had screamed at him that he doesn't understand.

I hide in the laundry room at the end of the hallway. I hide from the people I love, people who are just trying to help me. I hide like something pathetic, not even someone, but something. I hate myself right now. I wish I had the courage to face them, but I only have the strength to pray that they won't find me. I can hear them at my front door. I can picture the look on Rick's face as he realizes that my door is now unlocked, proof that I had been home. I thought it would be anger, but it's relief I hear in his voice.

"Oh, thank God. She's letting us in…Kara," he says my name softly like someone would say if they were trying to wake you up from a lazy afternoon nap.

"It's just us. You okay in here, sweetie?" I hear the door close to my apartment, and I know that I should use this moment to leave, but instead I sit, morbid curiosity at what will happen next. I kinda feel like someone at their own funeral.

The door opens and bounces against the wall. The noise echoes down the hallway.

"Kara!"

Rick is screaming into the hallway, running out of my apartment. I wish I hadn't stayed; nothing is worse than having to witness this.

"Kara!"

Stephan is right behind him. Together they go running down the hall back toward the elevator. Katie seems stuck to the spot. I hear a small sob escape her lips.

"Kara, no…" Then her footsteps slowly fade away.

I can't take listening anymore. I peek out the door, and once I see the hallway is clear, I run to the back staircase, passing my apartment (the door is now wide open). And I walk down the stairs to the street.

The bonus of city living is that none of them know where my car is parked. It's never in the same spot twice; it's hardly on the same street two days in a row. I throw my bag in the back and pull out.

In my rearview mirror, I can see the three of them huddled together. Rick looks up just as I start to turn off the street. I see him raise his arm and break into a run trying to chase after me. I turn and floor it, heading straight for the expressway. From there, who knows? I can feel tears streaming down my face, dropping off my cheeks. It blurs my vision, making the cars in front of me appear like dancing ghosts made up of tail lights. My phone is ringing, constantly ringing now.

I reach over and turn it off. I see the sign for the expressway, and I need to make a decision. Do I head north to Wisconsin or south to Indiana? North is home. North is the way I know. I have no choice but to act quickly. There are cars behind me. They won't wait while I sit here and make up my mind of where to run away to. North is what I know. North is my family, my high school, my friends.

North is my past.

I head south. How many times have I dreamt about driving? Just driving, no idea where I was going, how I was getting there, or what life would hold once I got there. It's sure as shit not the way I envisioned it, but now that little daydream appears to be coming true.

CHAPTER 20

I t was 9:45 p.m., Monday, November the twenty-sixth when I saw the last of the lights from the city in my rearview mirror. Now it's just past 2:00 a.m. I've been on the road for a little more than four hours. My head is pounding from crying an ocean of tears. I don't want to remember those first few hours on the road. I don't want to remember the way it felt watching Rick chase after me, the way it felt when I realized that I had left Stephan; I abandoned him just like his dad did all those years ago. I still can't believe I'm capable of that, that I'm capable of any of this. How could I put him through that much pain when all he wanted, all he begged for was to help? I'm so much worse than everything I hate in other people. I don't want to think about what that makes me. I sit here, knowing full well what I'm putting my family through, what I'm putting Stephan through. I hate myself for it, yet I still can't make myself turn the car around.

I'm far past the point of being able to focus. The windows are down, but the cold November air stopped helping to keep me awake an hour ago. I watch as the dashed yellow line dances in the middle of the road. I don't know how I'm this tired after I slept almost the whole day away. It feels like one hundred years ago that I made the decision to turn off the alarm clock.

I'm just plain exhausted, deep in the bones kind of exhaustion. I have nothing left in me. I think I'm still in Indiana, but to be honest, I'm not sure. I see a sign for a rest stop up ahead; I need some caffeine or some cold water to splash on my face, something. It's dark and lonely as I pull into the parking lot, empty but for one other car. I can see the family of four heading toward the bathrooms; two little boys rubbing the sleep from their eyes, one still clutching his teddy bear; it's clear they are either heading to a vacation or on their way home from one.

The last thing I remember was watching the family of four pulling out of the rest stop, waving goodbye to the little boy with his bear as they drove away. I must have fallen asleep almost immediately after that. I wake up to the sun shining brilliantly, but I'm freezing. How the hell had I slept while I was this cold? I hadn't brought a blanket with me, just what I was wearing and my jacket. No hat, no gloves, and it's November in the Midwest. I thank my lucky stars that this week the weather's been unusually warm. But even so, it must have gotten down to the mid-30s last night. I had obviously turned the car off, so it's not like there was any heat for me; if this had been a typical November night, I don't even want to think what could have been.

What I really want right now is to brush my teeth, but I'm so cold. And I know it has to be even worse outside. Turning the car on, I shiver at the initially blast of cold air; but after a few minutes, it has warmed up enough that I'm able to blast the heat. Once I can feel the tips of my fingers and toes again. I turn the car off and head to the bathroom to brush my teeth and pee.

I know, logically, no one is staring at me, but it certainly doesn't feel that way. It feels like every person I pass knows what I'm putting my family through. I try to be as quick as I can, record-breaking teeth brushing over here. I grab a coffee from one of those vending machines that pours black liquid into a cup. My hopes that it resembles coffee are dashed as I take my first sip, but really I'm just glad it's something that can warm me up. I get back to my car and head out to find some place for breakfast. I can't even remember the last time I ate.

I find a diner at the side of the road about twenty minutes past the rest stop. It has a name like Ruth's or Betty's, something like that. I didn't pay enough attention to know for sure. Sinking into a tall booth, I turn the mug over in hopes that I will soon have some real coffee in my system. Despite being in the car for twenty minutes, with the heat on at full blast, I'm still freezing. I'm out of it too, like I can't think right. I feel like I'm decently buzzed, but I haven't had anything to drink. It scares me a little, sleeping in the car like that when it's this cold out, feeling this out of it. I can all but hear Rick's voice telling me I should head to a hospital to make sure that I don't have the start of hypothermia; but that could also make it easier for them to find me. I'm hoping that as long as I'm in the heat now, as long as I'm drinking hot liquid and warming myself back up, I will be fine. I just can't allow myself to fall asleep in my car again. Stephan's right. There's something seriously wrong with the decisions I'm making right now. I want to pretend like I don't care what their outcome is, but I do. I try to think about something else instead, anything else.

Didn't I always dream of this, each and every time I drove back to the city when there was nothing to do but daydream? The not stopping, just driving, not being the Kara I was supposed to be but being out there—out here—trying to find adventure somewhere. The breakfast at the diner filled with truckers, the "who knows what the day will hold" adventure; I swear this is something right out of my head, right out of every long car ride I had after playing the "this is who I'm supposed to be" Kara role. Somehow in my dreams, it had seemed more glorious, more romantic in a way that could only live in dreams. Reality is always just a little dimmer, lonelier.

My reality is that I had run away from home. I'm twenty-five years old and a runaway. What the hell does that make me? It's the most pathetic thing I've ever heard, a twenty-five-year-old runaway.

My self-brooding moment is interrupted with a "What can I get ya darlin?" A waitress with curly hair and way too much makeup is smiling down at me; she's the exact stereotype of what I would expect at Ruth's trucker diner or wherever the hell I am.

"Coffee, pancakes, and bacon please," I respond, barely looking up at her. I don't want to be mean, but I want to remain someone unspecial, someone she won't remember.

"Sure thing, honey."

Pulling my wallet out of my purse, I start to count my cash; I need to think this whole thing through a little better. I'm almost out of gas, and it appears I only have $56 on me. I will need to stop at an ATM, and I'll need to use my credit cards. But I'm not sure if my bank would report where I am to my family.

I'm not a kid who's missing; there's been no sign of foul play. I even left a note. I'm an adult who left on my own. Would my family have rights to that information? I don't think so, but I'm not positive. The last thing I want is for them to know where I am right now. It's not like I'm going to stay gone. I just need some time to be left alone, and no one wants to give it to me.

"Here ya go, sweetheart. Let me know if you need anything more."

The pancakes taste better in my romantic dream version of the trucker stop too. I put my wallet back in my purse and notice my phone. A small black rectangle shouldn't lead to such panic. Picking it up, I hold it, turning it around and around in my hand, trying to decide what to do. I can only imagine what messages and texts are on here. I don't think I'm ready to listen to them yet. I need to have a plan first. I need to know what it is that I'm doing. I don't want to hurt them anymore than I already have, but I don't have any answers for them either. I finish my bacon—I'm not eating the watered-down flour they call pancakes—take the last sip of my nasty coffee, and head up to pay. When I ask the cashier what town and state this is, he looks at me like I have a third head.

"You okay, girly?"

What is with this town and the honey, darling, girly, sugar sweet, "gotta put a pet name at the end of every sentence?"

"I'm fine, just been driving all night."

"Well, um, you're about halfway between Indianapolis and Louisville. Another hour or so and you'll be in Kentucky."

Hmmm. I've never been to Kentucky.

It's eleven twenty-two Tuesday morning as I cross the Kentucky border. Somewhere between the diner and now I'd formulated my plan, thanks in part to a billboard advertising the lush open spaces of the Smokey Mountains National Park. I'm roughly six hours away, I think. I'm pretty used to the GPS on my phone—type in an address and done. I can't remember the last time I had to look at a real paper map to try to figure anything out. But I can't get to my GPS. I'm just not ready to turn the phone back on. So my newfound plan relies on my hope that my paper map reading skills don't get me lost.

I need time, just a little time where I don't have to be what people expect of me. I can't lie my way through my own life anymore. I can't pretend that the alley didn't scare me or that it never happened. I have to face that I lied to Stephan, to come to terms with the fact that he had to wake me up out of pill-and-booze induced sleep. After running last night, there's no more pretending, even if I wanted to. I might as well have made a giant float and driven through the streets of Chicago saying "Look here, look at me! I can't be what you want. I'm just not strong enough."

I know I'll have to face it all soon. I just want to put it off a little longer. I'm not ready to face the fear that was in Rick's voice last night after he read my note. I don't even want to think about my job, my dream firm gone, Stephan…the life I fought for gone.

I need some "Kara's gotta breathe" time, some space, just for a little bit. The picture on the billboard looked beautiful—wide open spaces, green meadows, and trees that are old enough to remind me that time will heal all wounds—beautiful. And it's down South, so it's gotta be warmer than the Chicago winter I'm used to. So down I go, heading toward Tennessee and the wide open; gotta be easier to breathe, Smokey Mountains.

Six more hours to the Smokey Mountain cabin from the side of the billboard, and then I can figure the rest out later. The image that sitting in that cabin, at the base of the mountain, and under a clear blue sky creates seems like perfection. Dear God, please let it be someplace I can just breathe. I couldn't do that anymore in Chicago, not really. My apartment had stopped feeling like a home. It became nothing but a box to escape in, to hide away and hope no one can see me. The problem is, there is no escape when what you're running from are your own thoughts and fears. Now that I'm physically gone, an escape seems like something that might actually be able to happen.

While driving past open farm fields and long lines of semis, I've come to the decision that when I stop for lunch, I'll call home, just a simple call, a message on a machine. I don't want to talk to anyone; I just want them to know I'm okay. I'll find a phone I can use so I don't have to turn on my cell, some random phone so they can't recognize the number. I'm hoping this way, they won't pick up. I'm not sure yet what I would say to them if they did.

My anxiety is getting worse as I drive; it's the attempt to figure out how I'm supposed to begin the conversation that I know eventually has to come that is bringing me to the brink of pure panic. My breath is coming harder now, quicker now. I know if I can't calm down I'll soon be blinking away tears, desperately trying to stay in my lane as I drive. The truth is, I don't want to explain it. I really don't want to say anything about the alley out loud. It would make facing my reaction that much more real. Nothing happened. Nothing happened, and now I'm a twenty-five-year-old runaway.

I lose another hour, driving while lost in my own head, as I try to sort it all out. I have to figure out how I'll explain myself, to make sure I understand how I ever let it get this far to begin with. It seems like that night in the alley is a snowball that has grown into an avalanche. Now I'm buried in the snow with no idea which way to even try to dig to get out.

An hour lost, and I'm no closer to knowing what to say than I was when Rick knocked on the door last night. I'm hungry, emotionally drained, and I know I've got to stop. I'm not going to feel better until I at least let them know I'm okay. I can't focus on the rest of this while I know they are sitting, scared about where I could be and what I might be doing. I let the car veer into the lane for the next exit ramp. I need to find a place to pump some gas and get something to eat, although I'm done with diners at this point.

I can see the yellow glowing sign before I even get off the exit ramp, at least I know what to expect from McDonald's. The closer I get, the more nervous I become. Fuck nervous, I'm terrified. What if Dad picks up? What if Rick picks up? Can I say I'm okay and hang up? Can I actually do it? Do I call Katie instead? Do I call Stephan?

Should I turn my cell on just real quick and send one text and then turn it back off?

My hands are sweating, and my throat feels like it's closing. This whole car seems smaller than it was just a few moments ago. I'm sitting in a McDonald's parking lot, in the cold of winter, having a full-blown panic attack, well, at least as much of a panic attack as I've ever had before. I'm not yelling at inanimate objects now, so that's gotta say something. In between gulps of air, I find myself staring at the radio as if some random DJ will come on and give me the answers that I need.

It's one nineteen when I finally calm down and my fingers can work well enough to dial the phone. With the time difference, it means it's twelve nineteen in Chicago. It's Tuesday; so Rick, Dad, and Stephan should all be at work. I don't want to risk Mom picking up, so I'm thinking I'll call Rick at his apartment and leave a message there; that should be safe.

My little panic attack, here in the parking lot, has left me feeling weak. Instead of spending any more energy driving around to find a pay phone (Do those still exist?), I give in and decide to try my cell. Taking a deep, "attempting to be calming" breath, I turn my phone back on. I close my eyes as it powers up and take a minute to try to center myself the best I can; I have to wait through all the beeping and vibrating, reminding me about all the missed calls and new texts anyway. I don't have the energy required right now to deal with any of them. I know they will break me, and my resolve is weak enough without it. "Tomorrow," I chant to myself, my new little mantra. Tomorrow, when I'm sitting in the fresh air surrounded by the mountains, that's when I'll deal with all of these. Tomorrow I'll be strong enough.

The cell phone feels dangerous in my hands; it actually feels unsafe. I don't know how else to describe it. I've never felt scared when thinking about my brother before, when thinking about my family.

It's just a phone call Kara.

Hell, it's not even a phone call. It's just two words spoken on a machine. "I'm okay" and then quickly hang up. *You can do this.*

I take a deep breath and dial Rick's number. I have to do it twice before it goes through. The first time I dial all wrong. It rings two times, and as I take a breath to leave my message, Rick picks up.

"KARA!"

Automatically my hand opens, and the phone drops. My heart's pounding. Tears pour down my face. I'm sobbing, and between giant gulps of air, I can hear Rick screaming.

"Kara! It's Kara! She's alive! Mom, it's Kara!"

I'm trying to reach for the phone to hang it back up, but my body can't seem to move fast enough.

"Kara, where are you? Are you okay? Are you hurt? Where are you? I'll come get you! Kara… Kara, are you there? Please say something, please!"

My mom must have grabbed the phone away from Rick because it's now her voice I hear, her crying that fills my car as I try to reach the phone. "Kara! Baby! Kara…please!"

I get my hand around it and hastily hang up. I turn it off and throw it out the window of my car. I never even said a single word to them.

I'm shaking, out-of-control shaking. Tears are pooling onto my chest, and I have never heard the noises that are coming out of my mouth before. That was ten times worse than anything I'd imagined than everything I thought I'd prepared myself for. I can't even calm down enough to get my key into the ignition of the car. I want to drive as fast and far as I can. I want to run my phone over and break it into a thousand tiny pieces. I want to be gone from this place, gone from these emotions.

Instead, I sob as I sit alone in my car underneath the electric yellow McDonald's M. I curl up onto myself as much as I can from the driver's seat of my little Nissan. Closing my eyes, I try to block out the sound of their voice, the fear and desperation I heard as Rick cried out that I was alive. Alive… What the fuck is that about? I left a note! I didn't want to hurt them. I left a damn note! How could they think that I was dead, that I would have died?

I don't know how long I have sat here like this, but eventually I'm cried out. I have physically run out of tears, and my throat is raw from screaming. My hands are still shaking as I try to put my key into the ignition. I focus, gulping in deep breaths, counting them in my head as I start to drive away. I'm calm enough to realize that I need my damn cell. I might be losing my mind, but I don't want to be stuck on the side of the road with a flat and no way to call for help. I drive over to where I see it sit, shining white on the blacktop of the parking lot. Thank God it didn't get run over. I slowly get out of the car and walk over to it. I feel like life is in slow motion. I watch my shanking hand as I reach down, pick up the phone, and put it into my jacket pocket. My hands are still shaking as I drive away.

It's two thirty-eight when I hit the expressway again. I don't know where the time has gone. I'm hungry. I never actually made it into the McDonald's. I just want away from this place; I want out of Kentucky. I want something different; I need something new, someplace where I can't recognize myself. I'm emotionally done and totally drained. Each breath seems to take such effort and control. I'm not sure how I'll make it all the way there, even if it is only another five hours. Right now five hours seems like a week. I turn the music up a little louder and open the windows. Maybe, if I'm lucky, the cold air will help me focus.

CHAPTER 21

With about forty-five minutes to go, I get off the highway. I need to fill the car up again and splash some water on my face. I'm not sure where I managed to get off at, but it's empty as hell around here, empty enough that it has me questioning if I know how to read a map at all. If it wasn't for the constant billboards I keep passing, advertising the joys of mountain life with children playing in streams while deer look on, I would have thought I was lost. It's pretty here, wide open space, giant sky, kind of pretty. The stars are so much brighter than at home. Even this close to the highway, it's quiet, no loud music, or people talking, no sirens in the distance. I'm utterly focused on the bed I imagine on a road as dark and empty as this one. I need some sleep, a pillow and a blanket, a real bed and room with a hot shower in the morning. The yellow warning light reminds me that first I need a gas station, a bathroom, and a cup of coffee. What I wouldn't give for my own little coffee pot with coffee the way I like to make it. I open the windows a little wider to keep me going and keep looking for this gas station that the highway sign has me believing should be right here.

●●●

I wake up as the car crashes. My head bounces off of the steering wheel and then back, hard, into the headrest of the driver's seat. My chest burns from the strap on my seatbelt.

Gripping the steering wheel as if my life depended on it, I try to figure out what just happened. I knew I was tired, but I've never

136

fallen asleep driving before, never even come close to it. And it's only 7:00 p.m., not two in the morning. My eyes are watering, and I'm seeing spots. It hurts to turn my head, but I know I need to look, to see what I hit, to see whom I hit. I don't know how I would face it if I hurt anyone else.

It seems to take forever to open the door. I already hurt everywhere. I feel like I could trace a line of pain from the base of my skull, down through my shoulder blades, and into my back. My seatbelt has come unplugged by itself, but I still struggle to get out from under it. The headlights from my car shine brightly over a large ravine as I half fall, half stumble out of my car to see the damage.

I'm all alone. No other cars are here, and no one has seen the accident. Thank God.

My car is banged up but drivable. A decent-sized dent digs into the passenger side bumper, and the door is pretty scraped up. The guardrail I hit barely has a dent in it. I look down into the ravine I would have ended up in if I had swerved a little too late or a little too early. It's deep, and in the dark, it appears that it never ends. It's not something I would have survived. It's like a grave awaiting a body, a coffin covered in stars. My head is pounding as I get back in my car; my thoughts are stuck in what could have been.

I watch the movie that unfolds in my mind. What it would have looked like as the young officer, in his crisp blue uniform, rang the bell to my parents' home; what he would have said as he informs my mom that her only daughter had died in somewhere-ville Tennessee? I picture it as her face distorts, and tears begin to fall. I see my dad standing silently behind her, one hand gripping her shoulder. I imagine all of this as I put my seatbelt on and drive slowly away.

I'm no longer worried about falling asleep. I'm wide awake. I give up trying to find the gas station. I know my car; even with the warning light on, I can make it another fifty miles. I have to get to a hotel. I have to sleep. The next hotel, wherever it is, as long as it has a bed, it's going to be good enough. I sure as shit no longer need the coffee or the water to splash on my face, although a couple of Advil sound pretty damn good.

Within about fifteen minutes, I find a hotel up ahead. There's a gas station on the corner, and I pull in planning on filling up and making a quick run inside to get some Advil. I seriously need some; my head and neck are killing me. Before I get out of the car, I pull down my rearview mirror to take a quick inventory of what I look like. My eyes are bloodshot from two days' worth of tears, and I have a welt forming on my forehead. It's going to be a nasty bruise by tomorrow. A line of blood has dried under my nose, and I brush at it, trying to make it disappear. I tuck my hair behind my ears and find a pair of sunglasses to hide my eyes; who knows what the clerk will think of them since it's already dark out? But at least I look a little better. Nodding to myself, I get out of the car.

As I walk into the gas station, the first thing I see is booze. I'm barely inside the door; and I'm staring, face to bottle, at the vodka. Part of me honestly doesn't want it. The good girl Kara, the wholesome me, is reminding myself that this is a big reason as to why I'm currently standing in Tennessee, reminding me that this is why I'm alone with a pounding headache instead of lying in Stephan's arms watching a movie.

Another part of me is thinking back over the day I've had, of waking up freezing at a rest stop somewhere in Indiana, the fear at calling home, the panic in my brother's voice as he yelled that I was alive. Then I remember the black hole of a ravine and the accident that almost was.

Remembering the way my head hurt as it bounced off the steering wheel makes my decision for me. I grab two bottles of vodka, a bottle of Advil, and a bottle of Tylenol PM. My sleeping pills are somewhere roaming around my apartment. I didn't stop to grab them in my mad dash to pack. I can only imagine what Rick and Stephan are thinking about them. Rick especially, he knows I've never had a problem falling asleep anywhere in my whole life.

The guy at the front desk in the hotel wants to make small talk. It's a "Welcome to Tennessee. How y'all doing tonight? How long ya planning on staying for?" kind of conversation. I just want my room key; I want to collapse into the bed and forget, just forget everything. Why is he incapable of understanding that? I try to play nice, but I'm sure it just comes off as bitchy. I've pissed off everyone that means anything to me. You mean nothing to me, so why should I care if I piss you off too?

The room is simple; it's nice. It's clean and warm with a big bed right in the middle. I throw my gym bag on the floor, put my keys and phone on the nightstand, and grab my little ice bucket. Heading down the hall, I try to find some place to fill it.

The sound the ice makes as it clinks against the side of my glass has me feeling better already, not my head, mind you, but at least the rest of me relaxes a little more. I'm already calmer. I'm in a room, out of the car, and tonight I can sleep for real. I swallow four Advil with a couple sips of vodka. I put the Tylenol on the nightstand by my cell just in case I can't sleep later. It hurts my neck to lean back against the pillows, but eventually I manage to get comfortable. I pour another drink and start to drift.

●●●

When I open my eyes, I find myself staring at the ceiling. The room is dark; no light breaks through the sides of the heavy curtains. My head hurts, but at least it's a dull pain now. I feel awake, not really rested, but awake. I start to sit up, and the pain in my neck multiplies; I collapse back down onto the pillows instead. Rolling, carefully, onto my side, I reach for the Advil. While throwing back a couple more of them, with the remnants of my melted ice drink from the nightstand, my fingers brush against my cell. It takes a few minutes of maneuvering before I can finally grab onto it. Drawing my knees up toward my chest, I take a deep breath.

It's tomorrow, and all of my "tomorrow I'll be stronger" bullshit is slithering its way through my head. I know I need deal with all the messages and texts from the past two days. After looking into that ravine last night, all of this, my reactions and theirs, are all so much more real. No matter how stupid and wrong I think they were to assume I could have been dead, I know I need to do something to let them know I'm okay. The least I can do is respond to them. I can text and turn it back off before anyone even wakes up to see it. It's two fourteen in the morning in Chicago. No one will be trying to call me right now, and I won't be tempted to call them and wake them up. If anytime is safe, it's gotta be now.

There are eighteen new text messages, forty-eight missed calls, and six new voice mails, plus the original ten from Monday. It's more than a little overwhelming. I close my eyes and count the rise and fall of my chest with each breath I take. Who knew that my phone could hold that many voice mails? After fifteen breaths, I open my eyes and delete all the voicemails without listening to them. I've heard enough fear and panic in the voices of people I love to last a lifetime. I clear all the missed calls without checking the numbers. The texts seem much safer, so I start to read.

> Rick: "Why won't you answer the door? I know you're home."
> Rick: "Kara, answer the fucking door!"
> Rick: "Fuck you, Kara."
> Rick: "What the hell do you mean you are okay but can't do this? What the hell does this mean?"
> Stephan: "Please, Kara, we're scared out of our minds over here. Please let us know you're okay.
> Please let us know you are not going to do anything stupid. I love you. Please, Kara, call us."
> Katie: "Kara, what are you thinking? Why didn't you talk to me about this? Are you okay?"
> Rick: "Kara, I called the police."
> Mom: "Kara, please come home, baby. Please tell us you are okay."
> Dad: "Baby girl, I love you. I'll always come get you. Come home to us safe okay."

Then you can tell they got my McDonald's parking lot call.

> Rick: "So you're alive. How nice you let us know."
> Mom: "Kara, please call back, baby. I'm sorry we didn't let you talk. It sounded like you were crying. Are you okay? Tell me where you are, and I'll have Daddy come and get you.

We will get you whatever help you need. Please, baby. I love you."

Stephan: "I'm with your family. I heard your call but couldn't find the words to say anything. I'm so sorry. I'm sorry about everything. Please call us back. We all love you and just want to be there for you, whatever you need. Please call, Kara."

Dad: "Kara, you know I don't do the whole guilt trip thing, but your mom is freaking out. She's afraid you'll hurt yourself. I told her you would never do that, but please let us know you are all right. We will give you all the time you need. Just please call us."

Stephan: "I'm sitting on the couch right now and thinking of you. I'm always thinking of you. I need you to tell me what you meant the other night when you said I wouldn't understand. Something is eating at you. This is not who you are. The girl I fell in love with would never hurt the people who cared about her like this. Talk to someone please, even if it isn't me. I love you wherever you are."

Stephan: "I'm sorry I left that night."

Stephan: "Please, Kara. Please pick up the phone for me. Please call me. I need to hear your voice. I need to know you're okay."

Rick: "You're killing Mom. I hope you know that."

Rick: "I love you."

The last text from Rick was only fifteen minutes ago. Stephan's was from an hour ago. I don't know what I expected to find, but this wasn't it. I've never seen Rick so mad at me before. And what the hell is with my family? Did they really think I would kill myself? Talk about dramatic! It was Stephan's text though that took me the most by surprise. I had really thought I had lost him with all of this. Does he really still love me, or is this a ploy to get me to call? I'm wide wake, half drunk and very bored. It makes for a brave combination. Well, somewhat brave, not phone call brave but definitely text message brave.

"Do you really still love me? Even after all of this?"

I hit send before I have the chance to change my mind. I don't really expect a text back, even if he was texting me an hour ago. It's the middle of the night. But I hold the phone anyway, hoping.

"Kara! Thank God! Where are you? Are you okay?"

And then another text. "What do you mean do I really still love you? OF COURSE, I love you! You have me scared out of my mind. Where are you?"

I sit holding the phone. The tears, that always seem ready, are running down my face. He still loves me. I don't really know what to text back. I'm playing with the idea of just turning the phone off, of falling back asleep knowing that he loves me and not having to deal with any of the reset. They know I'm alive. They know I'm at least somewhere safe. Do I really want to keep texting now? Can I handle what they have to say?

The phone is vibrating with a new message before I have the chance to make up my mind.

"Where are you?"

Just as I finish reading one, my phone is vibrating with another.

"Please, Kara…please. I'm begging you. Where are you? I love you. Please."

I can feel my heart start to heat up, and this time, it isn't from the vodka. How does he still love me even after all of this? Even after he's seen me crazy.

Maybe, maybe, he'll still love me if I tell him the truth, tell him how weak I've let the alley man make me. I decide to start with something much easier.

"I love you too."

A sob escapes my lips as I hit send. "I love you. I love you! I'm sorry I pushed you out of my apartment that night. I'm sorry I ran. I'm sorry."

I know he can't hear me, but I say it anyway, I say it for the sake of saying it. I cry as I type.

"I'm sorry I scared you. Yes, something is eating at me, but I don't know how to say it. I'm scared too, Stephan. I don't know how to face you, how to face Rick, and Mom and Dad. Please tell them I'm okay." I hit send.

Part of me really wants to turn the phone back off. I can't believe that I sent the last text, that I wrote anything at all. Part of me never wants to turn my phone off again. I'm sitting in my bed, wrapped in the ugly hotel comforter, deliberating if I turn the phone off when it rings.

I should have fucking known.

I sit just looking at it, watching it ring. A moment ago, I was wondering if a text was too much to handle; now I'm supposed to talk too? The caller ID says it's Rick. He's gotta be with Stephan. How else would he have known to call now? I'm just watching the phone ring, one more time and it should stop. I don't think I'm brave enough to answer it. A text comes across instead.

"Please, Kara, I'm begging you. Please pick up the phone. I'm not angry anymore, I promise. Please." The ringing starts all over again.

It's when he calls for the third time that I tentatively say hello. I hear him exhale for what seems like forever. Then it's silent. I don't know what to say, so I don't say anything at all. After a long and quiet minute, I hear Rick's voice.

"Kara, I love you. Please be okay. Are you okay? Do you need anything?"

I can tell he wants to keep talking, to keep asking questions. I can tell how hard it is for him to stop. I imagine it's Stephan's hand on his shoulder that keeps him quiet now.

"I'm okay, Rick." I have no idea what else to say, how to explain all of this.

"Where are you Kara? Can we come get you? I'm with Stephan. We'll come get you right now, I mean, if you want us to. We can give you time too, Kara…if that's what you need. I just, we just…we don't understand."

The last part he says so quickly it's hard to make out the individual words. "I'm a little too far away to come and get right now, Rick. I just need some time; I think…" My voice is starting to crack.

There is only so long I can keep my hysterics at bay. "Honestly, Rick, I don't know what I need right now."

"Can you tell us where you are? We'll come to you, and if you need us, we'll be there. If you want time, we'll leave you be. Please, Kara…please tell us. Where are you?"

I'm thinking this over, mulling it around in my mind. I'm not really sure Rick will be able to leave me be. I'm starting to think that Stephan will give me whatever it is I tell him I need; but Rick, I'm just not sure. I'm not sure he has the ability to turn off his, "older brother gotta step in to save the day" mentality.

"Are you sure you can leave if I ask you to?" I'm not sure I should have even said that much. I can hear the hope in his voice now. "I promise, Kara, pinky swear, just like when we were little. You say the word, and we'll disappear."

I take a deep breath and let in slowly back out. What I really want is a good long sip of my drink, but I'm not sure what the sound of the ice in the glass would do to this calm that Rick is trying so hard to show me. Am I really considering this?

"Just you and Stephan, no one else right."

His answer is immediate; he's already thought this through. "Kara, we'll leave right now, and I won't even tell Mom and Dad that we've left until morning. I'll tell them we talked to you, and we're on our way to you. That's all I'll say. I promise. Please, Kara."

"I can't handle the whole family right now, Rick. I'm not even sure I have the strength to face you and Stephan."

"I know you do. Kara…I know you can." He's pleading with me to tell him, desperate for a name of a town where he can find me. I can hear it in his voice, and I hate it. I hate that I put it there.

"I'm in Tennessee."

CHAPTER 22

"Tennessee? What the he…" I can hear all the emotion in his voice. It's raw with pain. I think he was expecting me to say something more like Lake Geneva, Wisconsin, or even Rockford, something much closer to home. He takes a deep breath, swallowing down everything else he wants to say right now.

"Where in Tennessee?" He has regained the control of his voice, but barely. I can hear him purposely breathing even deep breaths. I can picture him counting them in his mind, his little trick to control emotion he had taught me all those years ago.

"Um, well, I'm not really sure, I'm at a—"

"Kara! How the hell do you not know where you are?" The control is gone, and he's yelling at me. This is exactly what I feared. He can't seem to control it for long; he's just so damn angry. Why the hell did I tell him where I am? At least he doesn't know enough to be able to find me, maybe with a team of detectives; otherwise, last time I checked, the state of Tennessee was rather large, so I should be all good. I'm getting ready to hang the phone up when I hear Stephan's voice in the background.

"Shut the hell up, Rick! Do you want her to hang up? You want her to run again? Give me the phone… Give it to me." His voice is so sure, so strong. I wait just a minute more. I tell myself I should hang up now, but I want to hear Stephan's voice again.

"Kara…baby." He's totally calm. He's totally in control. His voice is smooth. His voice is like a warm blanket, and it feels like home; it feels safe.

"I'm coming."

It's not a question; it's not someone asking for permission. It's just a statement of fact. Stephan is coming. It makes me smile and has me terrified all at the same time.

"Is there a number on the phone in the room or maybe some stationary with the address on it?"

I pause thinking this one through. I wasn't even planning to talk to them tonight, and now I've told them I'm in Tennessee. Do I really want to tell them the address of the hotel?

"Please, Kara…please."

"I'm in the Smokey Mountains, at a little hotel off Rt. 441." The words come out barely louder than a whisper.

"Thank you, Kara. We'll find you. Can you call the front desk and have them leave me a key? Just so I can get in if you're asleep when we get there, so we won't have to wake you."

I know it is more likely that they're afraid I won't let them in again. I answer with a type of grunt and hang up the phone to the sound of him saying, "Thank you…thank you, Kara."

I believe them that they won't tell Mom and Dad, but I still can't handle a chance phone call from them either. I know I'm going to turn the phone off, put it in a drawer, and forget I ever bought it; but first I Google how long of a drive it is from Chicago to the Smokey's. When you actually start out knowing where you're going, not when you drive for half a day before heading here. I should have at least eight or nine hours.

It's still the middle of the night, not much to do now but wait. The vodka bottle looks seductive in the glowing light from the small lamp on my nightstand. I close my eyes to keep from looking at it. *Something other than drinking, Kara. Do something else.*

I decide on a hot shower to try to calm my nerves. As the hot water flows down my back, I feel my neck start to relax. My shoulders drop. I do feel better, a little more like the Kara I thought I had lost, a little. I didn't tell them what town I was in. I don't know what town I'm in. I know they'll call around until they find my name listed at one of the hotels. One will drive, one will call. It shouldn't take all that long before they figure it out. I sit on the oversized chair in the corner of the room wrapped in a small white towel, and I'm shivering. I wish I could figure out if it as from being cold or from being terrified. My head is still pounding. My neck is still stiff, and the bruise above my eye is starting to form. What am I going to tell them? How am I going to explain this?

I could run. I could pack up right now and leave the phone here this time. I wouldn't have to stop; I could just drive to the edge of anywhere. My mind is already picturing it though, the anguish that would be on their faces, the total disappointment. Rick and Stephan would arrive, after driving all night, to find the hotel room empty and have no idea where to go. It seems beyond cruel, as if I saw this like some sort of game, some personal torture for them. I hate that I even had the thought. It would be unforgivable for me to do that to them, again. Today is going to suck. There's no way around it, but I have to face them, to face what leaving two days ago has done. I try to reverse it, if Rick had been the one to leave like this; what would it have done to me?

I know what it would have done. It would have broken my heart; it would have killed me until I got to hear his voice, to know he was okay. Great, now I feel even worse.

The room phone is on the desk next to me. I don't even think about what I'm doing. The next thing I know I hear Rick pick up.

"Hello." His voice is so unsure; I'm not used to that. Rick has always been strong. I can't think of a time where he seemed unsure or weak. Every scared or lonely childhood memory I have, he was there letting me know we could handle it together, that I wasn't alone. Why didn't I let him handle this with me? Why did I try to do this alone?

"Kara…"

I haven't said anything since calling him. I think he's afraid I'm going to tell him not to come, as if that would stop him. I called from the room, so now they have the hotel's information, no hiding anymore. I take a deep breath, trying to settle myself. I picture him in his mad dash to the car. I picture him holding the phone trying to figure out why I've called, the look on Stephan's face as he's waiting to hear what I want. I don't even know what I want. I just know how it felt when I reversed it, when it was Rick leaving me.

"I'm sorry, Rick." and I'm sobbing into the phone. "I'm so sorry." He doesn't say anything; he just lets me cry.

I don't really know how long I cry for. Rick keeps quiet. When I finally cry myself out and my gulps of air are quiet enough that I can hear him, he reluctantly responds.

"We'll figure it all out, Kara. You're not alone. We're on our way. We'll be there as soon as we can."

I notice he doesn't say it's okay, it's all right, or any other form of trying to make me believe he forgives me. I don't blame him at all. I don't have anything else to say, so I just hang up the phone. I pour a long, tall drink and fall asleep where I sit.

CHAPTER 23

It's nine thirty-three when I wake up. You know that feeling after you cry really hard, where you just feel refreshed? Ya, I so don't have it. Sleeping on this chair instead of the bed, sleeping in the car the night before and after the car accident yesterday, well, let's just say the chair wasn't the best idea. My head is still pounding, and my neck is a solid ball of pain that now shoots down my back as well. I take a couple more of the Advil.

I still have at least two hours before Rick and Stephan arrive. Realizing that I never called down to the front desk to have them put a room key aside for them, I head down to the lobby for the last of the free breakfast and to arrange for the key. The chatty receptionist from yesterday is gone, thank God.

With everything arranged for Rick and Stephan, and with coffee in hand, I head back up to my room. Even if I get ready slowly, there will be way too much time left alone. As I walk, I'm trying very hard not to think about what today will hold. I feel like I know what to expect from them, and that scares me; it's like a false sense of security, one of total panic and fear, but security nonetheless. I thought I knew what leaving a phone message was going to be like when I called Rick from McDonald's. I thought I knew what to expect when I texted Stephan last night. Everything I had thought was wrong. Everything I do lately is wrong. It seems to be the theme of my life right now. I'm six hundred miles away from my family and Stephan, no job, and I have the newfound knowledge that I have the capability to torture people I love—sounds pretty damn *wrong*, in every sense of the word, to me.

I place my coffee down on the small, stained piece of counter-top just below the mirror. I don't recognize the person reflecting back at me. It's the eyes that scare me the most. There's no life left in them. My eyes are flat. I have become flat, empty, and hollow.

I can't let Rick see this; I'm ashamed to admit it to myself, but I'm sure Stephan knows this look well. I didn't bring any makeup with me, just a hair brush. I must brush my hair about a hundred times before I get dressed. I pick out the cleanest of the few items of clothing I have with me. There's not much I can do about the bruise forming on my face. The only thing that might hide part of it are glasses, and well, sunglasses while inside the room might look a little suspicious. I clean the hotel room, not that it's actually messy. I just don't know what else to do with myself. I suppose I should turn my phone back on. They might be trying to reach me. Then again Mom or Dad might be trying to reach me too.

It's 1:00 p.m. They should be here by then. If not, I'll turn my phone on. I sit on the chair in the room. Then I get up and sit on the bed. The room isn't big enough to pace, so I sit. My foot is bouncing to the beat of an unplayed song. I'm just too anxious to be still.

How do I want to look when they walk in? My neck and head tell me I want to be propped up on pillows with a blanket to hide in, but I think that will make me look weak. The chair makes me look anxious (and is damn uncomfortable). If I sit on the floor, I look like I am hiding. I could always just leave a note saying to meet me somewhere else. Meet me at the pool or at the bar, but then I don't really know how this is going to play out. Will there be yelling? Will there be crying?

Shit. Why did I tell them where I was? I decide to decide later. For now, I curl up in my bed with the blankets piled over me, trying to block out what's coming. I open the bottle of Tylenol PM and take one in hopes of falling back asleep.

I'm not really sure if I slept or just tossed and turned. But eventually I give up and turn on the television. Nothing is really on, so I start flipping through the channels, seeing how fast I can make it through all of them. It's on my fifth attempt through all eleven stations that the door opens.

I sit up, completely startled. The blood rushes to my head and leaves me feeling dizzy. I hadn't really even started to prepare myself for this. They must have raced the whole way to get here this quickly. Rick looks worse than I do. His eyes are huge as he takes in the room. They stop when they reach the bruise on my head.

"Are you hurt?" His voice is cold and calculated.

"No, not really." I reach my hand up to the bruise automatically. He's standing in the doorway, just looking at me. There's not much emotion left on his face.

"Where's Stephan?" I ask.

"He's parking the car. He thought I should have a minute alone with you first." I see a crack in his carefully placed mask, his lack of emotion. He walks over to me and kneels down on the floor. He slowly reaches out to touch the bruise on my head but never quite makes it. Instead, he wraps his arms around me and gives me the tightest big brother hug a girl could ever hope for.

"Kara," his voice starts to break.

I'm hugging him back with all my strength. I can't take the thought that he's crying, but I can't handle pulling away from him and seeing the tears on his face even more.

"Rick, I'm okay... It's okay." I talk into his shoulder as we hug.

Pulling back, he holds me at arm's length. "Kara, you are a lot of things, but okay is not one of them." He's looking at me, looking for an explanation, and I don't have one to offer. I don't know what to say.

"What's going on, Kara? This is not you. I never would have thought in a million years you could do this." He rocks back onto his heels, trying to take everything in.

"It doesn't make any sense at all. One minute everything is fine, and the next you are driving away from me as I chase your car down the street after reading what was a...what...a runaway note? A suicide note?"

I can't take hearing this again. It was bad enough hearing that they had actually thought I could have committed suicide the first time I called.

"Rick, I was never going to kill myself! How could you even think that of me?" I push him away and stand up. I'm furious.

"Damn it, Kara, none of this is something I would have thought you were capable of! How would I know suicide isn't something you could have done! 'I can't do this. I love you.' It sounds like a damn suicide note to me. It sounded like one to all of us!"

I turn my back to him as I walk to the window thinking about how big of a mistake this whole thing has been. Starting with the moment I didn't answer the door in my apartment to my decision to tell them where I was.

"I…" I slowly turn to face him. I want to tell him I can't do this. I want to tell him I never should have answered his call, that he shouldn't be here. I want to slap him for thinking I would kill myself, for letting Mom and Dad think that. Instead I just turn back around to face the window. I can feel Rick behind me.

"I'm sorry, Kara. I just don't understand this. Help me to understand this, please." Rick takes a deep breath and turns me around, so I am looking at him.

"Stephan told me that you've been acting weird. Drinking…I mean, really drinking." Rick runs his hand through his hair before he continues.

"He wasn't sure that's all you were doing. He said it's been over a month since you have really seemed like yourself. He hates himself right now for not speaking up sooner." I look up at Rick's face and see Stephan standing in the doorway of the room.

He walks in and closes the door. He doesn't take his eyes off of me. It's as if he's afraid that if he does, I'll disappear. He doesn't say a word as he walks over to me. His hand reaches up and brushes the hair away from my eyes. It sends shivers down my spine and leaves a trail of heat on my skin. He doesn't cry. He doesn't try to hug me. He just stands there looking into my eyes, letting himself see that I'm really here.

We're lost in our world, in this moment. My guard is down; there is no hiding anymore. There's no more pretending like everything is okay. I think he can see that in my eyes. Stephan takes my hand and leads me back to the bed. He sits me down and kneels in front of me.

"Start explaining please." His voice is tight but not as angry as I would have thought.

I can't look either of them in the eye, not if I am going to get through this. Instead I look at the pattern on the comforter I'm sitting on, thrown over the corner of the bed. One of them must have picked it up from the floor at some point because I swear it hit the ground in my moment of panic when Rick came walking into the room. Neither of them are saying anything, and I take a moment to just listen to all of us breathing. They both are here, looking at me, waiting.

"Do you remember the gym I joined, the one by my apartment?" I look up to see if they have heard my question, but no one wants to answer; I think they are afraid that if they talk, my story will end before it ever really begins.

"I really liked going there." My voice is shaky and quiet; I'm talking more to myself than I am to either of them. I know Stephan can hear me as he is kneeling on the floor next to me, one hand on my knee. But Rick is across the room. I'm not sure he can even hear my voice.

"I would go after work, maybe meet some friends there for a class. It was dark out. The clouds had covered the moon. I knew it was supposed to start raining, so I didn't want to wait for my friends. I just said my goodbyes and left."

Stephan and Rick are silently watching me. I take a deep breath and focus on the window. I don't see the mountains of my dreams. Instead it's Stephan's and Rick's reflections that are looking back at me. Somehow the reflections are easier than looking directly at them.

"I only made it a couple of blocks before I felt his arm on mine."

Their reflections are stiff; Stephan's hand tightens on my knee. His other becomes a fist at his side. Rick holds onto the desk as though it was holding him up, or maybe it was like he was holding the desk to the ground.

"I could feel his hot breath on my neck. It smelled like cigarettes, but he smelled like my gym. I'll never forget how he smelled, dirty and sweaty. He smelled like the gym on a humid day when the smell has nowhere to go." It's like my mind is remembering the stupid details, focusing on those, so it doesn't have to remember the rest. I take another breath and close my eyes. I don't want to see their faces at the next part. I don't want to see their reactions, the "and… where is the part that causes you to lose your mind," the "nothing really happened."

"He pushed me up against the brick wall of an alley. My head bounced off the brick, and he pushed so hard." My voice begins to shake. I'm trying to calm myself, but nothing is really working. In my mind, I'm back in the alley alone, waiting.

"My head was forced to the side, and the brick cut at my cheek. It wanted me to bleed too. He kept saying that, whispering it in my ear. 'Bleed for me, bitch.' It hurt."

I can feel the tear escape from my eye, and I brush it away quickly. I hope before either of them have noticed. I don't think Rick and Stephan have moved once. I can't hear anything in the room but the sound of me breathing. I'm not even sure they're breathing.

"He held my arm against my back and kept twisting it, pushing it higher and higher. I didn't know what he wanted. I didn't know if he was trying to kill me or just scare me. I couldn't find my voice to scream." I'm shaking now, even worse than before; I wrap my arms around myself trying to stop the shaking.

"He started to whisper in my ear. He wanted me to know what was coming…what he was going to do before he ever did it."

"Oh god. Kara…" Stephan is on his knees trying to look me in the eyes, but I won't look at him. I won't look into his eyes; I'll never get through this if I do. Rick still hasn't moved. Stephan is trying to hug me, but I'm not moving. I don't wrap my arms around him the way I want to. I don't lean my head against his shoulder the way I know it would fit just right. I don't move. Stephan pulls back to look at me again.

"You don't have to finish the story, Kara. You don't have to say it. I'm sorry, I'm so sorry. I didn't know. I never imagined. I should have figured it out that night in the bar, the way you reacted when that guy touched you. I'm sorry. You don't have to say it."

"But that's just it, Stephan. I do have to finish the story!" I'm up now, my sudden movement has thrown Stephan to the ground. He's sitting, ass flat, on the floor looking at me, bewildered. Rick starts to move toward me like he's afraid he's going to have to tackle me to keep me from running. I start to pace in my little room. Five steps to the window, five to the bed.

"He never did anything other than keep me pinned up against that stupid wall. He kept pushing himself against me, forcing me up against the wall. He kept whispering what was coming, but he never did them. He held me like that for ten hours, ten minutes. I don't even know how long."

I take a deep breath, trying to calm myself down again. Stephan's in front of me, blocking my way, trying to stop my caged animal pace. He's still trying to force my eyes to look into his. Rick is frozen in his spot again, not sure what to make from my actions.

"Don't you get it?" I'm getting angry now, desperate to get my brother to move from his statue like pose. "Don't you see? Nothing happened!" I take another breath and look to the ground; I'm speaking more to myself now than to either of them.

"Nothing happened…nothing happened, and I still can't handle it." It's barely a whisper, and then I start to cry.

CHAPTER 24

S tephan stands, wraps his arm around my waist, and sits me back down on the bed. He turns to sit next to me, wrapping his arms around me, and this time, I fold into them. I'm crying into his neck as he holds me. Rick still hasn't moved. Stephan starts to rock gently back and forth, like a mother trying to get her newborn baby to sleep. I have become a newborn baby that won't sleep. I hate how weak this makes me. I take a deep breath and pull myself away from Stephan.

"I'm okay, Stephan. I'm okay."

From the other side of the room, the desk lamp shatters against the wall. "Stop saying you're okay, Kara!" Rick is shaking. You can feel the anger rolling off of him. "This is not okay. What happened is not okay!" He is screaming. I feel frozen.

Stephan jumps up and runs the two steps to my brother. He grabs Rick's shoulders.

"Stop it. Stop it, Rick. This won't help anything. Do you think I'm not angry too? Stop it."

He is standing there, shaking Rick as his words slowly sink into me. They are angry. They're angry with me. After all this, I knew that they would be. I knew Rick was angry from the moment that I saw the look in his eyes as I left him chasing my car back in Chicago. Hearing that Stephan is angry too, hearing him say it out loud, it's so much worse than just thinking it.

"I'm sorry!" Now I'm screaming back. "I'm sorry, okay!" They both stop what they are doing and stare at me.

"Kara?" It's Stephan talking. Rick is still just staring. "Do you think it's you that we're mad at right now?" His voice sounds like he can't believe he even has to ask the question out loud.

"I know you are." I'm up again. I feel like I'm on a teeter-totter tonight, up and down and up and down. I walk over to the window and lean up against it, the cold glass cools the burning heat I feel running over my skin.

"Rick always yells at me for going out on my own. I should have waited for my friends. We should have all gone together, but it doesn't matter." I close my eyes. "I'm the one that did this. I'm the one that ran. I know you're mad at me. I know you have every right to be."

"For running, Kara, for whatever reason you felt like you couldn't share any of this… For the pain of the last two days. Yes, I'm angry. But that is nothing close to the anger I have for the spineless piece of shit who pulled you into that alley. I want to kill him, Kara. I want to hunt him down and kill him."

The last sentence echoes in my mind. Stephan is angry at *him*. As stupid as it sounds it's like someone just gave me permission to be angry too. *Focus, Kara.*

All I've heard is that Stephan is angry. It warms my heart, the way it did the first time he told me he loved me. I stand silently for a few minutes, just enjoying the warmth, how it spreads throughout my body, reaches the tips of my fingers and toes. I hate how much that feeling contradicts the heat I feel rolling in waves off of Stephan. I have to calm him back down. I have to remind him.

"I told you, Stephan. I told you nothing happened." He left me standing there. He just walked away.

"Please, Kara. Please stop saying nothing happened. It makes me want to shake you, force some sense into your head. Please stop."

I look from Stephan's eyes to the floor. "But nothing did happen."

Rick was suddenly at my side. I hadn't heard him move. "Why didn't you call us? Why didn't tell anyone?"

"I told you…NOTHI—" Stephan's hand is over my mouth before I can answer my brother.

"Don't, Kara. I can't take it. Don't say nothing happened."

"How did you get home? I want the rest of it. What the hell else aren't you saying? I didn't drive this damn far to not get the whole story." Rick seems to be spitting the words at me. Stephan is glaring at him as he slowly picks up my hand.

"Kara…"

The tears are silently rolling from my eyes, cascading down a trail they have etched into my face. My breath feels like it is stuck and with it my voice. What else do they want me to say?

Stephan raises our joined hands, holding them in front of his face, waiting for my eyes to focus on them…on him.

"What else happened, what happened once he left?"

I look from our hands to his eyes before I turn my head away. I need to pretend I'm alone, just a voice in a box talking to the dark. No one is here to hear me, no one to question me.

"I just stood there. He could have come back, and I was still waiting there. It was like I was waiting for him to come back."

I can't hide the shudder that racks my body, I can't help the way my voice raises.

"I did everything wrong! I didn't fight him. I didn't yell. I didn't even run! I just sank to the ground and sat there in the fog. I just sat there." They may be angry at him, but I'm angry at me, at how I did nothing to stop him, how I let him do this to my life.

I get up and walk to the mini fridge. I start to make myself a drink. I have no idea how either of them will react to this, but I don't care at the moment. I pour the vodka straight into the glass, and I swallow it down in one long, hard gulp. It's when I start to pour another that I feel Stephan's hand over mine.

"No more, Kara, not tonight."

I want to push him off of me, to push him down to the floor and pour the drink. I will do whatever I damn well please too, thank you very much. And with the two of you sitting in my room, yelling at me, well, what I damn well please to do is drink. But no, I look up and see nothing but love and concern in his eyes. I think about the nine-hour drive they somehow made in seven. I think about what that must have been like for them, not knowing if I would even still be here when they arrived, about what they would find when they got here. I think about how they thought my note, which was meant to keep them from worrying, made them think I would kill myself. I thought of all of this, and I put my hand down. I let Stephan lead me away from the fridge and back to the bed.

He sits me down on the edge and turns to Rick.

"Why don't you take a minute, Rick? Go check us into a room or something." Rick is still fuming. He's still standing next to the desk; you can tell he's trying to regain his composure. He doesn't answer Stephan. I'm not sure he even heard him.

"Rick," Stephan said his name louder this time. "Go."

Rick looks at me and then looks to Stephan and walks out of the room.

"It's okay, Kara. He's not mad at you. He loves you. It's okay." Somehow the words *it's okay, I'm okay* have become my new mantra.

Oh, Kara, she's okay. It's all okay.

Stephan leaves me sitting on the bed and walks around to the other side. He starts to pull back the covers and arrange the pillows. I stand back up and watch him.

"I don't want to sleep." He looks up at me. "Then don't, but you're freezing cold and dead on your feet. If you don't want to sleep, then don't. But please get in the bed, so I don't have to worry about you falling over and getting another bruise on your face."

I can tell he wants to ask what happened, but neither one of us wants another story right now. I don't want to tell one, and he doesn't want to hear one. I let him put me to bed. He tucks the blankets all around me and kisses the top of my forehead. It makes me smile.

"There's room for two in here."

He looks down at me. "You don't have to do that, Kara." I smile again, thinking I will do as I damn please. I pull the covers next to me down. "Just hold me, okay? Just make me feel like despite all of this, things might be okay."

He's looking at me trying to decide if this is what I want or what I think he wants. You can almost see his mind working. What's the right thing to do here?

"Your brother will be coming back soon. We might just give him a heart attack if he opens the door and finds us in bed together." He raises the covers back up but sits on top of them, his back up against the wall. He opens out his arm, and I snuggle up against him. For the first time in a long time, I feel safe. I let my eyes close, but I'm still awake.

Stephan is petting the top of my head, brushing my hair back and humming something soothing. I'll have to ask him what it is. I'm almost asleep when I hear the door to my room open back up. I keep my eyes closed. I don't want to get all worked up again. I'm emotional drained and not ready to deal with my brother again tonight.

"Is she okay?" Rick's voice sounds dead.

"Yeah, she fell asleep about twenty minutes ago. Are you okay?"

I hear Rick sigh, and the chair to the desk pulls out. "When she finally called, when we left to drive out here, I didn't know what to expect." I hear him sigh. "I don't think I really believed you, when you told me what she's been like lately. I mean, I'm her brother! I always knew her better than anyone else. If I couldn't see what was happening, well, in my mind that meant it wasn't happening. I knew something was off when she ran. I just…I wasn't prepared for this."

"No one was, Rick." Stephan starts to pet my head again. "I hate that she thinks this is her fault." He whispers. "Did you call your parents?"

I listen closer now. "Yeah, but I didn't know what to tell them. How do I explain all of this? How do I explain how she is? I couldn't tell them she was fine…she's not. She's not acting like herself at all. She hates to cry. I've never seen her cry like this before. Then when she started drinking vodka, straight, not even with ice. Kara was always a one-glass-of-wine-with-dinner kind of girl."

I hear the mini bar open.

"I want this gone." Then I hear the remnants of my last bottle of vodka pour down the drain. I want to sit up, to stop him; but I know if I do, he'll stop talking. And I desperately want to know what he's thinking. "What the hell…" I peak, just one little peak, to see what he is talking about. Rick has found my other empty bottle of vodka in the garbage can. I close my eyes again. Shit.

"When did the front desk say she checked in? It was last night, wasn't it?" I hear him sit down. "What do we do, Stephan? This would break Mom's heart to see. What do we do?" I hear him sigh again, a long heavy sigh, the kind that takes some of your soul with it. I took a piece of his soul with this great sister I am. I vow, in this moment, in this soul-stealing moment, to fix it. I just have no idea how.

"What did you tell your parents?" Stephan asks.

"I told them she isn't hurt, but she isn't really well either. They asked what that meant, and I had no answer. I told them I would try to get her to call soon, that it might be awhile before we can get her home. Mom cried." I hear Ricks voice start to break.

"Can you believe she thought we were mad at her...for what happened? She's been carrying that around for who knows how long and then to think that you can't tell someone because they will be mad at you." I can feel Stephan shaking his head in disbelief as he says this.

"I am mad at her, Stephan. She knew better than to leave on her own. I taught her how to fight. It could have been so much worse. He could have raped her; he could have killed her. He could have taken her from us forever." Another deep soul-stealing sigh. "He kind of did take her from us. She is like a shell of who she was."

I feel Stephan shift underneath me. I imagine it's to look at Rick better.

"Rick, you weren't in that moment. She must have been terri-fied. You can't let her hear you think that for one minute this is on her. If she had fought back, maybe he would have killed her. Maybe the fight is what does it for him. Maybe it was her lack of fight that kept her alive at all. We won't ever know...but if she is going to survive this moment"—now it is Stephan's turn for the soul-stealing sigh—"if she is going to get through this at all, it will only be because we decide here and now not to be mad. That we decide to forgive her for running, forgive her for not trusting us with this sooner."

"I don't know if I can do that, Stephan."

I fall asleep wondering if things will ever be normal between my brother and I again.

CHAPTER 25

When I wake up Stephan's gone, and Rick is sitting at the desk watching TV with no sound. I have a feeling I won't be left alone at all anymore. I look to the counter and find my empty bottle is back in the garbage. Maybe I'll be lucky, and we won't have to have this discussion today. I start to sit up. My neck is finally starting to feel better, and my head doesn't pound like it has for the past few days. I actually feel rested, for the first time in such a long time.

"Good morning, sunshine." There is no anger in Rick's voice. He must have decided to agree with Stephan and not to be mad at me anymore, or at least to not let me see the anger. I just look at him. Angry or not angry, I still don't know what to say to him. It's never been strained between us before, never been awkward.

"It's okay, Kara. It was just the shock of hearing what had happened…of hearing you try to say it was nothing when it clearly was—" he cuts himself off. He shakes his head as if to shake the thought from his mind. "It's okay. I'm not mad at you. I'm just so relieved you've let me back in, let us come and get you." I'm still just looking at him. I really have no idea what to say.

"I called Mom and Dad." Rick continues talking; I think it's just to keep there from being an awkward silence. "I told them I would have you call when you could."

I get up. I'm still in my clothes from yesterday. "I don't think I can do that right now, Rick. I don't know if I could face them. It was hard enough to face you and Stephan yesterday." I pause and look back at Rick from the bathroom door.

"What did you tell them about…about what I told you yesterday?" I can't hide the anxiety in my voice. I'm not sure I want them to know, to hear my mom gushing about this like it were a soap opera, to have my dad know the things alley man whispered in my ear.

"Nothing, it's not my story to tell, Kara. It's something you get to decide whom you share it with. I'm just happy you decided to share it with me."

Wow, where is the Rick from last night? Angry Rick is gone, and now I have understanding and gentle Rick. It's kinda weird.

"I'm going to take a shower and get ready. Do you think we could go for breakfast? I haven't really had a decent meal in days."

That brings a smile to his face. "Absolutely. Stephan is asleep in our room right now. I'll call down and wake him up."

"No, let him sleep, Rick. He needs it too."

Rick looks up at me. "Not a way in the world, Kara. Neither of us want to wake up and not know where you are."

I turn away so that he can't see the look on my face. What have I done to them by running? I was so focused on what I felt or didn't feel; I wonder if I'll ever understand what I put them through.

When I come back out of the bathroom, they're both standing in the room waiting. Stephan walks up and wraps his arms around me.

"Good morning, beautiful." I melt into him.

"Good morning," I mumble as I laid my head against his chest. Rick clears his throat, and it makes me smile. It's as if this is a normal moment, like we're all back in Chicago going out to breakfast together, not in some hotel down south waiting to feed me my first whole meal in days.

"We'll wait for you in the hall while you get dressed." Rick grabs Stephan's arm and makes a show out of dragging him into the hallway. I laugh, and it startles me. I think it's my first laugh in weeks. It brings huge smiles to the faces of both Stephan and Rick. They look at each other and walk into the hallway, leaving me to get dressed. Maybe things really will be okay. I take a deep breath, the cleansing kind, and get ready.

As I walk into the hallway, Rick takes one look at me and starts laughing.

"I know, I know." I look down and laugh at myself. Nothing matches. I have on my black work pants, gym shoes, white socks, and a navy Nashville sweatshirt. "So I packed in kinda a hurry."

"Yes," Rick says as he put his arm around my shoulder. "Something I can't wait to hear all about."

I'm no longer laughing; I know I still have a lot of explaining to do. "Why don't we take your car? I'm just about out of gas."

My car, I'm not ready to explain the dent and the scrapes. It will be hard enough to explain why I ran without having to explain what happened when I ran.

"I, umm, I'm totally out of gas too. Guess you're stuck driving after all, Rick." I try to play it off with a little laugh, but I catch them looking at each other. And I know I just raised even more questions that I'll have no choice but to answer. It's going to be a long morning.

CHAPTER 26

The coffee arrives at the table, and I couldn't be more thankful. I can tell from the rich brown color it turns as I pour the cream that it's going to be good. The steam rises off the cup, and I let myself be momentarily fascinated watching the patterns it makes in the air.

"Kara, earth to Kara."

"Huh?" I look up to find them both looking back at me rather amused.

"It's coffee, you drink it, not stare at it." Ah yes, there is my smart aleck brother whom I love so much.

"Ha ha, Rick." I take a long over exaggerated sip and burn the inside of my throat.

"Hot, hot coffee!" They both smile.

"Dork" and Rick pushes a glass of ice water at me.

Breakfast is nice; no mention of what I know is still to come. Stephan's quiet. He spends most of the time watching me while Rick and I joke back and forth, stealing food off each other's plates. He holds the door open for me as we walk back to the car.

"It's beautiful out today. How about a little hike on one of the paths? I mean, we are in the Smokey Mountains. You did come here for a reason."

I hear the coming questions in what he just asked me. You came here for a reason, as in, why did you come here?

"Do you think we could stop somewhere so I could get a clean pair of jeans before we go hike the mountains?" Give me a little time to come up with something.

That was two hours ago. Now I sit on a rock, wearing my new jeans, looking out into the forest on the mountain. It's beautiful. I take a deep breath, filling my lungs with the crisp mountain air, my whole reason for choosing the Smokey Mountains to begin with, a place I can breathe.

They're watching me again, watching and waiting. Constantly being watched like this is going to take some getting used to. I sigh. It's not a soul-stealing sigh; it's more of a face-the-music kind of sigh.

I can tell Rick is nervous; he can't seem to stand still. I don't want to start. I don't want to have to explain even more. Wasn't last night enough? I move to sit on my hands in order to keep them warm. I look into the trees and refuse to be the one who starts talking. I know it's immature, but I don't care.

Rick finally caves; he can't seem to hold it in anymore. "Why wouldn't you answer the door when I came to your apartment?" I can hear the hurt in his voice.

"I don't know, Rick. I…I guess I didn't want you to see me like that. I just wasn't ready for it."

"And this is easier?"

I don't have an answer for him.

"Why did you come to my apartment?"

Rick looks at Stephan but says nothing. It's Stephan that answers, "I called him and begged. He wanted to leave you be, said you were probably just sick. But after your outburst about me not understanding"—he pauses—"you didn't show up to work. You didn't answer the phone for anyone. I knew something was wrong. Maybe I shouldn't have pushed it. Maybe if I didn't beg for Rick to go over there, if I had just given you time, none of this would have happened."

I see Rick trying to hide the look in his eyes, not wanting Stephan to know that he feels the same way. I stand and walk over to Stephan; I hate the guilt that's etched onto his face.

"Stephan, this is not your fault." I say it slowly so the words have time to sink in. "I'm the one that did this. This isn't anyone's fault but mine." I use my fingers to try to smooth away the worry lines that have formed across his forehead.

"That's not true, Kara." I turn to look at Rick. His voice is like acid. "This is the fault of the asshole who pulled you into the alley. This is his fault."

It would be so much easier to just let Rick stay mad, to blame the alley. It had been easier to pretend that the alley never scared me. It had been easier not to face Rick at my apartment the night I ran. Just look where all my "easier" ways have led me.

"Rick." Once I see that he's looking at me, I let my eyes close; the truth is always so much easier to say when you don't have to look it in the face.

"This is my fault too." I hear Stephan start to argue, and I shake my head no.

"I'm not saying the alley is my fault, but if I didn't pretend that nothing had happened, if I didn't pretend about everything…"

No one is arguing with me now.

"Why, Kara? Why didn't you say something? Why did you pretend everything was fine? You knew it wasn't fine. You knew it every time you went to the bottle."

When I open my eyes I can see both of them studying me, waiting.

I sit down on my rock and put my head into my hands.

I'm trying to calm myself back down. Rick is standing, still waiting, still trying to figure out why. "You didn't see me that night. It shouldn't have scared me the way it did. I couldn't even think straight. All I wanted was him off of me, the smell, the feel of him off my skin."

I start to play with a twig on the ground, trying to break it into a thousand little pieces.

"The way it felt, it shouldn't have felt that way. People go through way more…it shouldn't have felt that way." My voice is barely above a whisper.

"I wish you would have told me." Rick squats onto his heels to look into my eyes.

"I wish you had come to me instead."

I smile at him. "Telling you would have made it that much more real. I wasn't ready for that; I'm still not ready. I just don't really have a choice now."

"Kara, I don't understand that. Why the hell would booze make it easier than telling someone who loves you? Help me to understand…please. Why?" Hearing the pain and anger in his voice strips away the last of my control.

"Because it makes it go away, okay! I can forget. It turns off my head, makes me stop trying to figure out why. I can stop feeling guilty."

"Feeling guilty? Until you ran, what the hell did you feel guilty about?"

Rick and Stephan are staring at me. I just want to go ten minutes without someone staring at me.

I draw my knees into my chest and balance my chin against them; I take a deep breath trying to force myself to calm down. "For being scared, for still feeling like I was living and breathing stuck up against the brick."

My hands cover my face. This is it, the heart of it. I'm ashamed for feeling anything at all, for not being able to forget.

We sit in silence, three people on the edge of a mountain. I don't think they know what to say. I wouldn't know what to say. Stephan has his arm around me, and I lean my head onto his shoulder. Rick is lost in thought. I know I just unloaded on him; I know the amount of shit I have told him in the past twenty-four hours has to be taking a toll. I focus instead on the scene before me. We didn't hike that far up the path, but it's far enough that I can look down into the trees below. There's something peaceful about looking down on nature. It helps you see the whole picture, not just the individual trees, the individual problems in life.

"Kara, didn't you hear me?"

I'm surprised to see that Stephan is no longer next to me. The two of them are already headed back toward the path. Stephan has his hand out, waiting for me. Rick is walking away.

"Let's head back. You might be able to stare at the sky all day, but the rest of us are cold. And we want some lunch."

Rick still hasn't said anything about what I told him, or at least nothing that I heard.

CHAPTER 27

Rick's silence is eating at me. Through the trees ahead, I can see we're getting close to the parking lot. I need more time; I'm not ready to head back to the small hotel room that feels even smaller since Rick and Stephan got here. I pull my hand away from Stephan and start backing up the path. Just a few more minutes.

"Kara? You okay?"

Rick stops walking and looks back to see why Stephan is asking. I nod my head yes but keep walking backward up the path. There's a tree that's twice as wide as anything you could find back home, and one thick branch had fallen. I use it as a bench and sit, facing the tree, my back to them.

"I just need a minute, guys. Please…just let me breathe for another minute."

My head is starting to throb, and my neck feels like it's holding up a forty-pound rock. I reach my hand around to the back of my neck and start to rub it. I don't hear Stephan come up behind me. I flinch as his hands try to replace mine on my neck. I turn my body quickly, quick enough that he doesn't have time to hide the look on his face. He clearly thinks I flinched because he touched me. He doesn't know it's because it hurt. Just once I want to look up at him and not hate the look that I've put onto his face. I know the only way to get the look off his face, the only way I can once again make him feel comfortable to touch me, is to tell them the rest of the story. Will today ever end?

"I'm sorry, Stephan, it's just—"

He interrupts me. "I know, I'm sorry…after what you told us… the alley, I shouldn't have touched you without you knowing it was coming."

"Stephan, stop it. I'm not afraid of your touch. Your arms make me feel safe. They always have." He smiles down at me. "There is no place safer to me in the world than being in your arms." I reach for his hand and place it, purposefully, on my shoulder.

"I flinched because it hurt. My neck and head are killing me."

His smile is gone. He reaches up to touch the bruise on my head. "Does that have anything to do with this mysterious bruise you won't talk about?" He gives me a half smile, one made to reassure me that it's all right to tell him. His eyes are tight, and the smile never reaches them. I might as well tell them now, at least here I have wide-open spaces. It would be harder back in the room, no place to move around, no real place to breathe. I have no idea how they will take the rest of my story.

"I didn't really sleep good the night I ran and then that phone call to Rick."

Rick looks weary, clearly upset that there could be more. He closes his eyes when he sees me glance up to him. I assume he's remembering the call.

"I wasn't ready for that. I had just planned to leave a quick message. I thought you would all be at work. I never thought you would be at Rick's apartment sitting by the phone."

Rick opens his eyes. "You seriously thought I would head to work when you were missing…that Dad or Stephan would head to work?" He looks at me like I have lost my mind, but there is no anger in his eyes. He might be thinking I'm stupid but at least he isn't angry.

"And we weren't at my apartment. We all had our home phones changed to ring on our cells, just in case you called."

"Oh."

"The police suggested it." He looks toward the ground and gently kicks a rock down the path. "I told you, well, texted you, that we called the police."

"Ah huh." Knowing they did it and hearing about it are two very different things.

Stephan reaches forward and brushes his hand across my forehead again, bringing my attention back to the story at hand.

"The bruise?"

"Well, that call took a lot of me. After I turned the phone off, well, threw it out the window actually… I just sat in my car and cried. So like I said, I hadn't slept good the night before and then combining that with all the emotions of that call."

I look back up at Rick. "Hearing you shout I was alive, like you thought I might really be dead. I wouldn't do that!"

"Kara." I can tell Stephan wants me to get to the point. "Why were you so tired? Where did you sleep the first night?"

I thought that by explaining the alley I would be done. How would they react to me sleeping in my car somewhere in Indiana?

"Kara." From the tone of his voice, I think he already knows.

"I slept in the car at a rest stop in Indiana."

Ricks hands form into fists at his side. I see Stephan nod "and the bruise?" There is fear in his eyes.

I look to the sky, focus on the clouds, anything to keep me from having to see their reaction.

"The bruise." Not knowing is driving Stephan crazy.

"I fell asleep driving about half an hour before the hotel." I hear them both gasp. I close my eyes. "I had gotten off the highway to try to find gas, splash some water on my face. I woke up when I hit a guardrail. The bruise is from my steering wheel."

When my eyes open, no one is moving. No one says anything. Rick's hands are on his knees as if he's trying to hold himself up. Stephan is frozen next to me. I can't take seeing them like this. I close my eyes again.

I can hear Rick's feet on the path as he moves closer to me.

"Look at me, damn it."

His voice is like ice. I open my eyes; he's standing over me. His anger is barely contained.

"I'm trying really hard here not to be mad at you, Kara, over and over again, more information…more of this damn story. I'm trying…but you're making that damn hard to do." His hands are fists at his side; he walks away down the path. I look over at Stephan. I'm waiting to see how he'll react. He's silently watching me; after about a minute, he stands up and offers me his hand. He doesn't say a word as we walk, hand in hand, after my brother.

By the time we catch up to Rick, he's pacing back and forth on the driver's side of the car. He looks up at us as we walk toward him. I can tell he's doing everything he can to control the anger he feels. He looks at me but doesn't say a word; he just climbs into the car and waits for us. Stephan opens the door to the back seat and watches me as I sit down and put my seatbelt on. I feel like a child who is about to be grounded for the rest of summer vacation, except it's almost December and I'm twenty-five years old.

Stephan turns around to look at me as Rick pulls out of the parking spot.

"Should I assume, based on your current decision making capabilities, that you did not go to a doctor to have your head looked at?"

I can barely look at him. I shake my head no. "Didn't you think you could have a concussion or maybe whiplash?" Again I shake my head no. At the time, what did I care if I had whiplash or a concussion? Looking back, I wish I would have gone just so that now I would be able to tell them I had done something right in all of this, that I had made at least one decision they could be happy with.

"Rick is right, Kara. You're making it hard to not be angry with you." Stephan turns back around and looks at Rick.

"Find us a hospital."

I wish he would have yelled at me, screamed at me. That would have been easier than the calm way the two of them are handling me at the moment—*handled*, what a great word for this. I'm being handled. Maybe it's what I need; maybe I need to be handled. I'm silent as they use their phones to find directions to the closest hospital.

"Do you have your insurance card on you?" Rick is looking at me in the rearview mirror.

"Yes." He looks back to the road and is silent again. I lean my head back and close my eyes.

I think I must have fallen asleep. Before I know it, we're at the hospital. Stephan is gently shaking my shoulder and asking me to stand up. I really don't want to do this. Will I be in trouble for not reporting an accident? Is that something you get a ticket for? Is that something you get arrested for? Will they think I was drunk? Do Rick and Stephan think I was drunk?

It's suddenly very important to me that they know I wasn't, that I really was just tired. I have my arm on Stephan's shoulder as I am getting out of the car.

"You know I wasn't drinking right? With the car accident, I mean. You know I was just tired right?"

I look up him, and he's looking at Rick. He doesn't answer me. He just bends down and kisses the top of my head softly. They don't trust me. They don't believe me, and I can't do anything to prove to them I had been sober when I hit the guardrail.

Stephan and Rick follow me back to the exam room in the ER. I keep trying to tell them they can leave. It's just going to be a doctor shining a light into my eyes or maybe a couple of x-rays. It hits me as I look from Rick to Stephan when I see neither of them respond; it's like I didn't even speak. It hits me then that I had better start to enjoy the time I have while I go to the bathroom because that's all the alone time I'm going to get. After repeating my story for the nurse and then the doctor, after x-rays of my head and my neck, after lights being shined, and reflexes tested, after any energy I had being zapped away, after all of that, I'm allowed to leave, a concussion and whiplash.

"Watch her for excessive sleeping. She will be very emotional and may not act like herself. If she starts to vomit or lose consciousness, you need to bring her back."

I can hear the doctor going over my discharge paperwork with them. I'm in the exam room changing back into my jeans and sweatshirt. I walk out as they hand Rick a prescription for pain and a muscle relaxant. I'm staring at the prescription, wondering how they are going to handle this. I am staring at the prescription, and they are staring at me.

CHAPTER 28

We get back to the car. I half close my eyes and pretend to fall asleep. I don't want any more awkward, angry silence around me. At least now I have an excuse for excessive sleeping. I can hear the two of them talking as we drive back to the hotel.

"I never thought I would have to ask this, but after last night… after finding the empty bottle in the trash, do you think she'll be able to handle the meds?" Rick is staring straight ahead, waiting for Stephan to answer.

"I don't know…I just don't know." I can hear the exhaustion setting into Stephan's voice. They drive in silence. I've almost fallen asleep when I hear Stephan. "I think we keep the pills, all of them, the Advil and Tylenol in her room too. I think we need to give her the muscle relaxants, but we need to be the ones to control it."

Not that I don't understand why, but this just confirms it—handled. I'm definitely being handled. "What about the pain pills?" Rick asks.

It takes a long minute for Stephan to answer. When he does, the anger in his voice is raw, "Maybe a little bit of pain will be good for her." I'm glad that he's hiding this from me. It's breaking my heart to hear it when they think I can't. It would be almost impossible to have to face it.

We pull into the parking lot of the hotel. Rick stops the car along the side of the lot over by the grass. "Kara, are you awake?"

"Hmm."

"Kara, wake up. Where's your car? I want to see it." I sit up straight in the back seat. Shit.

I take them behind the hotel, the last spot in a long row. The best spot I could find where no one could see, not that some stranger passing by would know, but hiding it from view makes it easier for me to forget. I don't want to get out and look. I know what it looks like. Rick and Stephan leave me in the back seat and begin to walk around my car. They stop when the see the damage on the passenger door. Looking back at me, they slowly start to make their way to the front of the car, where the real damage is. I can see them talking, but I can't hear what they are saying. They look from the car to me and then back to the car.

Stephan stays where he is at the front of the car, just watching me. My eyes leave him and begin to follow my brother as he walks over to the driver's side door. He gets into my car as though he were going to drive away. He runs his hand over the steering wheel and stops. He just sits there for a minute, not moving at all.

Stephan is still looking at me, and I can't place the look on his face. He walks back over to Rick's car and climbs into the front seat. He doesn't say anything to me. He just watches Rick. Rick finally starts to move. I see him looking around the inside of my car, reaching his hands under the seats and along the floor. I know what he's doing. He's looking for signs that I had been drinking when I got into the accident. Well, go ahead and look, asshole. I told you I was sober.

"Humph," I half groan as I lean back and lay my head along the top of the seat. Stephan looks at me in the rearview mirror, and I stare right back. I want to smirk at him, that teenage "I fucking told you so" kinda smirk. I want to, but I don't. I just sit there watching him watch me.

Rick climbs back into the car with us. His face is drained of color.

"There's blood all over the steering wheel."

What! I sit up so quickly that I feel dizzy. *I don't remember blood!*

I'm running my hand over my face, trying to feel for a cut or a scar, anything that could have bled. I remember the line of blood from my nose, but could it have bled the amount that has Rick clearly freaked out?

They look at me, waiting for an answer to their silent question.

"I don't remember blood." I say it quietly yet defensively. After everything I have spent the past two days telling them, did they really think I would start to lie now?

"Kara, if you can't remember the blood, then how can you be sure that you hadn't been drinking?" Stephan turns to look at me. The look on his face, he's daring me to lie to him.

"I wasn't drinking!" There is no doubt about it now; I am defensive, damn fucking defensive, and they know it. Rick puts his hand on Stephan's shoulder.

"There were no loose bottles, no pills."

I'm glaring at them; I feel so fucking betrayed. How can they still be questioning this? Who cares if I don't remember the blood! The damn doctor *they* just dragged me to told them there are things I may not be able to remember, that it's a side effect of a concussion. Why can I remember that when they can't seem to? I'm pissed off, and I'm no longer worried about what I put them through. I no longer feel guilt; I just feel anger.

I open my door and slam it fast and hard behind me as I storm away. They are both up and out of the car almost instantaneously. Rick yells out to me, clearly panicked, "Where are you going?"

"To my room, asshole! You can babysit me there!" I hear Stephan laugh, and it stops me cold. I turn, glaring at him from across the parking lot. "You can go fuck yourself too."

I start the walk back to my room. They stand there watching me go like two idiots with their jaws hanging open from my little temper tantrum. Once I get inside, I lean against the wall and try to calm myself back down. I don't even know what it is I'm feeling, not completely. I just feel so out of control from it all, so distant from everyone, like there is an actual wall that separates me from them. I hate feeling like they won't ever believe me, that they will never trust me again.

They could try to understand, if they were willing to; they could try to do more than blame me. They think that some stupid side comment, some stupid "can you believe she has been walking around feeling that way" means something. How about imagine what it is to walk around feeling this way, feeling guilty for feeling anything at all, feeling afraid to be alone, but worthless when you are around people? How about you try to do it for more than five minutes without letting it drive you crazy, without needing a drink just to shut up your own thoughts.

With one last deep breath, I push myself off the wall, turn around, and walk calmly up to the front desk. "So where does one go for a drink around these parts?" I give the clerk my best "had a rough day and looking to unwind" smile, and she provides me with directions to a restaurant with a decent bar attached; it's close enough that I can walk. I head out of the hotel, feeling angry at the world. My one concern about getting through the parking lot without them seeing me proves unnecessary; they are nowhere to be seen. I feel a little guilty as I picture them in the room waiting for me, but it's not like they will have to wait long. One drink and I'll head back; that way, they won't be worried. I can be quick, at least that is what I am telling myself.

● ● ●

One hour and four drinks later, I stumble into my room. Rick and Stephan freeze when they see me. They look frantic; Rick's hair stands on end from how many times he's run his hands through it. Stephan looks at me and half sits, half collapses onto the edge of the bed. His movements are a weird mixture of exhaustion and relief.

I'm looking at him through drunk eyes. He looks cute and kinda fuzzy. I take a step toward Stephan, but my eyes are drawn to the pile that sits next to him on my bed. My gym bag is open and the shirt I had been wearing during the accident is thrown across the top. It has blood spattered down the front. The sight of the blood, the proof it really was there, has stopped me in my tracks.

Rick grabs my arm, hard. "Where were you?" I start to answer but decide against it.

"Never mind, I can smell where you were."

I yank my arm away from him.

"Fuck off." I head into the bathroom, and when I come out, I'm alone. There's a glass of water and two Advil on the nightstand. I open the door to the room and find Rick sitting in the hallway, back against the wall, looking at his phone. He doesn't look up.

"You want to be all alone. Then be alone. But you WILL NOT have the chance to run again." I close the door and lock the dead-bolt. *Fucker*, I think. *Fuck you both to hell.* I take a deep breath and raise my head. I see the water; I see the two Advil placed next to it; my anger falters a little. I picture the look of panic that was in their eyes when I opened the door to my room. I picture the bloody shirt. I take a deep breath, and I fold; I reach up and unlock the deadbolt.

They're only trying to help, Kara, I tell myself as I walk to my bed. *They are as lost in all this as you are.* I swallow the Advil down with a sip of the water and fall asleep.

● ● ●

I can hear them whispering around me as I start to wake up. It pulls me the rest of the way out of my dreams and back into reality. I don't know how long they have been here, just watching me sleep. I'm too nervous to open my eyes. I can only imagine how angry, how disappointed, they must be in me right now.

"I know you well enough to know you're awake and just pre-tending. We brought you breakfast." It's Stephan's voice, and he sounds like he's right next to me. I crack my eyes open and see his face, just inches from mine. He's smiling down at me, smiling? Now I'm really confused.

"You unlocked the door. You let us in." As if that small action explains why he has decided to forgive me for yesterday, for the past three days? Four days? I don't ever know anymore. I tentatively smile back at him. If they can play nice, the least I can do is play along.

"We brought you coffee too, the good stuff."

"I don't understand?" I say it after my first long sip of coffee, let-ting my mind slowly start to wake up. "You should be mad. I would be mad. Why aren't you angry?" Stephan smiles down at me, but Rick sits in the chair looking like he a young child that has been put in time-out. He doesn't look at me, but instead seems to be staring at a spot on the wall just above my head.

"Who said I'm not mad? That we aren't mad?" Stephan is the one talking, but I can't seem to take my eyes off my brother. "We were terrified last night. You ran…again. We trusted you to be here. We even stayed away for a while to give you time." He pauses, with his hand on my chin. He turns my head to look into my eyes. "It felt like we were back at your apartment all over. We knocked on your door, and there was no answer."

I hear Rick mumbling under his breath.

"We came in, and you were gone, no note, no sign you had ever come back here at all. Then we found your shirt…covered in blood." He shivers. "It doesn't matter that we knew it was from the accident. To find you gone and then see your blood"—he takes a deep breath—"we were terrified."

I look into Stephan's eyes, silently begging him to believe me. "I don't remember the blood. I just…I just don't. I know I wasn't drinking. I didn't drink until I got to the hotel and only then because everything hurt…" I was a babbling idiot. The words just kept coming out. Stephan raises his hand to stop me.

"We know, Kara."

That's, sure as shit, not what I expected to hear.

"You know what?" I wait for him to answer, scared about what he might say next, but it's Rick who speaks.

"We believe you that you weren't drinking. Why would you have cleaned up the alcohol and not the blood? It wouldn't make any sense."

"You believe me?" I say it slowly. I'm shocked; as angry as I was yesterday that no one believed me, I find myself wondering why. Why would you believe me? I don't deserve to be believed right now.

Stephan reaches out to take my hand in his, "We know you weren't drinking when you got in the accident. But, Kara, it doesn't really matter. Drinking or not drinking that night, it doesn't change anything. You can't keep doing this. It will only be a matter of time before you are drinking and something happens. You have to understand, please…whether or not you were drinking that one time, it doesn't matter."

I look up at both of them, completely confused. "What do you mean it doesn't matter?" I ask it slowly, still not believing that they aren't screaming and yelling at me.

"It doesn't matter because you did what you had to do"—Rick pauses, and his eyes close—"with the…alley. You shouldered that by yourself. But now you aren't alone. You can lean on us."

Stephan picks up where Rick leaves off. You could tell they must have rehearsed this while I was sleeping. "But you WILL lean on us, Kara. That means no more booze, no more pills…no more running. The past is the past, but that WILL be your future."

Logically, what they are asking seems fair, especially after what they have seen from me lately and all; but emotionally…emotionally, it feels like a bunch of bullies trying to tell me what to do. I can feel myself starting to get defensive again. Defensive didn't work that well for me last night. The two of them are looking at me, watching me, waiting for a response. My mind is still trying to wrap itself around this.

No pills, that means sleeping will go out the window again—well, unless I keep getting concussions that is. No booze, it has been so long since drinking was something I did while out with friends; those weren't even the situations I was worried about. It was the dark of my apartment. It was nights where the fog rolled in. It was situations where there would be men I didn't know. Hell, even situations where they were guys that I knew, that maybe got just a little too close. These are the situations I'm worried about; how will I get through these without a drink?

My options lately have been drinking or let everyone around me see me go crazy. How would I keep from feeling like I'm going crazy all the time if I can't have a release? I can tell I'm breathing more rapidly now, my thoughts coming quicker and quicker. I hadn't even agreed to this, and I'm already starting to panic. They can see it on my face. One look at them, and I can tell. They go from watching me, to eyeballing each other.

Stephan walks up to me and puts his hand on mine.

"Kara?"

There really is no anger in his eyes, only concern, only love. It makes what they are asking a little easier to think about. Some of the defensiveness and fear I'm fighting starts to melt away.

"We'll do this together okay? One minute at a time. This minute, you can tell us you won't drink right? This is the only minute you need to think of."

I try not to think about anything else, just focus on this minute, just try to do what Stephan is asking. I take a deep breath.

"Rick?"

He sits down next to me and holds my other hand. "Are you still angry at me?" I sound like a little girl. I hate how weak and childish my voice sounds right now. I try to sit up straighter, to look stronger.

Rick looks me dead in the eye.

"I'm not angry. I'm terrified." A single tear escapes his eye, and he quickly brushes it away.

"I feel like I'm standing on the edge of a cliff holding on to you as you dangle off, like you're slipping through my fingers. And at any moment, it will be too late and I'll lose you."

He stands up and walks to the window. I can't see his face, but I think that's the reason he moved away; he doesn't want me to see him cry.

Stephan squeezes my hand, and I look back up into his eyes.

"We're here with you, Kara. We're not going anywhere, but we can't make you do this. You have to be willing. We can find you a treatment center or meetings, whatever you need."

My stomach is in knots. The second he says treatment I jump off the bed. It's the first real movement I've made since they asked me to agree to all this, and they move immediately by my side, afraid I'll run.

"No. No treatment. No meetings. No."

I'm in a panic. I'm talking more to myself than either of them. I'm pacing my new little track, five steps forward, turn, five steps back. Rick moves to stand in front of me. Blocking my way, he looks as though I've slapped him; but it's the moisture I see in his eyes that stops me.

Trying to sound in control, I look up at him. "No treatment center, no meetings. Please, Rick, no strangers." I have less panic in my voice, but anyone listening would be able to tell it was there just below the surface.

"I will agree to the pills and the drinking. I won't run. I swear, but just us, okay? No meetings, no therapy sessions. Please." Now the fear is in my voice. The words are running together as I'm speaking faster and faster.

Rick grabs my shoulders and forces me to look into his eyes.

"Breathe, Kara, just breathe."

He doesn't speak again until my breathing is under control. The panic is fading, but I notice he still hasn't agreed with my terms.

"Can you handle it without help?" He looks at Stephan now. "I mean, we're here, and we'll be here as long as you need us to." His eyes shift back to me. "But we don't know how to do this either, Kara. There are people out there that know what you will need. You're not the only one who has ever faced this."

I say the only words I know will get me what I want right now. I can feel the control coming back into my voice. I straighten my back and look directly into Rick's eyes. "If you make me go to meetings, if you make me go to treatment, I will run."

I turn and head into the bathroom. I feel horrible. I said the one thing that would work, but I hate myself for doing it. I look into my reflection in the mirror, and I know I'm starting to despise the person who is looking back.

I stand in the bathroom counting the seconds. I may have hated what I had said, but I still want it to work. After five minutes, I walk calmly back to the room. The two of them are standing next to each other talking. They have my car keys, my ID, credit cards, and money in their hands. Rick starts to talk, but Stephan stops him.

"Okay, Kara, we will TRY this your way. If you can't handle it, we'll look at other options." I note how he doesn't say what the other options are.

"So you're not angry, but you don't trust me." I point to my things in their hand.

"No, Kara, I don't." Stephan is looking me dead in the eyes. He speaks with no sympathy, no apology.

Hearing him say that, I can't stop the tears that start to fall. Stephan turns his head, so he doesn't have to see them.

"We need to figure some things out if we're going to do this your way. We're going to take you to the library. You can find some books to read, where we can see you, while we do some research. Understand?" Rick watches me as I nod my head, unsure of what else to do.

So this is what life's going to look like now.

CHAPTER 29

I'm a little manic right now, sitting here pretending to read while I watch two people pour over books and plan my life. Does it really matter that they're people who love me, who I love? I don't think I can sit still anymore; it feels like we've been here for hours. I push my chair back, and it squeaks against the floor like a warning alarm. Both of their heads jerk up. I never even stood up. I moved my chair for Christ's sake! Really, I mean, fucking really! This is so far beyond anything it needs to be. I lay my arm across the table and balance my head against it.

I'm back to my pretend life, pretend to read, pretend to be okay with this, pretend I can be strong enough to do this for them. Isn't this why I ran in the first place, to stop pretending, faking my way through my own life? I wasn't strong enough to live it before. What makes me think I can do it now?

God, please just make this day pass by quickly. This snail-crawling pace is killing me.

● ● ●

We're moving. Rick's still talking, but I'm not listening. I don't have a choice anyway. What does it matter that they think a change of scenery will be a good idea, some place that's not familiar, that's what Rick had said. *Since when is four days at a hotel familiar?*

Stephan is still in the library; he's calling on a house to rent somewhere. I'm sure Rick's mentioned where in this long drawn-out speech he's giving.

My knees are drawn into my chest as I sit outside the library. I can feel the cold from the concrete through my jeans. My hands are flat against the ground, and I focus on the feel of the cool steps, the roughness of it on my skin.

"Kara?"

Rick's watching me, shocking. I'm not sure how long ago he had stopped talking.

"What are you thinking?" His voice is careful.

"Does it matter what I think? It's not my decision anyway. I said I would do this, so whatever."

Ricks hand runs through is hair as he sighs. "I don't... We're doing the best we can here, Kara. I don't want you to feel like you have no choice in this. I'm not trying to be mean. It's just everything says that some place new will help. You can change your pattern, make a new one."

I tune him out again and focus back on the feel of the concrete. Eventually he gives up and sits next to me on the steps waiting for Stephan. So we're moving on, don't know where, just on.

Rick is as silent as I am, just looking out the window lost in thought as Stephan drives us back to the hotel. Stephan keeps checking the rearview mirror to judge my reaction as he fills me in on the plan. He's trying to sound excited, like this whole thing can be something to look forward to.

"It's not too far of a drive, Kara, about six hours or so. It's beautiful. I used to go there on vacations when I was a kid."

I think I'm hearing every third sentence or so. I meet his eyes in the mirror and smile. I can tell he didn't buy it, but he keeps talking anyway.

"We can leave tonight. Rick's already called your folks."

That surprises me. I don't know when he would have had the time to do that. I don't think he's left me yet today.

"Your dad will fly in to pick up your car and drive it home. We'll head down in Rick's car."

"What? No!"

It's my first real reaction since we left the hotel this morning. *Calm, Kara. They'll listen if you're calm.*

"Dad can't see my car, the damage, the blood. Please. Let's take my car. Dad can pick up Rick's…please." I know they can hear the panic in my voice. I don't even try to hide it. After way too damn long, Rick sighs.

"She's right, Stephan. We can't have him see that and not tell him anything. I think maybe there are some things that would be better if they didn't know. We can take Kara's car and have it repaired when we get there."

Stephan nods his head in agreement and is silent. The silence lasts the rest of the drive back.

I'm sitting on the bed in their room as they pack up the little bit of stuff they brought with them. I think we're all going to have to do some shopping to survive however long we're going to be gone for, wherever the hell it is we're going. I'm trying to be mad at them, to blame them for my current boredom. Don't they know I spend all my energy into not having downtime? But it's hard to be mad at them when I have to hear Rick call his boss to use the rest of his vacation time to be here with me. I have to watch as Stephan packs up his computer and client files he's been working on while I sleep. They're giving up so much for me. I'm stuck somewhere between anger at being handled and thinking I'm just not worth this.

Stephan stops as he's walking past me. He leans in and kisses me gently on the forehead. "What's that look for?"

He puts his computer bag onto the bed and sits next to me. "A couple of weeks on the beach not sounding good to you? Do you miss the frozen winds blowing at your face in Chicago?"

He's trying to be cute, to relieve the anxiety I can only imagine is in my eyes.

There's so much I want to say, but I suddenly don't know how to form the words. I want them to know I'm going crazy just sitting here, to know that I hate myself for them having to give up so much. I want them to know I love them. I want to know why they are doing this; but I have no idea how to ask. Instead I just lay my head onto Stephan's shoulder and let him silently hold me until I can start to feel the tension leave my body.

Can't this be the only part that's real, sitting in Stephan's arms with my head lying against him? I close my eyes and dream of opening them to find out I'm on my couch in my living room, that I've fallen asleep to some weird ass movie, and this was all just a dream. I imagine that Stephan carries me into my bedroom and makes sweet love to me until the nightmare is gone. I snuggle closer into his chest and move onto his lap; his arms hold me tighter. I can hear Rick opening the door to the room, coming back from carrying his stuff to my car.

"Kara?" When I don't answer he walks closer to us. "Is she okay?"

I don't want to move from Stephan's lap, from his arms. "I'm okay, Rick. Just tired of all this. I wish it could all go back to the way it was. I wish I never left."

"I don't."

What? I almost fall off Stephan's lap with that one.

"If you had never left, things never would have changed. I would spend my days trying to figure out what was wrong, and you would have kept pushing me away. Something was bound to snap, Kara, the way you were drinking…the pills…"

His voice drops to a whisper, "It could have ended so much worse than this. At least now I can feel you in my arms. You're talking to us. I wouldn't change that."

"I hate how it makes me feel, Stephan." I turn to be able to look at him. "To see how much you both are having to give up for me. I hate it."

"Well, don't." Rick walks up to the bed.

"I had so much vacation time piled up at work that I was getting yelled at for it anyway. I'm your brother, Kara. There's no place I would rather be. And besides, I've always wanted to go to Hilton Head."

I smile up at him. His line about vacation time really doesn't make me feel any better, but I appreciate that he's trying to lighten up my mood. If nothing else, at least now I know where we're going.

We leave around ten. I think they're hoping I'll sleep. Ever since it was agreed upon that I wouldn't do meetings or therapy treatments, life has been rather silent. They have all their research on what

I need to do and where I need to go, but no one knows how to talk to me. Little bits at a time, sure, but beyond the reassurance, it's pretty silent. I know they're trying here, trying to do their best in a situation they don't know how to handle; but the silence is killing me. There is far too much time where I'm left alone in my head.

It's too dark to say a proper goodbye to the mountains as we head down the highway. I have the back seat to myself while Rick drives, my jacket balled up like a pillow against the cold glass of the window. My eyes are closed, and I can hear them having a quiet conversation over the hum of whatever music Stephan has turned on. Six hours, I wish I could take something to make me sleep or at least something to relax my neck enough to get comfortable. Instead, I start to count how many seconds it takes to pass between exits.

I'm sure we stopped for gas. We must have, but the next thing I know, Stephan is lifting me out of the car and carrying me into a house. I can make out the shape of a palm tree above my head. This sure as shit isn't Chicago.

CHAPTER 30

I don't know what time it is when my eyes finally open. My room
has a faded glow of light that tells me I at least slept long enough
for the sun to come up. I have to give the guys credit for leaving at
night. Maybe they understand me more than I thought they did.
A six-hour drive during the day would have been torture. There's
only so much conversation that could have filled the time. Leaving
at night, I fell asleep as we drove, and I barely remember the walk
inside the house.

The house is bigger than I thought it would be. I follow the
smell of freshly brewed coffee until I find the kitchen. There's a mug
sitting next to the coffee pot with a bottle of half-and-half sitting
behind it. There are even muffins and a couple bagels sitting on a
plate.

I can see Stephan sitting outside on our deck overlooking a
small lagoon. The sight of palm trees in December is just weird. I
wrap a throw from the back of the couch around my shoulders as
I walk through the French doors. The cool breeze that hits my face
smells like the ocean and wakes me up even quicker than the coffee
in my hands. Stephan must have heard the door open because he
puts down his laptop and turns around in his chair.

"Good morning, beautiful."

I walk over and wrap my blanket around the two of us as I sit
on his lap and lay my head against his chest.

"How did you sleep?"

"Who says I'm done?" I snuggle closer into him and wrap the blanket around us even tighter. I can hear Stephan laughing as he wraps his arms around me.

"How did you find this place? It's so beautiful and quiet."

"We used to come here when I was a kid. It's one of the places we would vacation before my dad left. I didn't think I'd be able to find it. I must have been eleven the last time we were here. We were happy here. It was like everyone came down a level. My parents didn't fight. The chaos of life was gone. I was hoping it would have the same effect for you."

I don't know how to respond to that, here I thought I was asking a simple question, and I get this heartfelt "oh my god, I love this man" answer.

"Did you get to see the rest of the house?"

I smile to myself. "I never made it past the coffee in the kitchen."

"Figures." He playfully hits the back of my head. "Come on, you need a proper tour."

He lifts me off of him and places me gently on the ground. I pick up my coffee and take his hand as I follow him back into the house to begin my official tour.

He leads me through the kitchen with its eating area, into the oversized living room. There are board games lined up on the shelves next to a large flat-screen television: Scrabble, Monopoly, even Candy Land.

"I hope you're prepared to lose."

"Stephan, just let her win. You don't want to see the monster she becomes if she loses." Rick walks into the room and flops onto the couch. "Nice job picking out a place by the way."

I stick my tongue out at my darling brother, grab Stephan's hand, and pull him away.

"I want the rest of my tour please."

● ● ●

I'm feeling rather overwhelmed as I sit with Stephan trying to find something on television to watch.

Ricks gone out to drop off my car for repair and to pick up the rental. This house has to cost a fortune to rent. Three bedrooms, a lagoon, and we're only a few miles from the ocean. My car has to be repaired—who knows how much that's going to cost? I have no job; I have rent for my apartment, car payments.

"Penny for your thoughts." Stephan pulls me off the path my mind was wondering down.

"I can't afford this, Stephan. A couple nights in that hotel were simple, but this…" I wave my hand through the air.

"This is too much. I have to pay for my car to be fixed. My rent is due this week—"

"Stop."

Stephan's hands are on my shoulders, and his eyes are locked onto mine. "Breathe, Kara, take a deep breath and try to relax. You don't need to worry about it right now. We left my key to your apartment before we drove out to you. Your parents got into your place to get the bills. It's all been covered. This house, consider it an early Christmas present. I would buy it outright if it meant you were going to get better. Everything is covered. You have one job right now, one thing to focus on, and that's it."

I close my eyes and try to look at ease with everything he just said, but how is knowing that someone else is having to pick up the responsibility of my life supposed to help ease the guilt I feel?

CHAPTER 31

The fog is starting to build outside; you can see it rolling in as though it were a wave meeting the sand. I can feel the panic rising in my chest. Stephan and Rick clearly don't have a clue that it's coming on. They're still completely focused on the Scrabble game that they have laid out on the table. I don't want to give them cause for alarm; there's nothing they can do. It's just that I already know what tonight is going to hold, and all of my coping mechanisms are gone. I can't do anything to make sure I sleep deep enough, do anything that will keep the dreams at bay. I don't know how I'm going to get through it. The fog always brings it back, always leaves me trapped in a dream, face pressed up against the bricks.

Placing my book onto the table, I stand and Stephan glances up to me.

"Going to bed already?"

I put on my best and biggest smile. "You wish. I'm not going to bed until I see you lose. So sorry but no, I'm just going to get a cup of tea."

Stephan sits up just a little straighter, trying to judge if there's anything actually wrong. "It's a little late for caffeine, don't you think?"

No, dumbass, I think I don't want to fall asleep tonight; I think I don't want to wake up screaming, sweat pouring off of me. I think I don't want to find myself alone with a faceless monster in an alley. I think I don't want to see you look at me with pain and sympathy in your eyes ever again. I think I want you to treat me the way you used to treat me before I ever told you "my story." I think I want my life back the way it used to be.

I try to regain my smile, hiding any panic that I know must be creeping into my eyes.

"No, I have some new books I want to start, so I really want to finish the one I'm reading tonight."

He seems to believe me, but he hasn't looked back down to the game yet either. Rick glances up at him.

"Stephan, we've taken away so much from her this week. Let her keep the damn caffeine, man." He smiles to himself feeling like has come to my rescue, for caffeine; my life is sad. I smile back at Rick, silently thanking him. Stephan has given up and started to concentrate on words that start with the letter *q*.

The men folk finally head to bed about 1:00 a.m. I'm sitting in a chair with every light on in the living room of our little rented house.

Rick walks by and kisses my forehead. "Night, sis, not too much longer, okay? I don't want to have to answer to Stephan for standing up for your little caffeine habit when you are dragging ass tomorrow."

Stephan playfully punches him in the shoulder laughing. I look up at them. I never thought they would be so close, be such good friends. At least something good has come from all of this. Watching the two of them together warms my heart.

Stephan bends down for a kiss good night. Looking into my eyes, he asks, "Are you sure you're okay?"

He really can see through me, this man of mine. Sometimes I wish I could hide things a little better from him. But instead of facing the truth, I laugh and grab his shirt.

"Shut up and kiss me, old man." His kiss is warm and tender and must have lasted a minute too long because Rick starts clearing his throat.

"Dude, that's my little sister."

● ● ●

Everything is black. I know I'm in the alley. I can feel the brick slicing at my cheek. I can feel the blood dripping off my face, and I can hear him laughing at the joy of seeing me bleed.

"That's right, bitch. You're gonna bleed for me. You're gonna scream for me."

I can't move, and I can feel him pressed up against me.

"Kara!"

I turn my head to try to see where the noise is coming from, to find who is calling my name. I'm right here. Why can't you see me? Why can't you stop him?

"Kara! Wake up!"

I open my eyes, and Stephan is on top of me, my shoulders in his hands. He's shaking me. Rick is standing behind him, total terror in his eyes. I'm frantically looking from Rick to Stephan and back to Rick, trying desperately to control my thoughts, trying to remind myself I'm not in the alley. I'm in our house. I'm at the beach. I take a deep breath and then another. Stephan is still standing over me, but he's stopped shaking me. He's searching my eyes for something. I just don't know what.

"Are you okay?" I nod a weak yes.

Stephan climbs off my bed. He looks like he's moving in slow motion, like he's having to focus very hard at the task of moving at all. After a long and quiet moment, he turns to face me.

"Is that why you wanted caffeine last night? So you wouldn't fall asleep?" I nod my head again.

I don't want to talk about this anymore. I need to move. I need to breathe. My book falls to the floor as I stand up and walk out of the room. The sun is just starting to come up outside, and the fog is clinging to the ground. I stand still, staring out the window, shocked that something so beautiful can bring on such nightmares.

"What time is it?" My voice is scratchy, weak from screaming.

Rick puts his hand on my shoulder. "It's five thirty." He seems to be okay with my quiet moment. He seems to want one too; but Stephan wants none of it.

"Oh no, you don't. What the hell was that, Kara? The scream-ing...it was"—he pauses for a breath—"and then we couldn't wake you up. You wouldn't wake up. It was like you were trapped... What the hell was that?"

For the first time since we've been in South Carolina, I want to run, not to escape for a couple of hours but run, run far and run fast. I want to drown my memories in a bottle of vodka; I want to not know my name. I want to not know that alley; I want to burn the image of him, the sound of him from my head forever, and I think they can tell.

They are moving in on me, but all that it's doing is making me feel more trapped. My head is shaking back and forth as though, if I shake it hard enough, the memories will spill out. They are still moving, trying to block my path of escape. I'm standing still, shaking my head, when Rick tries to touch my arm.

"It's okay, Kara. We're right here. He can't—"

"DON'T TOUCH ME." It's not even a scream. It's a primal shriek. It stops both of them in their tracks. I need a drink. There has to be something here, something for them that they've hidden for after I fall asleep.

I run into the kitchen and start searching the cabinets, leaving a wake of destruction behind me. Rick stands in the doorway, watching, a look of shock on his face. Stephan walks up to me, hands in the air. He is talking quietly.

"There is nothing here, Kara, no alcohol, no pills. There is nothing you will find."

I don't believe him. He's lying. He has to be lying; there has to be something here. I run into the bathroom. They had filled the prescription for the muscle relaxers for my neck. I remember them talking about it. They have to be here, if I could just take a few of them, just enough to get the images to go away, to forget the dream, to forget the look on their faces when I woke up.

They just watch me as I run from the kitchen to the bathroom, from the bathroom to their bedrooms. I empty the suitcases onto the ground, tearing everything apart. Something has to be here.

I finally give up, falling to the ground I curl up like a baby. I can't stop crying. I lay on the floor, blubbering and rocking, while they look on. Rick seems frozen, but Stephan lies down on the floor next to me. Exceedingly carefully, moving painfully slow, he starts to put his arm around me. I turn into him and surrender everything I have left. I don't have any words to even begin to explain my actions.

I must have fallen back asleep because when my eyes open, I'm in my bed. Stephan has brought a chair into the room and sits next to me, like I'm some comatose patient in a hospital. I wish he hadn't seen my eyes open; I wish I was better prepared for what to do now. Brushing the hair away from my face, his hand softly caresses where my cheek had been cut from that stupid brick. "Are you okay?"

I nod my head yes, then slowly start nod no. "I don't want to be this person, Stephan." I feel like I should be crying all over again, but I don't have any tears left.

He's sitting silently, analyzing me, trying to figure out exactly what I mean and waiting for me to continue. The way he's looking at me, there's no anger in his eyes over last night, over the way I acted, and I can't understand why. Shouldn't he be angry?

It's suddenly very important for me to know—or maybe it's more like it's important for me to make him understand—I don't deserve someone like him right now in my life, and he deserves somebody who can do and be better than me. I sit up and wrap the blankets tighter around myself. I try to look calm. Tucking my hair behind my ears, I look straight into Stephan's eyes and ask the one question that I never want him to answer, but it's the one question I need him to.

"Why are you still here?"

He looks confused and opens his mouth to talk, but I keep going before I lose my nerve.

"I mean, Rick is my brother. I get that. But why are you here, dealing with all of this? You have to know that you can do better, that you deserve better."

He smiles at me, which is really the last thing I expect him to do right now. Taking my hand in his, he rubs his thumb over my knuckles. "I don't want anyone else, Kara. I want the you back that I fell in love with. Right now that means I'm here dealing with all of this. It means even if I have to fight you, for that Kara, I will."

"But what if she's gone? What if she can't come back?"

The calm I was trying to portray has vanished. My voice is now barely above a whisper as I put into words one of my biggest fears. "What if the person that I was is lost forever?"

The reassuring smile that was on his face is gone. Now he is the one trying to look calm and strong; he is the one looking me straight into the eyes.

"I know you feel lost, Kara, but I also know the girl I fell in love with is still in there. You are stronger than that alley. You are stronger than all these ways you have learned to cope with it. I only wish to God that you knew it too. I'm here because I believe you will figure that out.

He looks down at our intertwined fingers and is quiet for what seems like an hour. "I need to know something. The alley, it was the night you tried to cancel our date, wasn't it?" He looks at me for confirmation.

"The night before...yeah."

He closes his eyes and seems to try to take that in. Logically he must have figured that out a week ago. I guess hearing it is something different.

"I thought so." He reaches and softly traces the line of my lips. "The way I feel about you, it would take a lot more than this to change." He looks down at me, holding my gaze. "I understand why you didn't talk to me when this happened. Well, I'm trying to understand. I wish you would have. I wish you felt you could have. You can tell me anything, Kara. It won't change the way I feel about you. Something happened that was NOT your fault. I know you think that because"—he takes a deep breath and looks away—"because he didn't do everything he said he would, that because of that, you think it shouldn't affect you, that it shouldn't have scared you."

I can't look at him anymore, not when we're talking about this, not when I've been put in this bed weak from the dream and the following chaos. I look out the window, watching the leaves flutter in the wind as he continues.

"I think that you feeling that way is part of the problem, Kara. What happened, it would have scared anybody, terrified anyone.

How you had the courage to even try to pretend like nothing had happened—"

"I stopped going to the gym," I say it to the tree, to the leaves in the wind. With a sad little smile plastered in place, I look back over to him. "I never walked down that street again."

He looks back at me, not returning the smile. "Kara, I'm starting to think you never left that street. You can't move on until you do."

I don't know how much time has passed before I emerge from my room with Stephan. Rick is sitting at the kitchen table; he's seems mesmerized by his phone as he twirls it around and around on the tabletop.

"I think we need to call Mom and Dad." He doesn't look up; he just keeps staring at the phone. "I think this is more than we can handle. I think we were wrong to try to do this on our own."

He finally looks up at me. "You need help, Kara, more than we know how to give. Watching you this morning…"

I can tell he's on the verge of tears. He hates crying even more than I do. It breaks my heart to watch him try to fight the tears back.

"Rick, I'm sorry. Please…" My breath seems stuck in my throat, choking at the mere thought of having to see them now.

"Please don't call them, not yet. Give me a few more days. Give me a few more days, and then I will call them. I'll go with them." Both of them look at me as I say this, totally surprised, since the beginning I have been fighting them on bringing my parents into this with anything more than occasional updates.

"I can't hide from them forever, Rick. I don't know what I'm going to tell them. But I know, especially after this morning, I know that I can't be on my own yet either. You two have given up enough of your lives for now."

Stephan opens his mouth to disagree with me, but I raise my hand to stop him. "I know you don't mind doing this for me, that you want to be there for me, and you have been." I look up into Rick's eyes. "I have nothing left. You've seen me, seen parts of me that I never wanted anyone to see. I have nothing left to hide."

Rick is still playing with his phone, thinking this through. Stephan puts his arms around me and holds me. "Please, Rick?" Rick looks up from his phone to study me. I try to look stronger, to stand straighter.

"Fine." He backs away from the table and walks out of the house. Stephan looks down at me. "Let me make you some tea."

We are sitting in the living room now, my feet curled up underneath me on the couch. They are looking at me; after so much time alone with them, I can read the questions they want to ask simply by looking at the expression on their faces.

"You want to know about the dream." It's not a question as much as a statement of fact. I look at Rick. Stephan is sitting next to me with his arm around my shoulders.

"Only if you are ready to tell us." I lay my head on Stephan's shoulder and start.

"The fog always brings it on. On other nights, when I dream the edges aren't as hard, the dream isn't as real. But the fog...it was foggy that night too." I close my eyes, and the dream lays out in front of me. "It's dark, and I can't see. But I can feel. I can feel the bricks from the building I'm pushed against cutting my face. I can smell him, and I can hear him laugh. No one ever finds me. In my dream, people walk down the street so close I can touch them, but they never stop. They never see me."

I take a deep breath.

"When he's finished with me, he leaves me broken on the ground. People step over me; they leave me there. I lay there until I wake up. It's always the same." Stephan hugs me tighter, and Rick walks over to me. He kisses my forehead, something he does a lot lately. "Thank you." He walks away leaving Stephan holding me on the couch. I can see him standing outside looking at the water. He doesn't move for a very long time.

"This is hard for him, Kara. He blames himself that he wasn't there to save you. That he didn't see what was going on until it was almost too late, that you ever went to live in the city, that he didn't stop you." *What?*

"Stephan, that's ridiculous. You two keep telling me that this isn't my fault, that HE did this. If this isn't my fault, then how the hell can he believe that it's his?"

"I've told him that a thousand times, Kara. But it's how he feels, how we both feel."

What the hell?

I look up at him about to yell at him when he says, "Let me finish, I saw that night…that there was something seriously wrong. I knew you were lying about the fall, and I didn't push it. I could see the changes in you, how hard you tried to hide it. I thought"—he sighs—"I don't know what I thought. Then I found you that night in your bed, barely conscious. I was so angry." He shivers and takes a deep breath. "I was angry, and I was hurt you wouldn't tell me what was going on. Then when you told me I would never understand, I knew it had to be something big, but I had no idea."

He looks me in the eyes like he is trying to look into my soul. "I owe you an apology. I owe your whole family an apology. I should have called them sooner. I should have forced the issue with you. I was just afraid I would lose you, and then I did lose you."

Now Stephan is up and pacing. "Those two days when you were gone were the worst days of my life. We really were afraid that the note you left was a suicide note. When we searched your apartment and we found the pill bottles, two empty and one half full… When you called…"

He is looking at me now again.

"We had expected it to be the police. We thought they must have found your body… When we saw that it was your number, when Rick heard it was your voice…it was the greatest gift the world could have given me." I'm just staring at Stephan; I can't believe the words coming out of his mouth.

"Do you really think she needs to hear all this?" Rick is standing in the doorway looking at us. My head is still wrapping around everything Stephan had just told me.

"I don't know, Rick…but we're asking her to be totally honest with us, with every thought and emotion she's going through. It doesn't feel right to have us hide things from her."

200

Rick clearly isn't happy; he's glaring at Stephan. "I think this is something we should have talked about. Thanks a lot for making that decision without me." Rick stomps back into his bedroom and shuts the door.

● ● ●

"Kara?" I look up from the crossword puzzle I'm filling out. I have gotten very good at these lately.

"I think you need some time with just your brother." Rick has been in his room for the past hour or so.

"I think I'm getting in the way, and that is the last thing I wanted to do."

I put down the crossword and look up at Stephan. I can tell the hurt and fear I feel is reflected on my face.

"I think it's the right thing, Kara."

My heart is pounding in my chest. Rick is great, but he's not my rock in this. Rick has a harder time controlling his anger when I make a mistake, when they see me starting to crack.

"Please don't go, Stephan. I need you in this. I need you here... with me. I'm not strong enough yet." The words are running together again, the way they do when I am trying to control emotion that I have no hope in controlling.

"Take a deep breath, Kara. Calm down. I'm not talking about leaving permanently, just more like giving you the day. I know you don't think you are strong enough yet, the truth is... I'm not strong enough to leave you for more than a day. The memory of not knowing where you were is too fresh." He shivers as he plays with my fingers.

I look up at him, "Promise? Just the day?"

"I promise."

CHAPTER 32

S tephan left using some excuse about meeting a client nearby. I guess that's one of the nice things about having rich clients throughout the country. You can have a meeting even while on an ocean front escape. Rick is making me breakfast. I remember his cooking from when we lived together, and I'm slightly afraid. I walk into the kitchen only to meet him in the doorway as he attempts to block me from entering.

"Outta here, girly girl."

I can't help but laugh. This feels too much like the good old days to remain scared about what the day could possibly hold.

"Rick, do I smell burning pancakes when I should be smelling gourmet coffee?"

"Outta here!" He growls, and I can't help but laugh again. It feels good to be laughing like this, to be this carefree.

"Okay, okay. Sheesh." I go and sit patiently at the table, trying to prepare myself for burnt pancakes but hoping for the coffee.

I can't believe Rick is this relaxed when just two days ago, I was tearing the house apart looking for a way to burn the dream out of my head.

"Rick?" I place my napkin over my plate in hopes of hiding the uneaten food. "You said you didn't want me to hide anything from you, right? Hide what I'm really thinking and feeling?" Rick braces himself in his seat, straightening his back, trying to prepare himself for whatever I might say next.

"You can tell me anything, Kara. I love you, and nothing can change that. Nothing can drive me away."

You can tell he rehearsed it. For a minute, I picture him standing in his room in front of the mirror chanting it before Stephan left. He must have been just as nervous to be here without Stephan as I was. It makes me feel even better about what I want to say.

"That's good because this breakfast really sucked." And I'm laughing, deep belly laughing like a baby that doesn't know to be too embarrassed enough to stop. Rick throws his napkin at me pretending to be hurt, but he has a stupid grin plastered on his face.

"You're horrible."

This is proving to be easy, way easier than I ever imagined it would be. I think Stephan was right to let us have some alone time. Whatever the tension was that had been following Rick and I the past week, it's gone. We are just the silly brother-and-sister pair we've always been.

"So"—I turn around to face him as I dry my hands from doing the dishes—"what does the rest of this Rick and Kara day hold?"

"I don't know. Is there anything you want to do? Anything you need?"

"Nope, I got my coffee. Anything else is just a bonus."

"Then I say we go for a swim." He has that famous Rick West smile, the kind that means we are about to get into trouble. I love it. I haven't seen him smile like that since before I ran.

"A swim...where?"

"We are only a few blocks from the ocean."

"Rick, you're nuts! Besides, Stephan has the car. How do you think we get back from the ocean soaking wet when it's forty degrees outside?"

"Is that the only thing stopping you?"

"Why do I feel like I'm being tricked into something here?"

"Stephan rented a second car so we could go somewhere if we wanted to. You're out of excuses. Grab a towel. We're going for a swim."

I'm rethinking this whole plan as the waves break on the shore and reach my toes. The sand seemed cold enough; the water is freezing.

"Don't think about it, just run in and dive."

Rick goes running past me in a pair of sweatpants and dives under a wave. I don't want to wait to hear him shriek when he resurfaces. I take a deep breath and run for it.

The water takes my breath away. It's so cold. I can't help it. It's a reflex to try to catch another breath, and I swallow a large gulp of sea water. I'm screaming and coughing as my head breaks through the surface.

"Rick! I'm gonna kill you for this!"

"You have to catch me first!" He's running through the water, trying to get back to our towels that we had left on the sand. I chase him out of the ocean and can barely contain my frozen laughter as I wrap the towel tightly around me and slip my feet into my shoes.

"You're dead!" My teeth are chattering, so it comes out much more like "y-y-y-ou're d-d-d-ead."

In the car, we blast the heat and wrap extra towels around us. We can't stop laughing as we drive back to the house. I can't even begin to describe how wonderful it feels.

"That was your dumb ass idea. I get the first hot shower!" I'm out of my seat and inside the house before he has the car in park. The water burns my icy cold skin, but after just a few seconds, I'm heating back up. I haven't been in the warmth anywhere near long enough when I hear Rick banging on the bathroom door.

"Kara! Come on, I'm freezing out here. I want a turn with the hot water before you use it all up!" I reluctantly turn off the water and step out of the shower.

"I'm coming. I'm coming."

I dress in the softest sweat suit I have and throw my hair back into a ponytail. I'm in the kitchen making hot chocolate when Rick resurfaces from his shower.

"So…what's next?" I'm smiling as I hand him his drink. "Do you have any more life-affirming actions planned for the day?"

"Nope. That was it."

We decide we're just too damn cold to leave this house again. Our best alternative is a movie marathon while buried under a load of blankets. In the two weeks since we've been here, I've managed to see almost all the movies this house is stocked with. Rick, of course, wants Rocky. I throw out the idea of a chick flick, knowing that it improves my chances of a compromise and me not having to hear some half-beat-to-death-man-cry "Adrian" for the rest of my afternoon. As suspected, I got a firm "no way in hell" to that one. We settle on the *Rush Hour* series and sit with a bowl of popcorn between us.

Jackie Chan bloopers are playing after the second movie when I hear Stephan whispering in my ear.

"Hey there, sleepyhead."

I didn't realize I had fallen asleep. I shift trying to make room for Stephan while not waking Rick at the same time. "How was your meeting?"

"Faster than I thought it would be." He tugs on my "still damp at three in the afternoon" ponytail, the question reflected in his eyes. "How was your day with your brother?"

I can't wait to see his reaction to this one.

"Great. We had a nasty pancake concoction for breakfast followed by a trip to the beach and a quick swim in the ocean."

The look on Stephan's face is everything I had hoped it would be. "You went swimming, and I missed it? How was the water?" The smile on his face is more carefree than anything I've seen out of him in months. That alone is worth an ocean of icy liquid.

"It was cold." Rick tries to steal more of the blanket. "You two are noisy, go away."

Stephan and I both can't help but to laugh at Rick mumbling from under a pile of blankets. "How about I take you out to lunch? Get you some hot soup or something?"

Rick kicks at me with his feet from under the blanket. His voice is heavy with sleep. "Good, get your loud asses out of here and bring me back some chicken noodle."

He rolls over as I stand up to change into something more appropriate than a sweat suit.

The restaurant is cozy and more importantly warm. We have a basket of bread in between us and a steaming bowl of lobster bisque is sitting in front of me. I love how normal it feels sitting here like this with him. For a minute, it feels like we could be any other couple on vacation. I really want to be any other couple, here to escape the stress of the holidays at home with our families.

Holidays with the family. My mind races back, remembering days long before the alley, lying in Stephan's arms the night he told me he loved me for the first time, the unbelievable love I felt for him as he described why he was nervous for his mom to meet me when she flew in for Christmas.

Shit.

"Stephan?" I'm afraid to ask the question, afraid that I already know the answer.

"Wasn't your mom supposed to be coming? You need to leave, don't you?"

I hate the way that came out. It sound's whiny, like I'm already complaining when here he has stayed so long. I wish he had given me a little warning though. I'm sure my reaction the other day as he told me he was going to give Rick and I the day alone doesn't help the way he must feel about leaving now.

He reaches across our basket of bread and takes my hand in his, giving it a reassuring squeeze. "Kara, you need me right now more than she does. I told her not to come. I said—"

"Wait! You did what? Stephan, no!" My voice is rushed and a little too loud for our quiet seaside restaurant. The tables nearby have started to stare. It takes more focus than I care to admit to be able to control my voice, both the volume and the panic that it portrays.

"I don't want to come between you two, Stephan. She already has to think I'm crazy. I don't want her to hate me for this too."

"It's okay, Kara." His thumb is moving back and forth across the knuckles of my hand, and that little action helps to calm me down. "I told her work was too busy right now, that I had to travel for client meetings. I promised her we would come to see her as soon as we could."

She won't blame me. I feel selfish at how much relief I feel knowing that. I let out the breath I didn't know I was holding.

"I'm not sure about this, Stephan. I'm taking up so much of your life right now. So many things are changing for me. It doesn't feel right or fair."

"Then it's a good thing it's not your choice." Stephan's face shows no sign of doubt in his decision. He canceled on her, and he hasn't given it a second thought.

I try to put it out of my head. If it doesn't bother him, it shouldn't bother me, right? But it's so much easier said than done. I can't help but feel guilty for everything Rick and Stephan are giving up right now. They have lives that have been put on hold, friends, family, holiday parties at work. I sit up at night playing scrabble and reading a book like their lives haven't stopped, like this is somehow all how it's supposed to be. I have been able to forget what life is really like for Rick this time of year, even how life is normally for me during the holidays.

I don't mean to be quiet while we eat, but I know I am. Stephan plays along with it, giving me my space. Walking back to the car, he puts his arm around my shoulder.

"Kara, is everything okay? You've been silent since I told you my mom isn't coming. What is it?"

I don't know what to say. I promised him honesty, but I'm still not sure about the decision I think I'm coming too.

"Please, Kara, this silence is driving me crazy."

"I know you don't want to hear how I feel guilty about this, Stephan. I love you for everything that you and Rick are doing for me, for everything you have given up." I stop walking and look down at the ground. "I love you for it, and I hate me for it. I feel so guilty and unworthy of it. I feel weak for needing it, and I hate feeling weak. I feel like you're going to end up resenting me, that you will never look at me the same again, and you'll spend your time watching me and waiting for the next failure. How do I ever live this down? How do I even begin going about deserving to live this down?"

Stephan tilts my head to look up at him as he pulls me into his arms. "That's a lot to be worried about, Kara. Give it some time. This is so new to all of us. Just give it some time."

He starts to walk back to the car, but I stand still. I need to get this out while I still have the courage to do it.

"Stephan." He turns and looks back at me.

"What is it, baby?" His voice is apprehensive.

"I think I should go home."

CHAPTER 33

Stephan walks back to me and places his hands on my shoulders, he searches my eyes for something but doesn't say what. After a long and quiet minute, he finally speaks, "Why? Why do you want to go home? Yesterday, you were so against it."

I shrug, quickly dismissing his question. "Is this because you feel ready, or are you running again, only this time it's from guilt?"

"Can't it be a little bit of both?"

"No, Kara, it can't." He sighs, shaking his head ever so slightly from side to side. "You can't run from things. It's the easy way out. You feel guilty, as much as I hope you wouldn't. I understand why you do. Running from it won't change the way it feels."

He puts his arm back around me and steers me back to the car.

I can't help but see the irony here. Yesterday Rick was all but dialing the phone to have me sent home. Today when I say I'm ready, Stephan's telling me I have to stay. It's hard not to feel angry about it. I haven't felt handled since we got to South Carolina, not until this. Is he right? Am I wanting to run because I feel guilty? If we were back at home, Rick and Stephan could go back to their lives. Stephan wouldn't have to pay for our little vacation house. He could still spend the holidays with his mom. Of course, I feel guilty, who wouldn't?

If I go back to Chicago, well, when I go back to Chicago, I know it can't be back to my own place, not yet, not after the other night. I'm going to have to go to my parent's house. I still have to figure how to control how I feel. It's one thing to be able to control myself here; my panic-driven run through the house the other night proves I can barely do that; it will be another thing entirely to do it back in Chicago. I have to learn I can't run to a bottle in hopes of escape.

The South Carolina landscape has become a blur as we drive back to our temporary little home. It's even started to rain like some eerie Shakespearean fallacy. I feel as gray and weepy as the sky looks. All the laughter and fun of the morning with Rick has now been overshadowed with the feeling of responsibility over Stephan's mom and confusion over his one stupid question. Am I running from the guilt by wanting to go home?

"Kara, we're back." We're sitting in the driveway. The car is off, and you can hear the sounds of the rain hitting the windows. I don't know how long we have been sitting here.

"I didn't want to make you mad."

"I know."

I realize I should probably say more, but I'm not really sure what there is to say; I am mad. I'm tired of being handled. It's degrading to think he put his arm around me and steered me to the car, like "okay conversation done, I told you how to feel. I told you what you are doing, time to go. But on the other hand, I do want him to tell me what he thinks. I want that kind of relationship. I trust him, and if he thinks I want to go home because it's another version of running, then it's something I really need to figure out.

I'm still sitting in the car, only now Rick has taken notice of it too. He pauses in the doorway of the house before walking up and opening the car door. He looks over me to Stephan.

"What's wrong with her?"

It's the last straw for me. I'm already feeling shitty over guilt, not to mention handled by the man I love, and now my own brother is going to talk over my head as if I'm not even here.

"I'm right in front of you, Rick. Why don't you ask me that question?" I get out of the car in one quick movement. Pushing past Rick, I walk quickly into the house.

Grabbing one of the blankets from the couch, I wrap myself in it and sit outside overlooking the lagoon. Ignoring the cold drizzle that falls, I focus on trying to figure out how I really feel. If I were at home, by myself, this is the exact moment I would want a martini in hand, just one, just something to finish the scene, something to help turn off the cutting edge to my thoughts, to let me think a little more clearly. I watch as the setting sun changes the color of the sky. I try to lose myself in the dancing pinks and blues that peak out from behind the clouds and reflect onto the water.

It's dark by the time Rick joins me.

"Stephan told me what you said, how you feel guilty, how you want to go home."

He sits on the ground in front of me. "Kara, put it in reverse. If it was me who was going through this, wouldn't you act exactly the same way? I'm here because you're my sister, and there is no place else I would be. Please don't let the guilt from that control you. If you're ready to go home, then go, but Stephan's right. Don't do it because you're running from something else."

He stands and kisses me on my forehead before he heads back inside.

I think two of them know I'm waiting for them to go to bed before I head in. No one comes out to say good night. They just leave me be, sitting on the back porch wrapped in a blanket. I'm thankful for the alone time and for the trust it means they have in me. The house is dark as I head back in. I make it as far as my room before I turn around. I walk through the living room and down the next hall-way. Stephan's door in unlocked. He's lying in his bed working on the computer. He doesn't say anything as he looks up to me and moves his computer off of his lap. I don't think either of us know what to say, and that's kind of okay. I climb into his bed, pull the covers up and over me, and lay down to sleep. A moment later, I hear his computer shut off and feel his arm wrap around me.

"I love you" is quietly whispered in my ear as I fall asleep.

● ● ●

The bed is empty when I wake up. The house is quiet as I head into the kitchen to make my coffee. There's a note on the countertop from Stephan.

Went on a run—
be back soon.

This is the first time he's gone out for a run since I left Chicago. It reaffirms my decision to leave. He's taking his life back; I want to take mine back too.

I don't want to give Rick or Stephan the chance to talk me out of it. It's not that I'm unsure of the decision. It's the entire concept of seeing my family, of having to take ownership yet again that has me so nervous. It's exhausting and terrifying all at the same time.

I pick up my cell and lean against the counter. I've only talked to Mom and Dad a handful of times since this whole thing started, maybe ten minutes if you added all the conversations together. I can only imagine the work Rick must be doing to convince them to stay away. I don't know what to say to them. I don't even know where to start. I dial Dad's number and look at it on my screen. I don't have the courage to hit send. I know I'm being pathetic, but it's okay. I decide to embrace my pathetic ways and even find myself smirking at them as I type the text.

"I want to come home. Will you come and get me?"

No apologies, no I love yous, something is seriously fucked up with me. I put the phone back down, ignoring the alert that I have a text back. I pour myself a cup of coffee and head into my room to read. I need to get lost in something. Coffee and a book is all I have left.

CHAPTER 34

Stephan and I are standing together in the doorway when Rick pulls up with my parents. "Don't leave me alone with them, okay?" The anxiety I feel is obvious from the tone of my voice; he squeezes my hand to reassure me.

"It's just your mom and dad, Kara. They love you."

"But I have done so much lately to disappoint them. I can only imagine what they think of me. How do I do this, Stephan? How do I even look at them now?"

I try to turn around to go back into the house. I don't know how to handle this; I don't know what to say. At this point, I can't even remember what we had decided to tell them. Rick had been the one making the calls with updates. I spoke to them as little as I could get away with; I had no idea what to say then, and I still don't.

"No more running, Kara." He looks at me. "Rick and I are here. We won't leave you, I promise."

"What did we tell them? I can't remember." We had little conversations starting the week we came to Hilton Head. Nothing really important, just letting them hear my voice. Rick swore that was all mom wanted, to hear my voice, to know I was alive and getting better. It was the getting better part that worried me. What do they think is wrong?

Mom is looking at me through the car window. So this is where Rick had gotten his statue pose from; how had I never noticed that before? Dad keeps stealing glances at me while he tries to make sure Mom is okay. Rick is trying to pretend this is all normal. He's extra chatty with them as he gets out of the car.

"This is really such a great house Stephan found for us, and the weather is so much nicer here than in Chicago right now."

Neither of my parents are listening to a word he's saying; he could be telling them I was abducted by aliens right now, and they wouldn't have known. Rick seems to notice that he's being ignored, and silently he works his way up the front walk toward me. I'm standing now with Rick on one side and Stephan on the other; they would never admit it, but I'm sure it's to keep me from running. I take a deep breath and decide it's now or never. I square my shoulders and walk up to the car as Dad is helping Mom out.

"Hi." Mom is still looking at me, and at the sound of my voice, the damn deep inside of her breaks, she is sobbing. Dad is torn, wanting to hug me but also physically holding Mom up. I take a step closer and kiss him on his cheek.

"Hi, Daddy."

God, this is awkward, strained and so much harder than I could have ever thought. The sight of my mom in total hysterics has me ready to lose it myself. Rick takes one look at my face and steps in to intercede.

"Come on, Mom, Dad. Let's get this inside before we all freeze to death, it might be the South, but it's still cold." Mom seems to regain some use of her body as she shuffles into the house. She keeps stealing glances back to me as she walks.

"Rick, I don't think I can do this."

"Yes, you can, Kara."

He squeezes my hand and turns to follow my parents into the house.

He's giving me this moment to be alone with Stephan. I think he has come to notice over the past couple of weeks that Stephan keeps me calm, that, right now, he keeps me sane. I settle myself into Stephan's arms, and we're quiet. Neither of us want to face the truth, the knowledge that part of me still wants to run. I know he has to be able to feel it, yet he doesn't hold onto me like he's afraid I will. He holds me like a man who loves a woman.

I look down the driveway and picture my escape. I still have no money, ID, credit card, or car keys. Rick keeps them all in his room.

It's a type of unspoken agreement; I don't ask for them back, and he pretends he doesn't still control me with them.

I imagine myself hitchhiking down the highway, waiting for some stranger to pick me up and hoping that he isn't someone I have to fear. I try to envision the moments I would hate the most, a black foggy night, and there is no one I know, no place to feel safe. I picture the terror that would become my life, the constant anxiety and fear that I could never really run fast or far enough from. I try to live in that moment, to get enough strength from that imagined moment to turn around and walk back inside.

Nothing is at the end of the driveway, Kara. Its dark, and it's alone. Inside is warmth; inside are people who love you. Inside are people who want to understand.

I stand still, with my back to the house, taking the deepest breath I can manage, trying desperately to find enough courage to make it through the next few hours. Rick and Stephan seem to think I can do it; maybe I need to just have faith in them if I can't have faith in myself.

The three of them are sitting at the table as Stephan and I walk in. Dad stands to pull out a chair for me, inviting me to sit. I feel like it's so much more than just sitting at a table; it's an invitation to take a seat back in my life, back with my family. Rick has made me a cup of tea. Tea, coffee, anything hot in a mug with my hands wrapped around it has become a security blanket for me. It's not the same as the clink of ice against the glass as you prepare to sip the vodka, prepare for the burn, but it is what I have now. And I treasure that Rick and Stephan recognize that.

They wait for me to settle in, and I'm grateful for the time they are giving. I wish I knew what Rick and Stephan had told them.

"Are you okay, Kara?" My dad's voice is gentle and careful.

How do I respond to that? I have no idea what I should say, and my mind is a swirl of answers, a swirl of images—the alley, tall glasses of vodka, bottles of sleeping pills, the note, my car, the blood on the seat, my keys, and wallet hidden away from me, the scream that woke Stephan and Rick, the fog rolling in.

Stephan puts his hand on my shoulder to try to bring me back out of my own head. I realize I have my arms wrapped around myself, and I'm rocking gently in my chair. Mom and dad are watching me, their eyes weary.

"Not really." Can I even say that I'm getting there? How do I know when I'm always under guard, surrounded by people at all times with no real chance of drinking or running? Rick is right; I do need to get back to my life. It's the only way that I will ever know if I'm getting better or if I am just being good because I have no other option.

"Rick told us that you don't want to talk about it…about the reasons for all of this." Dad takes a deep breath. I'm sure his mind is thinking up a hundred horrors that could have driven his only daughter to become this weak person rocking in a chair in front of him.

"That's okay, Kara. We don't have to know. If you deicide one day to tell us, we will be here to listen. You're safe with us. There is nothing you could ever do to keep us from loving you."

I think he continues to talk only because he knows that I won't. Silence is always awkward. Rick and Stephan have gotten used to my silence. Mom and dad have not.

"We want to be there to help you. You said in your text that you want to come home, to live with us right now. Your brother said there are certain things that we'll need to do."

He doesn't want to say them out loud. I get that. Words have power, and to say that you have to empty a house of liquor, that you have to lock away prescriptions, it makes this more real than I think either of them want to admit.

"Rick said that there are nights you may want to stay with him or stay with Stephan."

Letting out a deep breath, I feel my shoulders relax, letting go of some of the stress I had been gripping tightly onto. Rick has given me a way out of having Mom and Dad see my dreams. On nights where the fog rolls in, I can leave. He really has thought this through for me, yet another gift my brother has given to me tonight. I look up at Rick and I know he can see the thank you in my eyes, and I can see how much he loves me in his.

"We just want to be able to help, Kara, to support you so that you can come home and get well." I don't want him to have to keep talking, to hear it again and again. "Come home and get well...get well...get well..."

"Thank you, Daddy." I silently hope it is enough to keep him from continuing.

I get up and walk over to my dad and give him a quick hug. Mom stands up and wraps me in her arms, her cheeks wet with fresh tears.

"I just can't seem to stop with all this silly blubbering." She is laughing through the tears, and I thank God for her laughter. These tears are so much easier to handle than the ones in the driveway were.

"You will be okay, Kara, just fine." She nods to herself as she pushes me to arm's length. She looks me over, clearly planning something. "Just fine, perhaps a little makeover fun when you get home. Everyone needs a good makeover once and awhile." Dad looks at me, shaking his head and smiling. After three weeks with Rick and Stephan—all this honesty, all the living in the midst of emotions and guilt—I forgot how much of a surface relationship I have with my mom, it's kinda weird to think it's a nice change. Things will be fine once we get a makeover. How could I not have thought of that?

I manage the rest of the evening without really having to say too much else. My mom is more than happy to pretend like everything is fine now. Once she has seen me with her own eyes, once she has stopped her initial crying, and once she has heard I really will come home, it is all onto planning a day of shopping at the stores in town, whom we still need to buy Christmas gifts for, which cousins have done what. And can I believe her next door neighbor put up that horrible wreath? It's nonsense, a bunch of nothing conversation, and it's great. It's the first time in weeks that every word and action hasn't been focused on me and my behaviors, my problems. I find that I'm wanting to go shopping in town tomorrow. I'm wanting to spend the day with my parents—and that is the last thing I would have expected when I first woke up this morning.

By about 11:00 p.m., I am far past exhausted, but neither Mom nor Dad seem to want to leave. I think it's my two hundredth over exaggerated yawn when Rick finally steps in.

"This has been a longer day than any of us has had in weeks. I don't know about y'all, but I am pooped. Kara, you must be done for over there; I know you were up even earlier than I was."

I love my brother; he knows damn well I slept a good hour longer than him. "Why don't I drive you back to the hotel so you don't have to wait for a cab?" Rick is already up and looking for his keys.

"Maybe Kara could drive us? She could just stay with us at the hotel. What do ya say, honey? We can have a girl's night! We can watch old movies on TV and eat greasy food from room service?"

Mom is clearly excited by the idea, but Rick barely gives her the time to finish the thought. He places his hand on her arm and gently starts to lead her to the door.

"Not tonight, Mom. I think we should still take it slow." She looks back at me, and the hurt is plain as day in her eyes.

"Of course, I'm...I'm sorry."

"Oh, Lil, there is nothing to apologize for. There are just going to be some new things to get used to. Right, honey?"

Dad looks over to me; he's looking for help with Mom, a little reassurance that things will be normal again soon.

"Mom, we have plenty of time for girl's nights. I will be living at home soon enough, remember? How about we just meet for breakfast instead, then we can have our day of shopping, maybe we can even squeeze in a manicure?"

She kisses my cheek. "Okay, baby, sure thing. Breakfast, shopping, and a manicure, that sounds wonderful."

Stephan closes the door once we have watched Rick pull out of the driveway with my folks.

"You did great, Kara." He wraps me into the kind of hug I can collapse against.

"It doesn't feel that way." I give myself a moment to just enjoy being wrapped in his arms before I start picking up the dirty dishes. He stops me, taking the glass from my hands.

"Cut yourself a little slack, Kara. You really are doing good. I know that must have been hard, that it must have been scary for you."

"Stephan, you don't get it." I push past him and walk into the kitchen, still talking but no longer having to watch my words register onto his face. "When Mom was wanting the girl's night, when she was saying movies and greasy food, all I could think was, 'I bet it won't be too hard to get her to order some champagne, maybe a late night martini.' I was sitting there, watching her cry and thinking of ways to convince her that none of this is as bad as her and Dad believe it is. You have to understand. There are still plenty of times I want to escape. I want some way to turn everything off that won't cause you all any more pain."

I see the mug of tea that always seems to be full, always seems to be within arm's reach. I pick it up and raise it to my mouth. But as I smell it, I have had my fill of tea, of all of this. The stress from seeing my parents, the exhaustion I feel, the false pride Stephan has in me, I'm at a breaking point.

"This…this shit does not do it." I throw the tea into the sink, and the mug shatters as it hits. I can't look at Stephan's face as I walk out. I lock the door to my room, something I haven't done since we got here.

He doesn't follow me. He doesn't knock. He just leaves me be.

●●●

I'm up early and more than a little embarrassed about my behavior from last night. The house is still quiet as I walk into the kitchen. Looking into the sink, I expect to see my broken mug still lying in pieces, waiting for me to clean it; but there is no sign it was ever there. Everything has been cleaned and tidied. It's as if the temper tantrum I threw before bed never happened.

Stephan stumbles in as I'm making the coffee. Walking up behind me, he wraps me in his arms, leans his head into my neck and mutters, "Good morning." He kisses me, and it sends shivers down my spine. I want to step into his arms even deeper and lose myself in him, but I know that we need to talk.

"You know it wasn't you I was mad at last night, right?"

"I know, baby. Don't be too hard on yourself. No one here expects you to be perfect. The point isn't what you thought about doing. It's what you did do. It's that you shared it with me at all."

He's still kissing me, his stubble tickling the crook of my neck. I push his head away and turn to be able to look at his eyes, and he can tell I need more.

"Kara, we have practically kept you prisoner in this place. So you had one little tantrum about it, who cares? You told us, and that is all we ever asked of you."

He moves away from me and sits at the table. "I'm proud of you."

Well, that's sure as shit the last thing I expected to have come out of anyone's mouth today. Wrapping my head around that concept is going to take more than just one cup of coffee.

"I would be more proud of you if you would bring me over a cup of that there coffee though."

How do you not smile? I woke up expecting this morning to be a bad one, filled with lectures and apologies, and instead I get kisses and humor? Maybe I should stop having expectations; I'm zero for two in the last two days.

Mom has already called. She has the day completely set; she wants to divide and conquer. The guys are to head out for a day of shopping for us girls while mom and I head out to start my Christmas shopping. I agreed because I didn't have the heart not to; the reality is I'm scared to death of being away from Rick and Stephan.

My goal is not to say anything that will stop this little outing of shopping terror. Situations are going to show up that will scare me. I'm guessing a day of shopping with my mother will not be the worst thing I'll have to face over the upcoming months. But as we pull into the parking lot of the hotel for breakfast, Rick looks back at me.

"We can come up with something if we need to, Kara. I prom-ised you we wouldn't leave you, and I meant it. You don't need to go off with Mom on your own."

"Yes, I do." I don't try to hide my anxiety from them. It would be pointless. "But keep your cell phone on you just in case." I try to smile at my pathetic attempt at humor. I'm hoping that it helps us all feel better about the hesitation in my voice and uncertainty in my eyes.

CHAPTER 35

You can feel the stress pouring off of my dad, but Mom is beaming like she won some prize at the fair. I'm standing between the two of them, getting ready to kiss goodbye to my safety net, to the two only people who really know me right now. I'm using every last ounce of strength I have to hide the pure terror I'm feeling about boarding this plane, about being stuck between Mr. Anxiety and his wife, Mrs. Won a Prize.

Rick offered to fly with us, but Mom would hear none of it. She had won her Kara prize and wasn't about to be told she needed to share. I think in her mind, when I called Rick and Stephan instead of her, it was like a slap in the face. She felt it was my way of saying she wasn't good enough. Now that I'm leaving with her, leaving Rick and Stephan behind, it's as though her feelings have been wiped clean. Great, we fixed Mom. But what the fuck about me?

I lean in to hug Rick goodbye.

"I can still get on the plane, Kara. I'm sure I can still get a ticket." He knows me too well now. I'm not sure if it's that he can feel my heart pound or if it's that he can see the panic in my eyes; but he knows I'm barely holding it together right now. I feel a little relief in knowing I'm not the only one who is worried about today, and every day from this point on.

I try to think of Dad and all his "fake it till you make it" ways. I put on my best brave face. "Rick, I'm going to be living there. If I can't handle a three-hour flight, then we are in a lot more trouble than we thought." I lean up and give him a quick kiss on the cheek. "It'll be fine. There is no other choice but for it to be okay. I mean,

I can't jump out of the plane or anything." I laugh a nervous, high pitched laugh. It was supposed to help hide what I'm feeling, but I think all it does is draw more attention to the awkwardness of this moment.

Stephan grabs me and pulls me into him. I can feel my heart-beat start to slow from its frantic march as he wraps his arms around me. I lean my head against him and match my breathing to the rise and fall of his chest.

"We'll be there by morning. I'll call you before bed tonight, and I'll be waiting for you with some good coffee by the time you open these pretty little eyes." The two of them are driving my car back. Their plan is to take turns, one sleeping while the other one drives. This way, they can make the fourteen-hour drive back to Chicago without much stopping. It's Friday afternoon, and Rick is out of vacation and sick time; he needs to be back to work on Monday. Even though Stephan can work at home just as easily as he can the office, it wouldn't hurt for people to see him at the firm at least once this month.

I don't want to think about the questions Stephan is going to have to face at work, about how he's going to answer them. He has told me repeatedly not to worry about it, that he will handle it and I will come out smelling like roses. I don't really see how that's possible, but I'm trying very hard to sit back and let him deal with it. After all, it's not like I work there anymore. Those are people I will never have to see again unless I choose to, and right now, I don't want to see much of anyone. The fact that Christmas is in seventeen days has me panicked enough, all those family members.

Stephan pulls me out of his arms and looks into my eyes. He must have been able to feel my heart begin to pound once again. "I would never leave you alone if I didn't know one hundred percent that you could handle this." One day, I hope to have the faith in myself that he has in me.

"I got you a little something for the plane ride." He reaches into his backpack and pulls out a very thick book. "It's always been one of my favorites. It's a book I think you could get lost in for a while." Dear God, I love this man whose knows me so well. I wrap my arms around him. I really don't want to let go, but eventually I feel my dad's hand on my shoulder.

"Come on, baby, we still need to get through security. You will see them both soon."

I peel myself away from Stephan as Dad puts his arm around me, and we head toward security. As I look back one last time, while clutching my new book to my chest, I see Rick give me a thumbs-up. I'm not sure, but from here, it doesn't look like he likes watching me leave any more than I like leaving.

I am officially sandwiched between Mom and Dad on the plane. (I think the two of them have an unspoken agreement that if I'm am constantly wedged between them, I physically can't run. Not that I didn't earn that concept, but damn is it annoying.) As we prepare for takeoff, Mom twists her body to be able to look at Dad and I.

"I was thinking we should do a big family Christmas this year, invite all the cousins and the kids, just like we used to when you and your brother were little. Don't you think that would be fun, Kara? We would have to go out and buy some more decorations, of course, and cook up a storm, but that would be so nice. You and I working side by side in the kitchen, I think I even still have the apron that you used to wear that matches mine."

I look at Dad, begging silently for help. How did I go from the peace and quiet of living with Rick and Stephan to becoming a Stepford wife when the plane hasn't even taken off yet?

"Lil, I think a big family Christmas sounds wonderful, but let her get home before we start handing her the to-do list. I'm sure Kara wants to relax and decompress a little before we hit her with too much."

I'm instantly four years old again. My head turns from Mom to Dad and back to mom. They are literally talking over me. No one has really asked me anything. I close my eyes and sink down into the chair, wishing that airplane seats could be a least slightly more comfortable. I decide to dream about a quite Christmas morning, one where Stephan wakes me up with coffee in hand and leads me down the stairs of his house, excited to show me whatever little treasure he has found.

Dad is getting our luggage out of the car, and Mom has gone to freshen up after the flight. I'm walking through the halls that I spent my childhood in. I'm sure that if I look close enough, I could even find a lone Barbie shoe or some crayon mark that never got fully washed away. I have obviously been here a thousand times since I moved away; but being back, knowing I will be living here again, it makes everything seem different, smaller somehow.

I stop outside my old bedroom door and take a deep breath. *Here you go, Kara. You put yourself in this moment. You made this bed, and now you have to lay in it.*

I open the door and look into the room. They have never even repainted. It's like a shrine to the Kara they had ten years ago, honor roll Kara, softball team Kara; my favorite books are still piled on the nightstand. At this point, I wouldn't be surprised to find an old retainer nearby too. I close the door and keep walking. That room, all it does is remind me of what I've lost, what I've thrown away.

At the end of the hallway is Rick's old room. I know, before I ever open the door, that it will be the same as it has always been. But at least in his room, it's not my failed life that will reflect back at me.

"Kara!" I can hear the worry in my mom's voice since I'm not where she expected me to be. How long will it be before people stop freaking out when they can't find me right away?

"I'm in Rick's room, Mom," I yell back at her. I hear the door to my bedroom close; I count the clicks of her shoes as she walks down the hallway. After thirteen clicks, her head peeks around the door.

"What are you doing in here, goofball?"

"I think I would rather stay in here, if that's okay?" I look up at her, hoping she has no problem with that. Why would she care where I sleep? They should be damn happy I'm here because really it's no place I want to be.

"But, honey, your room is so pretty. This is just so…blah. It's such a boy's room."

How do I go about explaining it to her? I don't really care what the hell the room looks like; I just don't want to be in the "look how far Kara has fallen" shrine.

"Girls?"

"We're in Rick's room, hun!" Mom yells back down the hall. These people should really get an intercom system or use cell phones or something.

"Whatcha doing in here?" Mom looks at him with a look that says, "You go and try to get her to explain it," I give up. She shakes her head and walks away mumbling something about dinner.

Dad comes up behind me. "It's okay, Karaboo. You can stay in whatever room you feel like."

"Thanks, Daddy." He kisses me on the cheek and heads down the hallway to find Mom. I know he doesn't understand it, but I know he doesn't have to. I also know he will do his best to control Mom. She means well. I know she loves me more than anything else; but for her, that means she needs to mold me into the image she feels I will be the happiest in.

All these things that "I know" leave me exhausted, not exhausted like you can sleep, but exhausted like your soul has suddenly aged and is too heavy to go on. I lean into the wall and slide down until I'm sitting. I do the only thing I have left; I take out my phone and call Stephan.

The phone barely gets the chance to ring before I hear Rick's voice.

"Hey, Kara! What took so long? We thought you would call a while ago. Stephan was starting to get nervous over here. Sorry, but he's driving, and we're going through a construction zone. We thought it would be better if I answer."

I love that they were holding the phone, waiting for me to call them. I love that they knew I would. It has me feeling better already.

"No problem, Rick. I can always talk to my brother too."

"How was the flight?" You can hear the apprehension in his voice. He knows, just as well as I do, how Mom can get.

"Fine, she started party planning, and I fell asleep. We just got home about half an hour ago. I decided to take your room instead of mine. I kinda felt like I should call and tell you."

"Ya, that's fine and all, no problem. But agh, bullshit on the reason you called. This is Stephan's phone, remember? If you wanted to call to talk about my room, you would have called my phone. Just because you aren't in the same house as me anymore doesn't mean any of this 'tell me what is really going on' shit goes away. No more I'm okay's, Kara. I'm serious."

If I plan on getting away with anything, any little white lie, I'm going to need to make some new friends.

"Nothing is wrong, Rick. I just needed to hear Stephan's voice. It calms me down, okay?"

"Oh. Well…damn, girl, you got it bad." I can hear the teasing tone coming through in his voice.

"Stephan, it's your girlfriend. She wants to kiss you. She wants to hug you. She wants to—"

"Dude, she's your little sister. Are you sure you want to finish that sentence?"

How do you stay in a bad mood when you can hear Tweedledee and Tweedledumber having this conversation while the phone is held in the air waiting for me to finally get to hear my boyfriend's voice?

"Hey, baby." His voice is like a warm blanket, and with the smile that's already on my face after listening to the two them, I feel better than I have all day.

"Hi."

"Are you okay over there? We should be home in about eight more hours. I can break you out, if I need to. You've never seen my ninja skills, but believe me, they're there."

Since when does a road trip bring out the idiots in these two?

"I'm o—"

"If you say you are okay, Rick is going to send police with sirens blaring. He just wants you to know."

"I'm doing fine. Is that better? It's just a little overwhelming is all. It's been so long since I've had to spend some real time around here."

"Just make it until morning, babe. Rick and I are trying to arrange it where you won't have much alone time over there."

"Stop it, you two. I appreciate it in ways you will never know, but you don't need to always handle me with kid gloves. I can do this. It's just my parents not some drunken frat party. It's just going to take some time to get used to is all. Just leave your phone on for me so I can call when I need to."

"Drunken frat party? Really? And you call me anytime, baby, anytime you want to."

CHAPTER 36

O nce that first day is over, life falls back into a somewhat normal pattern. I guess it's kind of like riding a bike. You never really forget how. I've spent so much of my life living in these rooms that it doesn't take much to fit back in. Mom and I wake up in the mornings, have coffee with Dad, and watch from the living room window as he heads out to the office. He's semiretired now, so he gets home on the early side—which is great, it helps to give Mom something other than me to focus on.

Trying to keep her happy is giving me something else to focus on too. We've been getting ready for Christmas and the huge party she wants to have. Our days are spent driving from store to store looking for the perfect tree topper or the perfect table cloth to serve Christmas dinner on. At least nothing there has changed; Mom's always been focused on image, on wanting things to look perfect so she can look perfect. That's what's gotten me worked up today.

I know it's a conversation we need to have, and Dad is heading out of town tomorrow; I will lose my "please help control her when she's like this" partner. Today is baking day, or at least that's what I've been told. Christmas Eve is only four days away, and she wants us to have enough cookies and fudge to feed the North Shore…for a year. We will both be in the kitchen, no distractions but the timer counting down on the oven. I need to know; I need to be able to prepare. What has she told the family? What are they expecting to find when they show up here Christmas Eve?

We're mixing the dough for Grandma's sugar cookies when I decide to stop being such a chicken shit.

"Mom? What are people expecting…from me…when they get here for the party?" My voice is quiet, and I'm playing with a piece of dough that has fallen from the bowl onto the counter.

"I don't understand, Kara. What do you mean, from you?"

"Well, what did you tell them happened…when I was gone?" I look up from my dough play toy to find her studying me like I have a third head.

"Nothing, baby. We told them nothing. No one even knew you had…left. We figured we would tell them if we needed to. But then you called Rick, and everything ended just fine."

"You didn't tell anyone!" I don't mean to yell, but I am.

Isn't this exactly what I was hoping for? Not having to have a single awkward moment during the party? Not having to answer Aunt Emma's thousand questions?

"Kara! Don't you yell at me, young lady! I may not be the person you called, but I am still your mother."

She puts the spoon down on the counter and walks out. Well, at least I know where I learned it from.

I turn and storm off the other direction. Waiting in the living room until I hear her bedroom door close, I head back down the hallway and slip quietly into Rick's old room. I refuse to think of it as mine. Thinking of it as my room would mean I intend to stay here, and today is but one of many examples of why that will never work.

I pace between his bed and the window trying to think and calm myself back down. She's embarrassed by me. It's the only thing that makes sense. I'm not really surprised by it, but that doesn't make it hurt any less. Dad would have gone along with not telling people because that's what Dad does. He goes along with things, but I refuse to be the thing in the back bedroom to be embarrassed by.

It's the middle of the day. Rick is at work, and so is Stephan. I've been enough of a drain on them lately anyway. I know if I call either one of them, they will leave work and come get me. But Rick is right. It's time I reintroduce myself to my life.

I pick up the phone and dial a number I should have called weeks ago. As I listen to the phone ring, I'm nervous; is she going to be mad? Will she want the whole story all over again? I should have found out what they told her, or did they call her at all? I'm about to hang up and accept my afternoon of hiding out in Rick's room when I hear her pick up.

"Kara!" The emotion in Katie's voice is overwhelming. "Are you okay?"

"I'm okay, Katie. Well, I'm getting there at least."

"Girl, I have been freaking out! What the fuck happened? Your brother called to tell me that they were with you…that they…found you and all. But damn, girl, don't do that to me again. I missed you!"

"I missed you too, Katie. I'm sorry I didn't call sooner. It's a really long story, but I'm okay."

I can actually hear the moment she relaxes. I picture her flopping back onto her couch with a smile on her face, and it brings a smile to mine.

"What are you doing? Do you wanna come break me out of my mom's house for a little while?"

"Hell yes! Let me call John and see if I can borrow his car while he's working. We can head back to the city and catch up. There's a new club by me that you have got to see. Can you stay out here tonight, and I'll drop you back off tomorrow? John would love it too; he keeps asking about you."

"I don't think it would be a good idea to be gone that long, and it might give Rick a heart attack to find out I'm at a club. I'm under pretty tight watch nowadays. So how about we start with lunch? I'm dying for some good sushi."

An hour later, I'm sitting in the front seat of John's car, feeling like Katie just broke me out of prison.

"You have no idea how much I needed this."

"Any time, girl."

She keeps glancing over at me while she drives. I'm not sure she fully believes I'm really okay; but it's not until my parent's house is far gone and the rearview mirror holds nothing but images I don't recognize that Katie brings up the pink elephant buckled into the back seat. "So are we going to talk about all of this or just call it 'water under the bridge and laugh about it one day a hundred years from now while we're old and drunk?'"

"Honestly, can we call it water under the bridge…at least for now? Not that I won't tell you, but right now, I am just so damn tired of talking."

I see the hurt flash across her face before she can put the "sure whatever" mask into place. "You got it, darlin'." She glances over to me and smiles. "So where does one find sushi in the suburbs?"

It's about half way through lunch that my phone starts to whistle annoying high pitched animal noises at me. Damn you, Rick, at least he thinks this noise is amusing. I think it's more horribly embarrassing. Everyone around me is looking around, trying to figure out who the asshole is. He knows it'll work though; he's got me jumping to check the text right away, anything to stop the monkey screech.

"Really trying to breathe here, Kara. Mom just called in a panic. She said you are gone."

I know better than to send back a quick text in response to this. He's going to want a phone call. He wants to hear my voice, to know this isn't a sad replay of last month. I'm impressed that it's just a text, that he and Stephan aren't taking turns stalker dialing me until I answer. Then again, maybe that's step two.

"Hold on a sec, Katie. This is Rick, and I gotta call him back." I get up and head outside as I dial the number.

"Kara?"

"Okay, Rick, before you even start, I didn't run. Mom and I got into this morning. She stormed off, and I called Katie. She picked me up, and we're at lunch. I'm being so good and healthy. I'm not even drinking a soda, okay?"

I take a deep breath trying to calm myself, but it doesn't do much good. Rick waits, just letting me breathe. "I left Mom a note, and I didn't call you or Stephan because you're at work. I CAN go out to lunch without security having to be alerted."

"Okay, psycho girl, calm down. I believe you, and I knew you wouldn't run again. I told Mom and Dad that." He goes from teasing to quiet in half a heartbeat.

"I knew you would never do that to us again, never make us feel that again. I knew that."

SIOBHAN NICOLE

Hearing the pain that is in his voice stops my little rant cold. I'm never going to get over the pain I caused him. I'm never going to be able to accept that I have it in me to hurt people I love like that.

"Rick, I'm sorry. I will make sure I talk to someone first next time I go out. I won't just leave a note."

"I'm sorry, too Kara. I know it has to be getting old, everyone always watching you. We're just so scared that something will happen to have you gone again, physically gone or just...gone to the bottom of the bottle."

My relationship with my brother has always been goofy, always been based on teasing or the inside joke that really was never funny to begin with. This new always honest, always deep, still catches me off guard. The way it feels to know that I made my family think I was gone, to think I could be dead, that they had to picture Christmas morning without me, birthdays without me, it hurts in a way that is so much more than anything that could have happened in that stupid alley.

My voice is barely above a whisper as I answer him. "I get it, Rick, I really do. I know I brought this on myself. I don't really blame anyone for acting like this."

I try to find a way to end this with more of the old Kara, try to show Rick she is still here too.

"It does get old though, this spy gear ninja action... Give me this little taste of freedom, okay? I don't have many ways left to rebel." Insert the appropriate little giggle here. "I gotta go, okay? Katie's waiting for me."

"Love you, sis."

"I love you too."

Katie can tell something is wrong before I even sit back in my chair. "Damn, girl, you look like you have aged a hundred years in one phone call." She has that nice person smile stuck to her face, the one you use when you pass by a homeless person in the street you're not going to give money to, but you want to acknowledge anyway.

"Do you need to head back?"

All I can think is no. I need a drink. I need something to make me forget what I have done to people I love. I need a blanket I can

232

put over my head and sink away to a land unknown. I need to run through the mountains screaming. But instead, I say, "Yeah. I think I need to go back." We pay our bill in silence and walk slowly back to her car.

"I'm sorry, Katie. I know you drove all the way out here, and that wasn't much of a good time."

I am so full of apologies lately that I'm sick of the sound of my own voice as I say them. "I'm just glad you're back. There will be time for longer lunches soon. At least we got to check out the waiter's ass, that kinda made the whole trip worthwhile." Her voice drops a little lower, as though she were talking to herself. "It was a good ass."

"Oh, Katie!" The laughter explodes out of me, out of the two of us. "It was a good ass! I bet he's got a good di—"

Katie hits my shoulder as she continues laughing. I wrap my arms around her in an unexpected hug. "Thanks, Katie." I try to look serious, which is hard to do while we're both still laughing. "Thanks for being there, for not making me explain yet...just thanks." She's hugging me in return. I can feel some of the anxiety the past month has held for her in her arms, in how hard she's holding on.

She mumbles in my hair, "Thanks for coming back."

Mom and Dad are waiting for me when I get home. They sit together in the kitchen and have the same look on their face that I learned to recognize from the early days spent in the hotel with Stephan and Rick. It's the look that says they weren't sure I was coming back. It's the hollow look of hope lost.

I hate that look, and I know it too well. As much as I feel bad that they had to think those thoughts again, I still feel like they need to know, that they need to understand, this is not how I'm going to live my life. I'm not the same person that Rick had to chase after, but I'm also not the same Kara that fit into some perfect country club mold. Mom can't pretend that everything is fine and that it's normal. I'm not some doll she can dress up in a yellow polka dot bathing suit and stick pool side while waiting for a drink.

Part of me is crazy happy I don't have to explain myself to everyone on Christmas Eve, that I don't have to relive those weeks over and over again. But it's damn hard to feel like the reasoning is shame.

I want to yell at them, "Why does everything have to fit in to some perfect concept of the family photo, green grass, sunny day, white puffy clouds? Why is it that everything has to be sunshine? When is it allowed to rain?'

One look at their faces, and I know I won't do it, that it would not end well. So instead I walk up to them and give them each a hug. I don't say anything, and I don't give them the chance to talk. Once the hugs are over, I head into Rick's room, lay on the bed, and toss and turn until eventually, I fall asleep.

My dreams are chaos, nails scratching at the window, people whispering my name; then two seconds later, it's all afternoon barbecues with Stephan, Katie, and John. I wake up not sure what was real and what was a dream and nowhere near well rested. I lay in bed regretting that I didn't talk to Mom and Dad last night. It clearly messed up my night's sleep, and now I know I'll have to deal with it today. Reluctantly, I get out of bed and head into the kitchen for my morning coffee.

I think that Dad must have said something to Mom, either that or Rick did. Mom is all sugar sweet lemonade and candies this morning; it's I love yous and "would you like to invite your friends over, it's your house too" kind of comments. But it's not, I just want my house, my little box with the white walls, the one where I can lock out the world and do my stupid Kara dance. There is no place for a stupid dance here, no place where I can hide.

CHAPTER 37

Mom and I wave goodbye to Dad as he drives off for his last business trip before his Christmas time off begins. Even though I know it'll just be the two of us until tomorrow morning, I feel a kind of peace settle over me. I think knowing that I won't have to explain anything to aunts and cousins has taken a huge load off my shoulders.

"We never did get that girls night." Mom puts her arms around my waist as we head back inside. "I have a little surprise for you."

"Mom, you didn't have to do anything."

"Consider it an I'm sorry for our little tiff yesterday."

I'm still more than a little pissed that she wants to cover everything up, to just focus on sunshine and rainbows. It's that exact attitude that has led me to this place in my life, this no booze, no pills, no privacy place. If I've learned anything in all of this, it's that you have to embrace the bad, as well as the good, that when you deny what you really feel, you lose yourself, and that's a dangerous thing to lose. All this "the strongest people fight battles we know nothing about" is bullshit. The strongest people are the ones that can stand up and own their battles, face their emotions and mistakes head-on. Don't get me wrong, I'm thrilled that I don't have to explain myself; I know I'm not strong enough for that yet, but that doesn't mean I don't recognize the strength it would take to do it.

Mom's arms are still around me, and I can feel the anger building up in my chest. It's a panic that doesn't fit the moment and not one she really deserves, especially since she's trying to make up for it now. I move out of her grasp and try to make the fake smile on my face seem sincere. "I'll be inside in just a few okay?" She looks like she wants to argue but bends in to give me a kiss on the forehead instead.

"Not too long now, Kara. It's cold out here."

I want to go back to the peaceful, relaxed in my own skin, feeling I had before Mom made me remember why she is being so nice and accommodating.

I take a moment watching my breath form into white swirls of mist, watching as they float away and fade back into the air. I look up at the brown branches of the trees, stretching toward the heavens as they sway in the gray Chicago sky. It's not the wide open spaces of the Smokey Mountains, and it's definitely colder than South Carolina. But the Midwest has a beauty all its own. Sometimes it takes leaving to know how good home feels. It only takes a few more minutes until I've gotten the "relaxed in my own skin" feeling back. I'm getting better at being able to control it, and it's a huge comfort to know.

There's a sudden movement in the trees as I turn and walk back inside. I love the burbs, but I liked not having to worry about animals watching me when I was in the city.

"Mom, I think you need to put out more salt licks for the deer." I shut the door quickly, and she's already laughing at me.

"I'll tell your father. But seriously they don't still scare you, do they, Kara? They are such cute little things."

"Yeah...cute, until Bambi wants to jump in front of your car and cause you to almost hit a tree."

"That was ten years ago. Don't you think it's time to forgive them?"

"Not really."

"Well, back to my little surprise, it's nothing really, so don't get your hopes up!"

I can tell she must be nervous that I won't like whatever it is she has planned. She's already walking away from me and into the kitchen.

"It's just a couple chick flicks, some nail polish, a little chocolate fondue...and well, I thought you have been doing so good lately that I got us the fixings for French martinis, just like we used to. I really don't think one martini will hurt, do you?"

I stop midstride. *What did she just ask me?*

I want to run back outside. I'm wondering how my breath will look in the hyperventilating mode I feel at this moment. But it's too late now; the thought is already running through my mind. The way the vodka feels as it warms you from the inside out, that first moment when the fog starts to move in and life blurs just a little. *Could I do it? Could I really have just one? Just make life a little less focused? Forget for a moment that no one trusts me, that mom is ashamed? Could I really do it?*

God knows I want to, if for no other reason just to prove that I can.

"Did you talk to Rick about the idea?"

"Kara. No. I appreciate everything that your brother has done for you, but something has died in you since you came home. You were always the one who lived life to the fullest."

She gently brushes a hair from my face.

"Now you stop and wait for permission. It kills me to see it. You make the decision, Kara. You say yes or you say no." Mom is standing in front of me. She seems so strong and sure of herself, and I suddenly feel like a little girl watching the mother that can do no wrong, the way your parents look to you until you realize they don't turn into super heroes and fly through the world saving lost kittens.

"But, Kara, please realize Rick won't be there with you forever. Eventually the decision has to be yours."

Mom walks away, yelling over her shoulder as she goes, "I'll be in the kitchen making a martini. Yours will be on the island."

Great, now I've hurt her feelings, the last thing I wanted to do. How do I keep from hurting Rick and Stephan and Mom? And what the fuck about me? Don't I count somewhere in that mix?

Turning around, I head outside. I'm dialing Rick's number before the cold air hits my face.

"Rick?" At first I think I've reached him, but it's only his machine.

"Never mind…it's nothing. Hope your night is going good."

I stand completely still while weighing the options in my head. Stand here and freeze, pretending like watching my breath dance on the wind is the same, that it's as relaxing as the sound the ice is going to make as it clinks off the side of a martini shaker. Stand here and pretend like the drink isn't what I want, pretend that I'm stronger than I really am. The movement in the trees is back, and I swear I can feel their beady little eyes on me. I feel like I'm awaiting an ambush, like some creature is ready to pounce. Call it an excuse, call it the reason. I don't care. It has made my mind up for me.

One sip... If I can't handle it, I'll throw it down the drain. It's that simple. By the time I make it into the kitchen, Mom is already in the living room. There is one lone martini glass, seductive in its shape, sitting on the island. No one is here. One sip and no one will ever even know. I approach the glass like it's an armed grenade. I reach for it like it's an old friend.

By the time I join my mom, I'm on my third sip. Damn, she can make a good martini. I feel like I've died and gone to heaven. I feel like I've let down Stephan and Rick. I feel like a liar. I take another sip, push all my "feelings" away and sink into the couch as we turn on *Mamma Mia!* and sit back to paint our nails.

Mamma Mia! is immediately followed by *Calendar Girls* and a large bowl of fruit and cakes with chocolate for dipping. My fingers and toes are looking awfully festive in a bright red polish. More importantly, my ONE martini sits empty on the table, and I'm damn proud of myself. Mom hasn't made me feel judged or bad for it. She hasn't watched me all night, no eyes staring holes into the back of my head that I'm supposed to pretend aren't there. I'm so used to it that I feel like Rick is watching me anyway.

The fear of disappointing him keeps me honest with my one drink, but I still did it. I made the decision, and I followed through with it. I feel a little buzz but just enough to stay relaxed, to stay a little less focused. It's almost midnight, and I'm not really tired. But I'm afraid if I stay up, I might break and have another, especially if Mom starts offering. I need to escape this room while I can still be proud of myself. Getting up, I head to bed.

"Thanks for a great night, Mom. It really was perfect." I kiss her on the cheek, and she smiles up to me.

"Night, baby."

It's a little late to call Stephan, but I really want to hear his voice; well, what I want is to fall asleep wrapped in his arms, but I would settle for his voice. I lay in my bed turning the phone over and over in my hands. Would he even be awake right now? I don't want to risk being the one to wake him, so instead I send him a quick text.

"Thinking of you. Love you."

I fall asleep still holding the phone. I'm not sure what brings the dream on. It isn't foggy outside. I'm not even in the city. I had spent the evening proud of myself, at peace, but that peace is long gone now.

I wake up with a jolt. Sitting straight up in my bed, my heart is pounding, the sound of his voice still fresh in my mind.

"You gonna scream, bitch."

There is sweat pouring off of me, but I can feel a cool breeze. The window in my room is open, just an inch. Mom must have come in and opened it after I fell asleep. I sit still, desperately trying to control my breathing. My cell is in my hand, and I dial Stephan's number.

He picks up on the second ring, "Kara… What's wrong, baby? What is it?" I instantly feel bad as I can hear the fear in his voice. Looking at the clock, it's three in the morning.

"I'm okay, Stephan. I just had a nightmare. I shouldn't have called. I didn't mean to wake you up."

I hear him release the breath he must have been holding. "Never apologize for that; it's what I want, for you to know I'm here whenever you need me." He pauses. "Do you want to talk about it? Were you back in the alley?"

I love that he knows me so well. It helps to push the dream out a little further. "It doesn't make any sense, Stephan. It's not foggy tonight. I'm not at home. There's nothing to bring it on. It just caught me off guard, is all. I'll be okay."

"Do you want me to call your brother? I'm in Atlanta, or I would come over now."

Atlanta? When did that happen? "It's just a last minute meeting, I'll be home tomorrow morning." He must have known I was wondering. "Sorry, I didn't tell you."

"Stephan, please. I don't want to be the kind of girlfriend you have to call to let know where you are every waking moment. And no, I don't need you to wake up Rick too. It's bad enough I woke you up. I'll be all right, just hearing your voice helps."

"Picture me there, baby. I'm lying down next to you, one arm wrapped around your waist. We are toasty warm under the covers. But you're mad that my feet are cold."

Laughing at Stephan has pushed the dream away. "Thanks, babe, that was exactly what I needed."

"Good night, Kara. I love you." I smile—a first-love, giddy teen-aged, kind of smile.

"Love you too."

I roll over and close my eyes. The cold air hits my face once more, and I know I will never sleep unless I close that damn window. It's pitch black outside, not even a star is visible in the night sky. The wind blows, and I shiver. It's as if the wind is calling my name. "Kaaaarrrraaaa…"

Okay, now I'm officially nuts. I'm terrified, but I also recognize I'm nuts. I can't call Stephan back. He can't do anything from Atlanta, and I won't have him worrying about me. It's the wind, just the wind. I lay back in my bed trying to get the feeling back that I had when I hung up with Stephan; picturing him next to me, his arm around me. I smile just as his face morphs in my mind to one much more sinister. "Biiitttccchhh" it hisses just like the wind.

No. Hell no. It's like I'm watching myself in a movie. I'm standing on my chair in a theater of Rick's and Stephan's, but no one will look at me. I'm waving my arms screaming, "No!" The me on the movie screen is in a dark room, alone and at the fridge reaching for the vodka. I'm watching that Kara, clearly she cannot be me, just another version stuck in the nightmare, stuck in the fog.

I'm watching her as the ice clinks off the glass, as she closes her eyes for the first sip. I watch her as she reaches for the bottle, as she walks away toward her room, glass in one hand and bottle in the other. She sashays her way down the hallway. I'm still on my movie theater chair waving my arms screaming, "Stop!" as she shuts the door to her room and the screen fades to black.

CHAPTER 38

I wake up to the sound of arguing voices. Rolling to my side, I pull the pillow over myself to drawn out the noise; it does me no good. Now they're knocking on the bedroom door.

"Go away... I'm still sleeping. Go and fight somewhere else."

I hear the door knob rattle as someone tries to get it.

When did I lock the door? I never lock the door. It's an unspoken promise with Rick, ever since that fate filled day he couldn't get into my apartment.

"Kara, open the door!" Shit! It's my brother and I can hear the panic growing in his voice.

"Let her sleep. Why are you acting like this? So she tried to call you last night. I'm sure she will forgive you for not being there to answer it. What is your problem?"

"Mom, stay out of it. Did you know she called Stephan too? Do you? She woke him up at 3:00 a.m.! Did ya know that?" Silence.

"What did you two do last night, huh, Mom? What did you do that had her calling both of us, that had her terrified at three in the morning!"

"Nothing! We watched movies, ate junk food. We did our nails and had a martini."

I'm listening closely now. I guess I'm going to find out what Rick thinks of this sooner rather than later; I just wish my head would stop pounding so I could hear easier.

"You WHAT!" Mom is silent. I can almost hear the sound of her breathing. "What did you just tell me? You gave her a fucking martini! Did you not hear me at all when I told you there could be no

241

booze in this house? What the fuck did you think that meant? Did you think that was just me being mean?"

"Rick…"

"Don't fucking Rick me, Mom! You didn't see her, did you? You didn't see her with bruises on her face and blood on her clothes, and she couldn't even remember where it came from! You didn't see that."

"Kara! Open this damn door now, or I swear I will break it down."

Groaning, I roll off the bed.

"Calm down, Rick. I'm right here. I'm fine."

I stumble as I walk; my head is like a thunderstorm over a volcano on an island during a hurricane. I open the door and Rick's eyes take in my face before they scan the room and stop at the nearly empty bottle of vodka on the floor by my bed. *Where the hell did that come from?*

"Get your shit. We are leaving."

Mom is staring at the bottle on the floor. She murmurs, "I didn't know." She whispers it over and over again.

"Rick… I…"

"I really don't want to hear it, Kara. Get your shit and get in the car now."

I think my head's going to explode. I grab my bag, throw my toothbrush, and a change of clothes into it. This feels far too familiar.

Rick and Mom stand in the doorway, silently watching me. Mom looks like someone has slapped her, and Rick looks like he's hanging on by a thread. It's not anger or disappointment I see in his eyes; it's rage, pure, unadulterated rage.

Neither Rick nor I say anything as we drive to his apartment. His knuckles are turning white from his grip on the steering wheel; if it had been alive, it would have died from strangulation five miles ago. He won't look at me; he just stares straight ahead as he drives.

I can't take it. "Rick…"

His eyes stay straight ahead, staring down the road. "Shut up, Kara. Please just shut the hell up."

When we finally arrive at his apartment, he silently walks to the bedroom that had once been mine. I follow, not knowing what else to do.

"Kara, if you leave this room I swear to God, I will never speak to you again." He shuts the door without saying another word.

I don't even try to argue with him. There's nothing I can say. I stand behind the closed door, looking at it and waiting. I sit with my back up against it, knees bent and my foot taping with anxious energy.

I stand up and walk from the door to the window and back to the door. Finally, I give up. I lay in the bed, pull my legs toward my chest, and allow myself to break.

I cry as though someone had died; it's as though I've died. I might as well have; it feels like I did. It's not like I recognize the sobbing, hungover, mess of a person lying here. The Kara I was would never do this to the people she loved, to people who love her. The Kara I was would have had some control. She would have at least known where that bottle of vodka had come from.

I try to think back to last night, but the pounding in my head makes it hard. I remember the dream; but I remember smiling as I talked to Stephan. I remember feeling better. I remember the voice in the wind "Bbiiitttccchhh" and I shiver. But I don't remember anything else.

I don't know if I've laid here for an hour; for all I know it could have been five. I'm so lost right now. I'm drowning in self-pity and the knowledge of who I've become. There's knocking on the door, but no one waits for me to say come in.

Three steps to the bed, and I hear a sigh; I feel him sit.

"Kara." It's Stephan's voice, not Rick, Stephan. He sounds empty and beyond exhausted. He pauses, giving me the time to turn and look at him. When I don't move, he stands and walks along the bed. Slowly he kneels on the floor until he can look me in the eye. At first, he just looks at me, studying me as if I were some financial profile to analyze.

"Kara, what happened last night?"

His voice is softer than I thought it would be, none of the anger that seems to never be far from Rick is portrayed in the way he sounds. I still can't seem to make myself talk. I shake my head no and feel a fresh batch of tears start to overflow. I can't imagine what I must look like to him right now. I haven't even brushed my teeth.

"Kara, you have to tell me. Please talk to me. Don't shut me out again." I say nothing. "Your mom gave you a martini. You woke up from...that dream. You called me and you were smiling when we hung up. I could hear the moment the smile reached your face. I loved that moment."

He reaches toward me and wipes away a tear. "What happened after we hung up?"

Closing my eyes, I find myself questioning if I can tell him. What would hurt him more, thinking I don't trust him enough to talk to him or knowing that what scared me, what drove me to drink was him? That last night, my mind had turned Stephan into the man in the alley?

"Kara, tell me. It can't be worse than what my mind is coming up with. Please, baby, tell me please..."

It's the sound of him begging that breaks me. Keeping my eyes closed, so I don't have to see the pain on his face I tell him, "You...I was smiling when we hung up. I had felt so much better. But I was cold because my window was open. When I got up to close it...the wind...I heard his voice in the wind."

I can't control the shiver that runs through my body as I remember just how much it had sounded like the voice in the alley. "I didn't want to call you, to make you worry from so far away. When I closed my eyes, I imagined you were there with me, holding me. It made me feel safe again. But then, you opened your mouth to talk and... and it was his voice that came out, his fucking voice hissing at me."

I'm sobbing. Before I ran, I never would have imagined a person could cry so much. It's like all the tears I had ever held onto were stored for this day in my life. I hear him take a quick deep breath as the realization of what I said settles in.

After a moment, he takes my hand. He's cautious as if he doesn't know how I'll react to his touch.

"Kara, I…I need to know. Are you afraid of me?"

I shake my head no, and now his arms are wrapping around me. He's gently kissing me, my head, my back, my shoulders.

"Shh…it's okay, baby. It's okay."

Eventually I'm quiet. I'm cried out, empty in so many more ways than just tears. I'm not asleep, but he must think I am. I hear him stand and walk quietly out of the room.

Rick must have been waiting right outside the door. I can hear the two of them talking.

"How is she?"

"You want to know how she is? Now I need a fucking drink. That's how she is…"

I'm not sure I have ever heard the edge that is in his voice before. I roll over and force myself to sleep.

CHAPTER 39

When I wake up, I have no idea what time it is. I hear voices, but I can't hear what they're saying. I have to pee.

I lie in bed thinking, *Do I risk it? Getting up to go to the bathroom? When did I become a person who was afraid to pee? When did the mere thought of running into my brother become a risk?*

I open the bedroom door. The voices are coming from down the hall. "Rick, it's not really fair to blame your mom. We never told them what it was really like when we got to her. We were trying to protect them. I think we were wrong."

I hear Dad. "What do you mean what it was like?"

I know that voice. That's the voice where he asks a question he doesn't want to know the answer to, the "why were you late coming home" voice.

Rick sighs. We have turned into the siblings of sigh; it feels like we sigh more than we breathe. It seems to take forever before he starts.

"She spent the first night in her car at a rest stop in Indiana. I don't know how she didn't freeze. I remember that night. I remember being so cold as we looked for her..."

I'm not sure I want to hear any of this; the quiet tone of Rick's voice makes me think he doesn't want to say it either.

"When she called from the hotel, by the time we got to her, she had already been drinking. There were empty bottles in the garbage, pills loose on her nightstand... She had a bruise above her eye. It took her a whole day before she admitted she had fallen asleep driving, that she had crashed her car into a guardrail and left. Her

246

clothes, her car, there was blood everywhere. She didn't even remember bleeding."

I hear a muffled cry escape my mom's lips. "We took her to the hospital as soon as she told us. She had never even thought to go. They said she had a concussion and whiplash. They gave us medicine for her, but we were too afraid to give it to her. We didn't know if we could trust her with pills."

"Why, Rick? Why wouldn't you give her medicine? Medicine that a doctor prescribed, why would you let her be in pain?" My mom's voice is angry and accusing.

"Mom, didn't you see them? When you were in her apartment, didn't you see all the pills? Empty bottles of prescriptions in the garbage, pills on her nightstand? Didn't you see the glasses everywhere? Did you ever check to see what was in them, or did you just wash it all away…pretend like there was nothing really there at all?"

"But those were prescriptions, Rick. It's not like there were drugs in her house."

I hear a chair screech as someone pushes away from the table to stand up.

"Damn it, Mom! Who cares who gave them to her! She was swallowing them down with bottles of vodka. Do you really think that doesn't sound like using them as drugs?" I can hear his footsteps as he paces across the room.

"What the hell is wrong with this family? Why does it take someone who has known her months instead of years to see it. Why the hell weren't we the ones who could see what was happening to her?"

"Don't, Rick." Stephan sounds so calm. I don't think I'll ever understand how he is able to keep his cool when everyone around him falls apart.

"Don't do this to yourself. I did see it, and I didn't say anything until it was almost too late. We can go around and around with blame, but it won't get us anywhere. And it won't help Kara at all."

"I still don't understand." Dad's voice is cautious; he speaks very slowly. "You're saying she has had no pills, no alcohol since you found her? Then what happened last night? Why all the panic last night?"

247

"Dreams, Dad... She has horrible nightmares. She woke us up once with her screaming. I will never forget that sound, not if I live for a hundred years. We couldn't wake her up. When we finally did, she was so scared. She lost it. She ran from room to room in a desperate search for pills and booze. She dumped out the suitcases, emptied the fridge. I have never seen anything like it before."

There is a pause, and I picture Rick and Stephan looking at each other; I imagine the concern, the look that's in their eyes. I put that look there. I keep putting it there.

"You know how she normally is, Dad. She's always tried to shake everything off, like it's no big deal. I saw the fear in her eyes that night, and I realized we never even imagined how terrified she really was."

"Why? Scared of what?" Dad's voice is getting louder and louder with each word he says.

"Damn it, Rick. I still don't understand!" He's yelling now. I can't remember the last time I heard him yell.

I can't take this anymore. I can't hear them explain this to my parents. Standing up, I walk slowly toward the bathroom and lock myself inside. I roll up onto the floor.

Please, God. Please make this stop. Make it all stop. I don't care. I don't care how, just make it stop.

It won't stop. Even with the bathroom door closed, I can hear my mom as she cries. I can hear my dad as his fist goes through the wall. I can hear too much. No. No. No. No. No.

●●●

I feel my brother touch my shoulder. "Kara."

Blinking back against the tears, I look up and see my whole family crowded into the tiny bathroom, Stephan pacing the hall behind them. What the hell?

Rick picks me up and carries me back into my old room; he tucks the blankets around me before he walks away. Sleeping is easier than answering the questions that are waiting for me. My eyes close, but not before my mind can remind my heart that this is not who I want to be.

● ● ●

One minute I'm warm, content, and fast asleep; the next minute the sun is blinding me. I shimmy back down into the bed, trying to get the orange color under my eyelids to fade back into a nice deep black. Somewhere nearby Stephan is laughing.

"Oh no, you don't, sleepyhead. Enough of this lying in bed all day. It's time to get up."

"What time is it?" I croak. I sound like a frog.

"It's 1:00 p.m."

He's sitting on the edge of my bed now; it feels like we've had far too many conversations that start with Stephan sitting on the edge of my bed.

The joking tone in his voice disappears, he's soft now…careful. "I know you don't want to get up and face this, Kara, but you have to."

I roll away from him, but as always, he just moves to the other side of the bed.

"I'll be right here with you."

I look up at him. "Why? Why would you still be here, Stephan? You don't deserve all of this." *Breathe, Kara.* "I'm damaged goods. You should be the one running instead of always worrying if I'm gonna be."

He's just looking at me, thinking, I assume, that I'm right.

Why did I have to say that? I mean, obviously it's the truth, but I don't want him to leave. I don't think I can do this without him.

"Kara, you're so much more than this moment, than that moment. Life attacked you, and you survived it. But now you're stuck. You're still living in that alley."

He's right; I know he's right. I find a spot on the ceiling and focus all my attention on the one scratch mark that's above me. I'm still in the alley. Only this time, this time it's so much worse because

I'm the one forcing me up against the wall. I'm the only one keeping me there.

"Please look at me."

I never thought it could be so difficult to fulfill one little request. I don't know what emotion is reflected in my eyes right now, but I don't think I want him seeing it.

I try to force myself to go blank, to take all the turmoil that I feel and tuck it away. I blink as I look back at him.

"I will be here as long as you're trying, Kara. But…I can't watch you give up on yourself." He closes his eyes and sighs.

"If you do, if you stop trying, if you give up…I will leave. My heart can't take watching you give up. I will always love you, Kara, but…but I can't sit back and watch that fucking alley kill you."

Stephan turns and leaves my room.

I stare at the door after he's left. My mind is a swirl of thoughts and emotions and of one image—a dark sky, dirty red bricks with my face pressed against them. Only this time, there is no one standing behind me, no voices from the sidewalk, no people laughing; it's just me, alone in the alley.

I don't want that stupid moment to control me, and I know right now it is. Right now, I'm standing on the border of life and nothing, not death, but nothing. I have no choice but to find a way to control this. I know if I keep it up, I'll lose what little of my life I have left. The dark reality of it all is if I keep living my life this way, running from people I love, drinking to avoid the way I really feel, not being able to stop hurting those around me, the reality is I might as well never have come home from the alley.

What happened was terrifying, feeling that out of control, that scared of what was about to take place; it was pure fear and panic. I'm not sure my mind even worked right the whole time. It was like something in me shut down. Some torturous part of my brain decided to slow time down until it was moving at a fraction of its normal speed, to make every individual moment last forever, each moment spent creeping through the words he was saying, wondering which of his promises he would fulfill first.

A shiver, I could never hope to control, runs through my body. What would have hurt my family more, one hate-filled act of violence, one moment that would have ended it all as he did the things he whispered or to slowly watch me fade like this, watching me give away a little life each day until there is nothing left?

I stare at the door and try to wrap my head around the concept that Stephan's not coming back. He's not coming back in. Rick's not coming back in. After last night, or was it the night before? They're done; no one is coming to force me back to my life. I'm the only one that can choose to walk through the door. They know they can't control me or my actions; they can't keep a bottle out of my hands or make me into the person they want me to become once again. Only I can do that. I know who it is I don't want to be. And that's this tear-stained, mess of a person who was afraid to get up and pee.

CHAPTER 40

B ut who is it that I do want to be? The question sinks like a rock into the pit of my stomach. I can't be the Kara that hides from her emotions. I don't want to be someone that has to pretend that everything is okay even as the walls come crashing down around her. I won't be someone that sits, full of anxiety and panic at the thought of someone she loves coming over, the fear that someone may see through me. I want whatever they see to be enough.

I want to be enough. I want to be able to be afraid and not feel like it makes me weak. I want nights where I need an escape and to have that be okay. I want to be able to lean on the people around me and to feel them holding me back up.

It sucks to realize I had all of it. The only person who was in my way of me seeing it was me. Is it too late now? Have I lost the ability to have it all back? I can't even imagine the desperation that my family, that Stephan, must feel as they sit and wait for what I will do next.

I think deep down I always knew. It wasn't the alley that I ran from. I ran from me. I did everything I could to escape myself and how I really felt. I had gotten away. I walked out of that alley without being raped, without any real injury. There are so many women that can't say that; women that go on with their lives without having the total breakdown that I seem to be stuck in. What I'm really escaping, what I'm really afraid of is one little question, Do I have the right to be this scared?

I feel so weak knowing that in the end, nothing had really happened, a few minutes of my life, maybe ten or fifteen total, a hand on my arm, a knee in my back, words whispered into my ear. Why is it some people have the power to face so much and still walk away strong? How I wish I could have been one of those women, maybe the kind to organize a neighborhood watch, shouting my story through a megaphone and handing out flyers while standing in the entrance to that damn alley, the type of woman who would have taken actions to make sure he never has the chance to follow through on his threats. Why couldn't I have been someone who could at least had said this happened, and it scared the shit out of me?

Nope, I'm the type of woman who cries into a bottle of vodka. I'm the type of woman who actually spent nights wishing that more had happened. If it had happened, then I would at least have a reason to feel like this. And there lies the truth of it all. That's who I really am, and it disgusts me. That's what I run from. I'm afraid of my own fear, afraid of what it makes me, of who it means I am.

I don't want to be this person, and only I have the power to change it. And that scares the shit out of me. I don't know how to become someone that's strong enough, someone that can be left alone with the hurricane in my head and pretend like it won't drown me. But I think there is a room full of people just outside this door that will help show me the way. I sure as shit hope they know the way.

CHAPTER 41

I slowly get out of the bed and stand on my own two feet. I feel more rooted in this moment than I've felt for so long, and that scares me too. It has to be fake; it has to be a deception my mind has come up with to survive the day. But behind that fear is a calm, the peace I had felt the night I drank at mom's house—it seems like a child's emotion compared to the serenity that I can feel growing, overtaking the fear.

I'm not stupid; nowhere in my mind is the thought that this will be easy, that only this feeling of contentment will remain. I know, without a doubt, I'll feel weak again. I know I'll feel hopeless. I'll feel the need to run, the need to hide, the need to drink. But I also believe I can force myself to lean on those around me, that I can learn to ask for help.

I walk to the door and quietly I open it. Rick is in the hallway sitting against the wall. He's barefoot and asleep. I smile to myself. He wouldn't come back into the room. He wouldn't pretend like it was all okay; but he never left me either. He sits here, still waiting for me.

It makes my heart swell for the love he has for me, but it also breaks my heart to see him like this. Will I ever know or understand the damage I've done to him with all of this? Will I ever deserve his trust again?

I sit down next to him, back against the wall, knees pulled to my chest, and wait. It doesn't seem to take long before I feel him start to stir.

"Hi."

He's looking into my eyes, searching for something. Eventually he blinks and sighs.

"You look better."

"I feel better. I'm sorry, Rick… I'm so sorry for all of this, for—"

"Kara, I'm so damn tired of your I'm sorrys. I really don't give a damn if you're sorry or not because no matter what you say right now, your actions never show that you're sorry."

He stands up and walks into the kitchen.

Stephan is sitting at the table working on his laptop. I didn't expect that; I didn't think he would still be here. He smiles at me and then looks at Rick's face, and the smile disappears.

"Do you want me to leave?"

"No! Stephan, please don't leave."

"I'm sorry, Kara, but I was talking to Rick."

"No, you stay here with her. I can't."

Rick grabs his keys and heads out the door, slamming it shut behind him.

"I've really made a mess out of everything, haven't I?" I move into Stephan's arms and smile as he wraps them around me.

"He loves you, Kara. But we all kinda feel like we're watching you die right now."

His honesty is overwhelming and heartbreaking. "I know Stephan. I really do, and I will make it up to all of you. I will earn your trust back. I'll give you a reason to have faith in me again. I'll earn it back, Stephan, I swear."

"Kara, I never lost my faith in you…even when you did. I know you're stronger than this. I just wish to God that you knew it too."

"I think I do…well not really, but more I think I can be."

"What…does that mean?"

He pulls back, arms on my shoulders and looks into my eyes. His eyes are guarded. It's as if he's afraid to be hopeful.

"What, exactly, did you figure out?" he speaks slowly. His voice is full of apprehension.

I take a deep breath, trying to put all the thoughts that have been rattling in my head into some type of order.

"When I ran, it was only because I didn't want Rick to see me like you had to see me that night." I close my eyes in an attempt to calm myself back down. "Then things got even more out of control. It was such a simple and totally stupid decision that I made out of fear. I almost opened the door for him so many times."

I turn away from Stephan and move to the couch. Following, he sits down beside me and takes my hands in his, his thumb rubbing slowly against the top of my knuckles.

"Once I left, things just seemed to roll together. I didn't want to hurt you, any of you. It was only the knowledge that I was hurting you that made me call. It was just guilt that caused me to tell you where I was. I wasn't ready to be found, but I couldn't hurt you any-more than I already had."

Deep breath, eyes close, and slowly open. One, two, three...breathe.

"I stopped drinking because it would have hurt you for me to keep drinking, because you wanted me to. I didn't want to stop. I still wanted to escape." I close my eyes and keep talking, wanting to get it all out while I still felt strong enough to say it. "Stephan, I still want to escape... I just want it to stop, to go away. I want me back. When I ran, I thought I was escaping the alley, escaping him. In the end, I think what I wanted to escape was guilt." I can't hide the tears that begin to fall.

"I feel guilty for ever having been scared. I feel like I don't have the right to feel that way because he never...hurt me, and I know there are so many people who can't say that, and they didn't lose it like I did. I still feel weak that I'm scared, that I ever think of that night."

My voice is barely above a whisper and that somehow makes it easier to admit everything.

"I feel guilty. I hate that I hurt you, that I hurt my family...that Rick can't even be in the room with me. I hate that I don't have a job, that I'm gonna lose my apartment...all because of this stupid shit."

Stephan is still watching me, silently. "But I get it...I don't want to be this person. I don't want to need an escape. That's all the drink-ing has been. It's my escape when I knew running would hurt you." I look up at him, instead of looking at our hands. The hope in his eyes has grown to a total soul-encompassing joy. He doesn't say anything; he's just looking back at me.

"I don't want to drink and it's the first time I can say that."

Stephan smiles. It reaches his eyes, and he's damn near glowing. He bends down, and his lips touch mine. He's kissing me, a thousand kisses; and in his kisses, I can taste the saltiness of tears.

Eventually he pulls himself away. "Finally, you do finally get it." He has the most stupid, giddy grin on his face. "I love you, Kara."

I bury myself into his neck and let him hold me. I never want to move from this space. "I think we should call your brother and your folks. This is something they'll want to hear too."

My peace in enjoying this moment with Stephan is dropped as I fall back to reality. I find my spot on the wall.

"I really have to go through that whole thing again." The thought exhausts me, but I'm laughing at the same time.

"Yep…and it was beautiful. Thank you for sharing it with me. I know being that honest with someone can be scary, even if it's just being that honest with yourself. Thank you for trusting me with it."

Now it's my turn to lean in and kiss him. He pulls back, quicker than I would have liked. He lifts my chin until my eyes meet his. "You are so brave. You are strong."

CHAPTER 42

Everyone is gathered back at my brother's place. There is so much tension in the air you could cut with a knife. They don't know why we called them, and the fear is evident on their faces.

Stephan still has a stupid grin on his face, and that seems to help break some of the tension. Rick keeps looking from Stephan to me. He seems stuck somewhere between hope and anger.

I take a deep breath, and Stephan takes my hand, a little reminder that I have done this once already, that he's here with me and that apparently, he always will be.

I start by looking at Rick before I let my eyes wander over to my parent's faces. "I'm sorry for last night, well, for so much more than just last night. I know I've hurt you. I know I don't deserve you're trust, and I'm not really asking for it. I just, well…what I'm asking for is the chance to earn it back."

I turn to look only at Rick now. "I know I've broken your heart with this, and I don't want to be the type person that could break you. I don't want to be this person."

I'm starting to shake, and I know I'll be crying soon. "It's the fear of hurting you, of all of you that ever made me run. It's that fear that made me call, that let you find me…that made me stop drinking."

Rick still won't look directly at me, and it's heart-wrenching.

"Don't you get it, Rick? It was never something I wanted. I still wanted something, anything, to turn off the fear inside of me. I still wanted to escape. I tried because of you. I tried to be good, to be right. I kept failing because it wasn't something I was doing for me."

Rick glances up to me, but all I see are questions in his eyes. I don't see the hope or the joy that was there in Stephan's eyes.

I look back to Stephan gathering strength so I can get through this. "I don't want to be that person anymore. I don't want to just escape. I want my life back. I'm not sure I'm strong enough to get it back on my own. And I'm sorry that I need to ask you all to give me even more, but I am."

The last part is almost a whisper. I know Stephan will be there with me, for me. I don't know about the rest of them. In theory, my family should have my back, but shoulds don't really mean a thing. Rick always would have before.

But in reality, I've hurt Rick so many times over the past month; I wouldn't blame him at all if he were to walk away now. As for my parents, I'm asking them for their time, and that's something they've never been good at giving. The fact is I have no idea what any of them will say, and it's torture to admit.

I look up to a room full of eyes, weary, bloodshot, haven't-slept-in-days eyes, eyes that want to believe me, but with one glance, you can read just how unsure they are.

It's Stephan that breaks the silence. "I love you, Kara, and I'll be here as long as you're trying." Apparently, that declaration is all that's needed.

My mom jumps up and hugs me. "Oh, Kara, of course, we'll help you."

Dad is right behind her. I can see the depth of his anger in his expression. "I wish you would have come to us sooner. What happened…what you went through on your own, I don't want you to ever face something like that alone again. Do you understand me?"

"I know, Daddy." And he's wrapping me in his arms like a little girl.

All eyes turn to Rick. He's standing apart from the rest of us, alone and leaning against the kitchen wall. I can see he wants to believe me, but he's unsure if he can.

I look down at the ground, suddenly finding interest in the pattern and swirls on the carpeting; I've gotten to know the patterns on carpets and blankets well these last few months.

"It's okay, Rick. I'll earn it back." I can't seem to force myself to meet his eyes. I know I deserve this, but I don't want him to see how it hurts.

He stays silent but wraps me into a hug nonetheless. I can smell the whiskey on his breath. I look up into his eyes, and he looks ashamed, not angry.

Oh god, what have I done to my brother? The tears I had been holding back while I talked break through now. "Rick…"

I'm sobbing. I've basically collapsed into his arms, and we sink to the floor. Rick's holding me, struggling to get back up and move us to the couch. He's having to comfort me yet again, and I hate it. Why do I always have to be so weak?

"I'm sorry." I try to control myself, to put a smile on my face. "I swear I can do more than just cry and say I'm sorry."

Find laughter, Kara. Find a smile. "It's okay, Kara." Instead of laughing or smiling, Rick cuts straight through to the truth I foolishly thought no one could see.

"We know how much fear and how much pain you've been holding onto. You will never heal if you hold onto it. You have to let it go."

He wipes the tears from my cheek with the sleeve of his shirt. "You have no idea how happy it makes me to see you let go, to finally admit it all to yourself."

I smile, trying to lighten such a tense moment. "It's a good thing you don't mind the tears, Rick, because I seem quite good at them lately."

He's looking at me, not letting me make a joke out of anything right now. I bury my head into his shoulder so I don't have to see his face. "I hate being weak like this."

"What? Kara…" Rick moves to look into my eyes, holding my gaze and with a lecturing tone he states, "No one here thinks you're weak."

"But I do."

He's shaking his head as he pulls me back into a hug.

● ● ●

260

No one seems to want to leave, like somehow if they do, this will have all been a dream. They will wake up and find me gone or find me drunk in a pile of nothing lying on the bathroom floor. I can see the exhaustion taking its toll on my parents. I doubt they have slept since Rick came bursting into their house to gather my drunk, still-sleeping ass.

"If it's okay, I think I'll stay here tonight…if Rick will have me?"

He's laughing for the first time in so long, and it's such a sweet sound.

"Umm, well, I did have this hot date…but okay."

I shake my head in a brother-sister banter "you're crazy, but I love you anyway" way.

Rick looks to Mom and Dad. "Why don't you two head home. I'll call you in the morning, and we can figure out everything else once everyone has slept."

They still don't move to leave. "I swear, Mom. I am okay."

Dad gets up and walks over to me. "Never again on your own. Swear it to me, Kara."

"I promise, Dad. It may not always be you and Mom, please understand that, but I won't deal with things on my own. I think I've proven that I can't."

Dad lets a long breath out, and I see his shoulders relax for the first time tonight. "I don't know many people who could have dealt with that on their own. You need to give yourself some credit."

I shake my head. I'm not foolish enough to believe that, but instead of arguing, I give him a kiss good night.

● ● ●

It's quiet now, just the three of us sitting on the couch enjoying the sense of peace that has settled over the room.

"Rick, I don't think I can make myself leave. I know it's your house and your little sister. But I don't think I could force myself out the door, even if I wanted to. Would you mind if I stay here tonight? I'll sleep on the couch if it makes you feel more comfortable."

"Right now, this is Kara's place again too. Just, umm, don't let me hear anything!"

I slap Rick's shoulder. I'm sure my face is fifty shades of red.

Stephan and Rick are laughing. I love this. "You got it."

Rick kisses me good night and nods to Stephan. He heads off, and we hear his bedroom door close.

"I'll sleep out on the couch, if it makes you more comfortable too."

I look up at him thinking of his lips, his warm embrace. "There's no place I would rather be than wrapped in your arms."

I reach out to him and trace the outline of his bicep through his shirt.

"There's no place I feel safer than when I'm wrapped into these, and I can't ever imagine that changing."

With a slight smile on his face, he reaches out and wraps his arms around me. "Can I ask you a question?" His voice is quiet and thoughtful.

I laugh nervously. "You just did, but sure."

"It's been killing me trying to figure something out." I feel my body stiffen at where this is going; and I focus on my breathing, trying to make myself relax.

"Why didn't you tell me that night? Why didn't you let me try to help you?"

"I don't remember." I'm ashamed to admit it. All of this could have been avoided if I had only told him, if I had only trusted both of us enough. "I remember I was cold walking home. I remember the smell of the alley, the way my cheek felt against the brick…the way his knee felt in my back. I remember the words he whispered into my ear."

I'm shaking now. "I remember feeling like I had to get away, my mind racing to try to figure out how to escape and I couldn't, not even after he left. I remember the disgust in the voice of the first person that found me, the way it sounded as he said, 'Drunk ass bitch.'"

I feel Stephan's body tense. "Someone…found you. You never told me that."

"After he left, or maybe he left because he heard them...I don't know. I heard someone coming. I thought it was him coming back. I thought he was bringing more people with him...that's what really got me moving. I though he was bringing more people."

The tears run freely down me cheek, and my words are mixing together.

"I remember how scared I was. I thought he was coming back to...to rape me, and he wasn't going to do it alone."

I'm not the only one shaking now. I can feel a shudder rip its way through Stephan's body.

"I couldn't walk. I was so scared my legs wouldn't work right. I was crawling my way out of the alley when they saw me. I don't know why they looked into the alley, but they did. They looked at me and walked away laughing. I could hear them as they left, 'Drunk ass bitch.' I was just so relieved it wasn't the same voice. It never occurred to me to ask for help."

I can feel the anger rolling off of Stephan like a wave. "I wish it was me... I wish I had been the one to find you"—his tone drops—"to find him."

The calculation in his voice, how icy cold he sounds, I've never heard Stephan sound scary before. I think he must have carried me to bed because I don't remember leaving the couch, but when I wake up, I'm wrapped in his arms with the sun shining into my room. I move carefully so as not to wake him. I find Rick drinking orange juice and eating cereal at the kitchen table. I love the comfort of this. It feels so normal. This was my life before I ever moved to Chicago, and I think this is what I need.

"Rick, do you mind if I were to move back in here? I know I don't have a job, and I'm pretty sure I don't have an apartment anymore either."

Rick smiles. "Stephan tried to save your job...but without telling them what was going on, he couldn't. I'm sorry, we really didn't know what to do. It felt like it wasn't our story to tell. I paid your rent last month... You still have your apartment, if you want it; but you are more than welcome to move back with me."

Guilt washes over me. They actually feel guilty they couldn't save my job, and then he paid my rent.

"Rick, you didn't need to do that. I don't have a job. I don't even know how I can pay you back."

"I don't care about that, Kara. I just want you back. Get better, that's how you can pay me back."

How am I ever going to get used to this guilt? How do I not let that drive me crazy? The guilt alone is making me want to drink. I can feel my breath start to quicken.

Rick is up and at my side. He now lives to watch me and my moods, at least that's what it feels like. He saw this coming almost as soon as it started.

"Calm down, Kara. Just breathe."

Once whatever the look that had been on my face, the look that alerted him to my panic, is gone, he starts to talk.

"What was it? What brought that on?"

This always honest thing is getting old.

"Guilt."

Breathe.

"I feel so guilty for the pain that I put you through. I saw how ashamed you were last night. I smelled the whiskey on you. I hate that I caused you to need to drink, that I made you feel ashamed for it. You don't have a problem. You should feel no shame in wanting a drink."

I run my hands through my hair.

"I hate that Stephan had to try to save my job, that you had to pay my rent. I hate it."

My head is in my hands, and it's like I am talking to the table. I might be able to be honest, but I can't do it while looking at him. I can't see the reaction on his face to my words.

"There is nothing you can do to change the past, Kara. This past month was what it was. All you can do is focus on today, on this moment. Don't live in the past."

There is a double meaning of sorts with that. Don't live in the past…the past month, the past three.

I stand up, kiss him, and walk into the kitchen. I know what he says is true, but it doesn't do anything to change the way I feel. I pour my coffee and lean up against the countertop.

This is me breathing.

CHAPTER 43

I'm okay…kind of okay. I'm not drinking. I sleep, kind of…I dream, kind of. I've decided that I'm borderline girl, borderline crazy, borderline sane. I'm borderline, and I'm okay with it.

● ● ●

"Are you sure you're ready for this?" Stephan asks me as we stand outside my apartment door. "You don't have to be alone yet. No one will think badly of you if you need more time."

The plan, my plan, is to spend one night alone at my apartment before they all meet me here in the morning and we pack up so I can move back in permanently with Rick. It has a kind of majestic closure to it. It's the start of the New Year. It's the start of the new me. I had made it through the family Christmas party. I had made it through New Year's Eve, quiet and tucked into Stephan's arms. It's time to make it through one more thing, one night alone to end it all, just like one night alone began it all so many months ago.

"No, Stephan, I want this. I can handle it." He opens his mouth to talk, and I put my fingers over his lips. "And if I can't, I know I can call you or Rick, and you'll be there no questions asked." He reaches up to take my hand off his mouth and smiles; taking my hand in his, he kisses the tips of each finger. Moving into me, he bends down to reach my mouth. His lips are soft, and I melt into the warmth of his kiss. I love this man. He's my rock, my safety net; and for some reason, even after I have put him through so much, he loves me too.

He looks into my eyes "We will always be there for you, Kara. I will always be there." I look up to him. "Always and forever."

Together, we open my apartment door and step through it into the living room. Mom had come while I was at Rick's this past week and cleaned for me. I know without looking that all the liquor is gone, as is any type of pill beyond an Advil, and I'm okay with that. A letter to help me through tonight, I assume from her, has fallen to the ground. I picture her writing it, a smile playing across her face. Picking it up and with Stephan's chin balanced on my shoulder, we read the letter together.

> Hello, little bitch.
> You haven't been home. You haven't been to work.
> Do you think that means I can't find you?
> I see you.
> I watch you.
> Why do you watch the sky?
> Is it so you can think of me?
> Because I'm thinking of you.

I drop the note to the ground and look up at Stephan. His eyes are wide, and I'm sure the terror I see in them is the same look he sees reflected in mine.

"We're leaving…now."

ABOUT THE AUTHOR

S iobhan is a designer, amateur photographer, mom, and someone who values the simple things in life, like the morning cup of coffee while sitting and staring out the window.

A good book happens to pair perfectly with that quiet drink and allows Siobhan to escape the world and to get lost in someone else's life. She has discovered writing can provide a similar experience, only with writing Siobhan can get lost in emotions as well, creating the experiences and thoughts she wants to dissect. In *A Quiet Kind of Crazy*, Siobhan invites you into the dangers of hiding who you are, what you have experienced, and the dark and twisted places the mind can take you.

CPSIA information can be obtained
at www.ICGtesting.com
Printed in the USA
BVHW041500160323
660599BV00002B/155

9 781684 984862